Kaelin's Evasiveness

DOMS of Titan Book Two

Cynthia P. O'Neill

Contents

To my soul mate, my friend, my inspiration, my forever love – Craig. Without your belief in me, this writing journey wouldn't be possible. I love you Truly, Madly, Deeply – Always!

To my family – a huge thanks for your patience and understanding in letting me pursue my dreams. You are the world to me.

To everyone who wished they had a knight ready to ride in and save you – this one's for you!

Song Playlist

T HE SONGS CAN BE found on Spotify: Kaelin's Evasiveness
"Hands to Myself" – Selena Gomez
"The Heart Wants What it Wants" – Selena Gomez
"Good to Be Alive" (Hallelujah) – Andy Grammar
"I Want You" – Savage Garden
"Alone Together" – Fall Out Boy
"Crazy For You" – NSYNC
"What Makes You Beautiful" – One Direction
"Something I Need" – One Republic
"Stay" – Rhianna, Mikky Ekko
"Every Breath You Take" – The Police
"Fresh Eyes" – Andy Grammar
"Shape of You" – Ed Sheeran
"Hungry Like the Wolf" – Duran Duran
"Follow You Home" – Nickelback
"Two Steps Behind" – Def Leppard
"As Long As You Love Me" – Backstreet Boys
"All of Me" – John Legend

Prologue

Van

Almost Two Years Ago...

"WHY DID YOU CALL me home, and why are we at this university? This isn't another one of your power plays, is it, Father?"

My brother, sister, and I thought of our father as nothing more than a sperm donor. He never gave a damn about us as children. Mainly our respective nannies and our mother raised us. The only men in our lives were those who worked around our house; they were the ones who taught us how to cook, repair cars, and so forth. Those men were more fatherly than the man walking next to me. He only became interested in my brother and me when we came of working age and could be brought into the company and shown some of the ropes. We were, in his words, "being groomed to one day take over the company and run it".

My brother was to become the President and CEO, and rightfully so; he was older and more business inclined than myself. I was to become the Vice President. As soon as we were old enough to go to college, we were shipped off and told to study business. My sister was less fortunate, deemed only marriage material, a bargaining chip for Father to use to finagle a merger deal with another company. Once she graduated high school, the wedding announcements went out, and she was forced into a marriage of convenience—one she detested with a passion.

Truthfully, we all hated our lives, but dealt with the endless difficult situations, thanks to Father, the best we could. Our mother promised to one day rid us of that horrid man. She was forced into marrying him but during their engagement was skillfully able to negotiate for the controlling interest in the stocks and to become a silent, but ruling, member of the board of directors for the company her parents had owned. Yes, it's the very same company that my dad renamed and was now running into the ground.

He stopped in his tracks and turned to me with the look of a bulldog sporting a permanent scowl on its face. His gruff voice was to the point. "I'm checking to make sure my orders were followed in regard to your brother. I discovered he was staying in the spare room above the coffee shop on the edge of the campus in exchange for working there. How he managed to invest in that place with his former flame, Mark, without my knowledge is beyond me. My assistant, Luke, informed Mark to fire your brother and kick him off campus." Father's eyes held pure malice, his voice contempt. "If he didn't comply, I've already made a call to the health inspector to potentially shut him down."

It'd been a while since Dad kicked my brother out of the company and onto the streets without a dime to his name. My father was one that if you didn't play by his rules, he didn't acknowledge who the hell you were anymore.

He continued walking at a brisk pace, causing me to almost jog to catch up to him.

"So how does this involve me, Father?" I still didn't understand.

"You're here to meet with the chancellor of the school. You'll continue your master's degree here, at this university, while you work for me."

I started to open my mouth to argue that I was perfectly happy at my current school, but immediately was cut off when he stopped and whipped around on me like a tiger ready to pounce on its prey.

"You'll do as I say and like it. No arguments, son."

Oh, joy of joys! Father was in one of his hissy fits today.

We stumbled upon the quaint little coffee shop where the masses were gathered outside , chattering away while imbibing their beverages. It was quite the sight to behold, as every last outdoor seat was taken and people were even standing around, conversing with one another like they had nothing better to do. I must admit, I found it rather comical that dear old Dad believed he could just waltz in here and shut the place down without any pushback. Ha! Fat chance. I'd be the first to admit, my brother was smart for investing in this establishment. Who knew that students and teachers were such suckers for their caffeine fix? Oh, the things we do for a simple jolt of energy.

We stepped into the shop and found it even busier than outside. There were students in every corner, studying and using the free Wi-Fi while sipping their lattes, espressos, or mochas.

I instantly recognized Mark. He started to smile and call me by name but realized my dad was with me and quickly shifted the attention to him. "I'll be with you in a second, Mr. Meyers. I'm just training a new employee how to work the machine and complete this order."

The employee he was referring to was a young woman, maybe early to mid-twenties. Cascading past her shoulders was her slightly curly, deep-brown hair with amber highlights. She wasn't paper thin like most of the college girls who worried about gaining an ounce. She had curves in all the right places, which enhanced her outer exquisiteness. But her eyes...when she looked up and offered a polite smile, my heart skipped a beat, and I almost forgot to breathe. They were two glowing emeralds, completely mesmerizing, reflecting an internal radiance with a touch of softness and determination. I wasn't one to believe in love at first sight. Hell, I'd dismissed that as nothing more than a fallacy created by women to explain away their weakness for men, yet here I was feeling weak in the knees just thinking about how much I'd like to get to know that beauty.

I heard someone clear his throat and looked over to my father, whose face held discontent. "Wipe that damn smile off your face, my boy. She's nothing more than trash compared to our circle. Once you're married to Heather Thresher, you can stick your dick wherever you want, but you only tap something like that as a mistress, nothing more. Throw those ideas of yours out the window, now, or you'll end up just like your brother: penniless and on the street."

Bastard! He'd truly thrown my brother out with nothing more than the clothes on his back and the money in his pocket. I could only hope Mom was gathering enough evidence against my father to kick him out of the company and out of our lives for good. As for his threat to make me marry Heather, neither she nor I wanted that, and we were looking for a way out. However, her father and mine had merger ideas on the brain. I wasn't a cynic, but did marrying for love even exist in the world anymore? I asked my father that once, to which he replied, "In our world, love doesn't exist. Your mother's family and mine arranged our marriage to expand our businesses. That's how it's done." He even snickered, scoffing, "Love's for fools."

All I knew was what I felt when I looked at that stunning creature behind the counter. This might sound whack-a-doodle, but my soul felt instantly connected to hers, as though we were meant to be together. I would stall for as much time as needed to finally meet this woman and find out everything I could with regard to who she was, what her interests were, and anything else I could learn.

While Dad was talking with Mark, I asked Kaelin—gotta love nametags—what she knew how to make on the espresso machine.

"A Café Mocha is fairly easy."

What are the odds she'd know how to make my favorite drink? Was it hers, too?
"I'll take one." I watched as she carefully performed each step before offering it to me, which required our hands to touch briefly, sending a spark racing up my arm and into my heart, as well as my groin. *Hey, I'm human. My dick often has a mind of its own. It's been as hard as a rock since I walked into this coffee shop and began thinking of all the different ways I'd like to romance this woman into my life and, more importantly, into my bed.* She seemed as affected as me, because she jumped back in surprise—an audible gasp escaping her mouth—and her eyes fixated on mine.

Kaelin held her breath as I took a tentative sip.

"This is the best mocha I've ever had." I would have told her that even if it tasted like tar, which, thankfully, it didn't.

She breathed a sigh of relief. "I guess since that's my favorite drink it kind of helps. Can I get you anything else, sir?"

I don't know why, but the word *sir* on her lips sounded amazing. It gave me visuals of her beneath me in bed. I shook my head and laid down a fifty on the counter. "Here's a little 'thank you' for a wonderful mocha. Keep the change, my sweet angel." *I don't know what possessed me to call her that, but it seemed to fit.*

She looked like a deer caught in headlights when she realized the amount of the bill in front of her, and then tried to insist on giving me change back, but I just turned away, noting Dad had finished his conversation and headed toward the door. I conceded to him for now and would stay away from Kaelin, but I'd spend every day, from that day forward, thinking about her and wondering how and where I'd run into her again. Call me a fool, but if we were meant to be together, then fate would lead us back to one another.

Current Day...

I, Donovan Meyers (a.k.a. Van), was now the provisional CEO of the family business, pending the completion of my master's degree. I often think about how our luck has changed now that the bastard is finally gone, dying from a heart attack while screwing his secretary. I managed to redo this entire office, turning a boring, cold room into a welcoming environment. I'd been going over the information regarding the last few mergers my father—*damn I hated that word*—had forced through the company. I couldn't understand the reasoning behind it. On paper, the companies he'd acquired showed them operating in the black, while the current and past financials of said companies had them losing money left and right. This made no sense. Even to a newbie in the business, you didn't buy a failing company unless it had potential to be turned around or sold off for profit.

I was definitely feeling frustrated from pouring through the financials to try and figure out how to turn things around and save my family's future in business. I'd already cut loose a couple of bad business deals and was looking to do more, when a knock came at the door.

"Come in," I yelled out, not even bothering to ask who it was. Luke, my father's former assistant and bodyguard, was due to update me on the morning's details, so I assumed that's who it was.

"Mr. Meyers? Is this a good time?" He peeked his head around the door.

I leaned back in my chair, running my hands through my hair in frustration and breathing out an audible sigh. I looked over at Luke and raised my eyebrows in question. "How long have we known each other, Luke? And how many years separate us in age?"

He walked in with a smirk on his face and closed the door behind him. "I'm only two years older than you, sir. I pretty much grew up with you and your siblings while my father provided security for your family, which I now afford, along with administrative services your father had insisted upon."

I raised my hands in exclamation. "Exactly! So what's my name again?"

He shook his head, smiling and half laughing. "Sorry, Van. I'm just so used to the formalities that your—"

I looked pointedly at him. "Don't say that name if you know what's good for you."

He corrected himself. "That the former CEO insisted upon."

"Thankfully, he's dead and, hopefully, rotting in hell for all the problems he caused in this company and in our lives." I truly did wish that.

"Are there any changes with the special assignment you and Marcus have been handling, and are the preparations in order for *her* to be moved up here to work with me?" I'd been waiting for this day for nearly two years. My father's abrupt passing helped me get out of the forced engagement to Heather, which was good news for a couple of reasons: her family's company would've caused hardship on ours by forcing us into a loss for the quarter, and then there's the fact that we were each enamored with other people, and it looked, hopefully, as if our desires would be coming true.

As luck would have it, Kaelin and I were taking several of the same classes to achieve our master's degrees from the private university. She was there mainly on scholarship and work programs and was one of the smartest people in our class. I moved heaven and earth to get assigned with her on group projects. I even had Luke pose as one of the company's representatives for hiring interns. We honestly did have to take an internship as part of our graduation requirements, so I made sure we both ended up at the same company, albeit different departments since her master's was focused on accounting and finance, while mine was focused on finance and management.

When the former CEO passed, I'd begged my brother to come back and work with me or to take the reins of the company and let me work alongside him, but he refused. He did, however, agree to do some consulting work for us, but his focus was elsewhere. He'd been "discovered" and was now working as a male model. He was enjoying the perks of his new life, and since several people had helped him, mom and myself included, he was paying it forward by assisting a local college student to achieve her goals in life.

He wouldn't tell me her name, but I managed to uncover it through a complicated process, which I won't recount currently. Kaelin somehow ended up meeting my brother and becoming best friends. I hoped that working alongside her would make her feel comfortable enough to talk to me, maybe even enlighten me about her roommate situation.

She had no idea I was her roommate's brother, not yet anyway. I was looking to resolve that today or sometime this week when the opportunity presented. I didn't want to scare the girl by coming on too strong, too fast. Plus, if she knew how much I knew about her, then that might spook her too. For instance, I knew she was currently dealing with a threat against her.

Luke cleared his throat, drawing me out of my daydream. "There were a couple more deliveries this morning. One was intercepted. The other, however, made it through to her."

I gestured for him to elaborate. "Marcus received a box containing pictures of her. Some were from her online webcast as Mystique, and some were of her walking around campus as Kaelin. This psycho figured out her true identity. Marcus bagged up all the evidence and sent it to the lab to be dusted for fingerprints and to try to discover the origin of the package. The other delivery was a dozen red roses. Kaelin pulled the note and read it, stuffing it in her purse before handing the flowers off to the concierge on duty. We don't know what the card said, but Marcus stated she was definitely spooked by it."

"Does my brother know?"

Luke nodded. "Yes. We called him this morning after the first delivery. He hired a driver and gave Kaelin a bullshit reason for it so she wouldn't fight the idea. You know how independent she can be."

I smiled and laughed to myself. "She definitely is that." I looked up into his eyes with concern. "Are we set to put things into motion around lunchtime?"

"Yes. Mr. Walters asked her to stay behind, and we'll go get her at that time."

"Wonderful! Thanks for your help, Luke."

He nodded and walked out, closing the door behind him.

I leaned back in my seat, smiling at the thought of her here in the office with me, helping me go through these financials to try and figure out what's wrong. For some time now, we'd been tasking Kaelin with errors on spreadsheets she'd done just days before to see if she could figure them out. Her mind was definitely photographic, fixing everything with perfect detail in record time.

The need to have her here with me was strong, to not only figure out what the former CEO had up his sleeves, but also to protect her from this stalker fiend. My brother loved her like a sister, and I was just head over heels for her but didn't know quite how to state it. We both had her best interest at heart and knew that she needed our help but wouldn't ask for it even if we forced it on her.

I'd reached out to Dr. Galen Christensen, who had passed our way recently to collect monetary donations and medical supplies for medical missionary-style work in South America. My father had always dismissed him, but I found his cause worthy and enjoyed talking with him any time he passed through town.

Galen and I were mutual friends with much of the staff at Prescott International and their subsidiary, Titan Security. I had heard through the grapevine that he'd had similar stalker issues with his girlfriend, now wife. He'd suggested I take measures to keep her close but not overwhelm her. At the same time he advised me to contact the head of Titan, Rick Caldwell, to see if they could offer up any suggestions. Currently, they were short-staffed and could only offer security systems, which we agreed to and already had in place.

Rick stated he'd try to pull some favors and get someone to investigate things should the stalker become more threatening. He was to the point and honest when he admitted, "Our hands are tied until he/she makes a more aggressive move that would put Kaelin in danger. Without them showing their hand, it would be like trying to find a needle in a haystack. There's just not enough evidence to show who her stalker is at this point."

Feeling a bit anxious, I picked up the remote to the hidden panel of security monitors—one of which was honed in on Kaelin working away in her department. I'd almost had the cameras removed from the office to spite the former boss; he put them in place because he was paranoid about people stealing from his company. He was a misguided fool. Granted, there's one bad apple in every crowd, but you don't have to treat people as though the whole bunch is spoiled, just weed out the bad cores and your morale goes up considerably.

Ironically, the former CEO was the spoiler. Once he died, everyone seemed happier. But truthfully, I couldn't repudiate the monitors; being able to take a quick overview of the company, or specific employees, any time I wanted was a nice perk.

Looking up at the clock, I realized I only had a few moments left before she'd be here. My heart began to race with excitement knowing she'd soon be sitting next to me. I just needed to remind everyone who knew my real identity to refer to me as Mr. Van Ellings—the name I'd been going by at school. If anyone there knew I was actually Donovan Meyers, every Tom, Dick, and Harry with a business scheme or other quick money-making solution would hit me up. Surprisingly, my father gave me some good advice and insisted I come up the back elevator where no one but Luke and the board members knew who I was. I preferred to remain mysterious, just like Kaelin's online persona; only, she wasn't evasive to me anymore. She was going to be mine.

Chapter 1

Kaelin

A DING SOUNDED IN the background causing me to shift from my state of slumber into semi-wakefulness and bringing with it one of the recurrent scenes from my past, my own personal hell.

"Why do you treat me this way?" I'd questioned, *"I've done everything you've ever asked, or rather demanded of me, just to try and get your attention. You treat my sister, Bethany, like a queen and me like I'm nothing more than the unwanted stepchild, except I'm your firstborn. Why, Dad? What have I done to warrant this kind of behavior?"*

I remember the rage in my father's eyes as he turned on me. No one has seen his anger like I have, and I was about to be on the receiving end of it once more. *"You destroyed my life, making it a living hell!"*

Wondering how I could've done anything he claimed, I was at a loss for words. I had rarely gotten into trouble, and I'd always gotten A's in high school, with the intent to go to college on a full scholarship. Dad, however, put me in a university of his choosing and dictated my career path. I accepted it just to try and get one ounce of unconditional love from that man. I did everything I could to please him, but never came close. To me, he was nothing more than a sperm donor for my mother.

There were just so many things I didn't understand about my father. With tears streaming down the front of my face and soaking into what was left of my torn shirt, thanks to an earlier altercation that night with a coworker, the only thing I could do was ask, *"Why are you saying that? All I've ever done is love you despite your love being based on whatever conditions you had in place for me at the time."*

I didn't know what evil looked like, but my dad soon showed me, as his facial features transformed to expose the hideous beast the lie beneath the surface, and his next words cut through me like a dagger to the heart. *"You were born. I begged your mother for an abortion but she refused, wanting to bring you into this world, and when my parents found out, I was forced to 'do the right thing' or forfeit my inheritance. So if you want love, get it from your mother, because you'll NEVER get it from me."*

He opened the door to the house and pointed to the outside world. *"You have three choices, so listen carefully and think long and hard about which option you want, because once the decision is made, you will see it through, or I'll make sure your mother pays for your mistakes."*

His threats were not to be taken lightly. I saw him do some truly reprehensible things, including backhanding my mother when she blocked him from going after me. That was the one and only time he exposed his hatred toward me in front of other people. At least we were smart enough to take pictures and use them against him that night to keep his rage to just below a simmer. He never struck either of us ever again. God forbid we sully his reputation as an upstanding citizen and bring shame to his family's name, which would cause him to face the one fear he held: being cut from his parents' will.

I silently stood there. The options he listed were abysmal to say the least. Basically, my life would be forfeited for his personal gain and my eternal damnation. I picked the option that left his jaw hanging wide open: I walked out the door. I held my head high, refused to shed a tear, and never looked back as he screamed, *"You're no child of mine. When you find you can't make it on your own, you will NOT be allowed back into this house. You're on your own now. You will never be anything more to me than a bastard child. You'll never make it as anything more than a whore, if even then."*

The hum of an electronic device made its way into my subconscious as my mind shifted to my most recent situation. I'd created a webcast out of necessity to finish up the last couple of semesters of college. I didn't stoop to anything illegal, nor did I compromise my virtue—yes, I was still a virgin at age 25—but remembering my father's words made me shiver with fear.

The webcast kept me elusive to everyone, because my roommate and I created a persona—with a wig, faux tattoos, decorative mask, and so forth—a complete one hundred and eighty degrees of my normal life so no one would be able to recognize me. Who knew watching someone get themselves off would go viral? I'd be able to make enough money to stay in school and finish my master's degree. Plus, I dropped back on the number of work hours at the coffee shop, until I finally made enough from the webcast to quit, allowing me to accept a paid internship at the company I hoped to seek permanent employment.

It wasn't something I was proud of, but it was a way to make some easy cash without sacrificing myself entirely...and I did like to get myself off to help relieve stress. My favorite client came to mind, as I recalled the words he used to make my heart accelerate and my lady bits moisten with desire for him.

"I want you to close your eyes, Mystique. Feel the heat of my body hovering over you as I lower my lips to the side of your neck and nibble on your skin just below your ear. I sweep my tongue down the side of your neck, down your chest and over to your nipple. Lick the fingers of your right hand and roll your right nipple with your fingers, imagining it's my tongue going over your flesh, teasing it to a hardened point while your other hand kneads and grasps your other breast. Can you feel me caressing you, my sweet angel?" DaLuvMaster's voice was sweet seduction personified.

"Yes, Master."

"Good. Now lower one of your hands to your clit. Find your hardened nub, the one desperate for my tongue, and begin rubbing it in circles as you grab the vibrating wand and gently place it on the outer folds of your vagina. Rub it in circles and imagine it's my tongue licking every inch of your warm center..."

The man was my favorite. He could have me worked up and ready to come within minutes. Only, I wasn't allowed unless I begged for it and until he gave permission. Usually dominance from the opposite sex scared the hell out of me, thanks to my father issues, but with this guy, it worked, and I was drawn to it, hypnotized by his sinful voice.

I was on the verge of coming that night, when my worst nightmare managed to kick DaLuvMaster offline and ruin our private session. A recent stalker, EagleEyes4U, was taking more and more risks trying to find out who and where I was. He'd taken control over my "other" life with tactics designed to kick people off my webcast, even in private rooms. Thankfully, DaLuvMaster took up most of my private sessions and paid whether he was kicked out of the room or not.

Eagle Eyes' words began to edge into my mind, *"You are meant to be mine, Mystique. You're pure for now, but I WILL have you. CLAIM you. OWN you. I'm coming for you, my precious slut."*

I had several rules when it came to my webcast; the main ones were no one would ever hear my voice or see my identity, and I wouldn't do anything to break my hymen. Granted, numerous viewers offered to "pop my cherry" for an amount of money that would leave me financially secure for some time to come, but I'd NEVER let my father's words of being a whore hold true. I wouldn't sell myself for actual sex, and I would reserve my virginity for the special man I hoped to one day find. If and when I decided to have relations, it would be on my terms and when I was ready. It was the one thing I could control in my life.

An alarm sounded, causing me to bolt upright in the bed and clench the sheets tightly to my chest. My breathing was frantic, and my heart was pounding out a faster rhythm than normal, making me feel it was ready to flee my body for its own safety. I quickly looked around trying to ascertain where the alarm was coming from. Was it the alarm on the condo? Why hadn't anyone called out over the intercom to see if I was okay? Then I realized how stupid and neurotic I was—it was the timer on my phone letting me know it was time to get ready for my internship.

I reached over to silence the device and wondered whether I should throw it against the wall for scaring the hell out of me or thank it for pulling me from my dark dreams. I leaned back against the headboard and saw the message light blinking. That was probably the ding I'd heard. I swiped the screen to notice a text from my roommate Trent.

Trent W:Hey, sweetie bear. My plane's delayed until the smog lifts at LAX. Be back later. Feel free to cook up or order in lots of sinful foods tonight. With the photo shoot over, it's carb-loading time.

A driver's been hired to pick me up when I get in. He's an all day deal, so use him to take u to work. No sense walking in the rain when u can ride in style, hun! Luv ya, T

My roommate was the best. He was my own personal fairy godmother or, in this case, godfather. He rescued this fairytale reject from disaster and in turn became my BFF. We grew up in different environments but share so much in common to the point it's scary. As he likes to put it, he's "my brother from another mother." Granted, we have had lots of questions and discouraging looks living together, but we're purely platonic. I'm into other guys and so is he.

With my heart rate finally calm, I jumped out of bed and scampered across the room to the window. Yep, it was already starting to drizzle. At that moment, I was so thankful for the use of the driver. Maybe the dreams of this morning were just that and my day was looking up. I needed to text Trent back.

Kaelin R:Hi, T-man. Woke to nightmares again. Wish u were

here to chase them away. Be safe.
Thanks 4 the ride - ur right -
raining today. We'll carb-load
ourselves silly and watch cheesy
movies. Luv ya more, K

I quickly showered and got ready to go to my internship with E. Meyers Corporation, or as we nerds liked to refer to it, the $E=MC^2$ company. They actually weren't half bad to work for, especially since the new CEO came onboard. No one ever saw him or knew what he looked like, but who could complain, with all the positive changes occurring at the company. He opened up paid internships to several of the colleges in the area, along with new programs that were increasing morale tenfold. Rumor had it that the former CEO was worse than working for Hitler himself.

Since my major was accounting and finance, I was assigned to the accounting department. I was looking to become a forensic accountant to help increase the efficiency of spending and resources within a company. One of my classmates, Van, interned with management, which was nice because we had a couple group assignments we worked on and often met over the course of lunch to discuss school and how our work was going.

Before I left my room, I, thankfully, remembered I needed to grab the baby shower gift for a coworker off my dresser, when I noticed the light on the webcast camera was turned on. I dropped the gift and quickly opened up the computer to see that I had indeed gone through the ritual of powering down my computer and other equipment needed for my webcast. I turned the computer on to check the log record, revealing the last show had aired for a few hours several nights ago. There'd been no evidence of an outgoing signal and no explanation for the camera to be turned on. *Maybe you bumped it getting into bed last night; you were pretty tired. Or was this the humming noise that started to wake you up after Trent's incoming text?* My subconscious might be right, or we could've had a power surge, only all the clocks and devices still held their correct times and didn't need to be reset. I didn't have time to deal with it at the moment, so

I unplugged the power cord and the USB connector to the computer, forcing the camera to shut down.

Grabbing the gift and shoving it into my briefcase, I headed to the front door, reset the alarm code, locked the door, and headed down toward the lobby where Trent had texted a driver named Davis would be waiting outside.

Arriving at the ground floor, I walked through the lobby toward the front when the concierge, Anthony, waved me down. "Miss Richards. I have a delivery for you." He was holding a lovely vase filled with a dozen long-stemmed red roses, and my mind immediately went to Trent. He was the only person to ever send me flowers. But, it wasn't my birthday, and I still had a month and a half left until my last finals before obtaining my master's degree.

Marcus, the head of security for our condo association, had been busy packing something up to hand off to a courier, when he asked them to hold on so he could take a look at my delivery. "Ms. Richards, it's my duty to check and ensure the safety of each of our tenants. If I could please take a look at the flowers before you take them, just to make certain they're okay"

He always seemed to be a bit anal—going overboard on things—but Trent said that's one of the reasons why he picked this place to live, so he could have privacy and peace of mind. I guess, with him on the verge of becoming one of the world's next great male models, he needed that kind of reassurance.

I yanked the flowers out of Anthony's hands and gave a look that just dared Marcus to touch them. "Geez, Marcus, take a chill pill. I'm sure the flowers aren't carrying any concealed weapons, bombs, or other items of malicious intent towards my person." However, I did have a shiver run up my spine, indicating something wasn't quite right, as I plucked the card from the center of the bouquet and opened it.

I gulped hard and tried not to show how shaken I was by this twisted freak's words. He found me. He now knew where I lived. I was never more thankful to know that Trent would be home soon; otherwise, I'd be too scared to come back to our place after work.

I pocketed the card inside my purse, but handed the flowers over to Anthony. I knew he had an upcoming anniversary with his wife of twenty years. "I'm not a big fan of flowers, so please feel free to give these to your wife with my best wishes."

Marcus looked annoyed by my actions, but Anthony was all smiles. "Thank you, Ms. Richards. Will Mr. Worth be returning soon?"

"Yes, he'll be back sometime today." I glanced up at the clock and realized I needed to get going. The downtown traffic in Orlando could be hell this time of morning. Even with the assistance of a driver, I'd barely make it on time. Once again, Trent was my lifesaver.

Starting toward the door, I raised my hand. "Have a nice day, guys. I'll see you later."

Anthony returned my wishes, but Marcus had already moved on, talking on the phone with someone and scowling, apparently not happy with their response. He sure was a peculiar person, who, coincidentally, came on board about the same time I started being stalked. He wasn't Eagle Eyes, though; Marcus's voice was very distinctive with a bit of northern grace, while my crazed fan's voice was polished yet rough around the edges, and when he'd get excited, there were Cajun undertones, suggesting he might be from Louisiana or another southern state.

The driver already had the door open and waved me inside. "To your work, Ms. Richards?"

Trent must have provided him with the information needed to take me to my internship. "Yes, please, Davis, and thank you."

The morning trudged on, probably because I was excited for lunchtime to come; the department was closing down and heading across the street to one of Gina's favorite Italian restaurants, Giuseppe's. We were all going to celebrate her last day at the company and the impending birth of her firstborn, a girl. She's been an accountant here but has opted to stay at home to spend time with her little one. She said it was something she'd always wanted to do, and the decision was easily made when her husband, Mitch, received a raise and promotion within the IT department here at Meyers Corporation.

I'd heard rumors that the company, under the former CEO, E. Walton Meyers II, had frowned upon employees having families. He didn't want to offer up maternity leave, provide a baby shower or party, or even wish the new family well. He sounded about as much fun as having hair removed from your entire body with wax—Ouch! Thankfully, the new CEO, Donavan Lane Meyers, was more in tune with social norms, even offering up this party and providing Gina's husband with a short paternity leave.

Mr. Walters, the head of the department and my boss, called me into his office. I was hoping this was to offer me Gina's position or one of the other spots that would be opening because of her not returning to work, but I was wrong.

He motioned for me to take a seat. "Kaelin, I'm sorry to have to ask this of you, but we really can't afford to have everyone in the department gone for lunch. Since you're our intern, would you mind sticking behind to help me with the phones and also handle any pressing matters that might come up while the others enjoy their little party?"

I looked confused at first and pointed toward him. "You mean you're sticking behind, too?"

"I'd like to join them and wish Gina well, but I've already given her my baby present and a present on behalf of the CEO. We're a little backlogged and have discovered discrepancies in some of our files. We're not sure what's going on and could use your help." He paused for a moment, looking straight at my face. "You've got a knack for remembering figures, and since you worked on the report a few days ago, I thought you might try your hand at finding what's wrong with it."

I know my face expressed my displeasure at being asked to stay behind, but I was the low man, or woman in this case, on the totem pole, so I couldn't really complain. "Sure, no problem, Mr. Walters."

I got up and headed toward the door, when he added, "Kaelin, I know you realize a position will be coming available. We're planning to move a few people around and haven't forgotten about your talents and how well you fit in here, but until you graduate, we aren't at liberty to hire you full time; however, maybe we can work something out for part-time employment once you're done with your internship requirements. I'll be reviewing them later this morning to see where we stand."

I tried not to let on how elated I was inside. I simply smiled. "Thank you, sir. I'd appreciate that and look forward to any opportunity to work for such an amazing company."

Returning to my desk, I busied myself with the tasks everyone had given me, along with the special assignment. I opened up the spreadsheet I'd worked on just days earlier and noticed instantly that several of the figures had been transposed to provide false information. This was happening way too often. I wrote myself a note to ask Mr. Walters if there's some kind of software we could use or specific measures we could take to prevent false entries into the financials.

The old spreadsheet I'd saved into multiple locations on the hard drive and network server was missing. *Something wasn't right here, but I couldn't place my finger on it. Why would someone keep doing this?* My subconscious was right. Someone was tampering with the system, whether internally or externally I didn't know, but I'd like to assist in putting a stop to it.

I completed the corrections. This time I printed out a hard copy, saved one to a USB stick, and filed away the others onto the usual locations. I wanted to be prepared should this happen again, because even with a vivid memory for numbers, recalling what you entered three days ago wasn't easy.

Some commotion in the area forced my eyes to drift over into Gina's direction. Mitch had come down from his department to meet up with his wife for her special luncheon. I was mesmerized with how loving he was toward Gina. He leaned down to give her a kiss on the cheek then helped her up out of the chair, all while caressing her belly. He bent down again to give his "Little Princess," as he called her, a kiss, stating he couldn't wait to meet her and hold her in his arms.

A small streak of jealousy ran through me, knowing my own father never showed any care or concern toward me. All he ever wanted was for me to be dead so I didn't mess up his life. *How could someone hate me so much but adore my sister once she was born? Why couldn't I ever get even an ounce of his affection?* As a result, I never dated and kept every man at arm's length, with the exception of my roommate, Trent. Thankfully, mom, her parents, and my paternal grandparents wanted me. They were the only ones to show me any form of love. If it hadn't been for them, I wouldn't believe love existed at all, and I would've given up the princess fantasy a long time ago. You know, the one where the prince comes in to save a lowly servant girl from a life of destituteness, falling instantly in love and sweeping her off her feet. I wanted the dream: unconditional love from a man I could trust with my life.

Careful what you wish for, honey, it might come true. I wish my subconscious would shut the hell up. Nothing in life seemed to work out for me no matter what I did. The only light at the end of my tunnel was Trent, his mother, and sister, who were a riot the few times we got together. Meeting his brother still eluded me, but maybe one day we'd finally meet. If he's anything like my BFF, I'd probably like him. Actually, I already did based on what Trent had told me. He always called him "Donny" and said it drove his brother nuts.

I watched as everyone piled into the elevators and out of the area. With everyone gone, except for Mr. Walters and me working at our computers and taking messages for the occasional phone call, it was quiet enough to hear a pin drop.

Lost in thought, I muttered to myself, "Where's *my* Cinderella moment? When will *my* prince come?" I wanted my happily ever after.

I shook my head dispelling the very idea, knowing it'd never happen, or at least not to me, when I heard a throat clear and someone different calling my name.

"Ms. Richards?"

Chapter 2

Kaelin

S WIRLING AROUND IN MY seat, I spotted Mr. Walters standing next to a man holding an empty cardboard box. Although I can't remember his name, I think that guy was the one who came to my class to talk about internships. "Yes?" I answered, a bit unsure of myself.

Mr. Walters spoke up. "Kaelin, I don't know if you remember Luke Kincaid. He's the assistant to Donovan Meyers and has been with this company for years. Anyhow, we need you to collect your things and..."

His words began drifting off without being heard, because I was fixated on that empty box. Was I about to get canned and, therefore, have to repeat the internship all over again, extending my time until graduation? My heart rate spiked, my breathing increased, and I nearly fainted from the idea. Had the discussion we had in his office earlier been a lie? Was Mr. Walters one more man I couldn't trust? Was this why I was kept behind, to get rid of me quietly?

I guess my boss realized I was panicking, since he held his hands up in surrender. "There's no need to worry, Kaelin. You're not being let go, instead you're being reassigned. This is all positive news."

He stepped forward, kneeling down to my line of sight. "Mr. Meyers has been called away on business and has Van Ellings, from your class, working on a special assignment. You've impressed the CEO with your ability to correct spreadsheets from memory, so he'd like you to assist to see what else you can do."

I didn't know what to say, except, "What about my internship?"

Mr. Walters spoke up. "I looked over the school's stipulations and you've completed all the required hours and then some, so your professor has already received my grade for you along with positive, glowing comments about your performance. We'd definitely like you to continue working here and move into a full-time position in the future, but only if you're interested. For now, however, you're needed elsewhere within our organization, and we're asking for your help."

His words soothed me. For once in my life, someone was praising me, and I wasn't quite sure how to take it. Luke stepped forward to put the box on my lap. "If you'd please help us. Van is using the conference table in Mr. Meyer's office to spread out all the financials and look for the items his supervisor has dictated. Would you be willing to assist him? He can't do it by himself."

I could only utter one word, "Sure." I liked Van. He and I clicked in class and worked well together on group assignments. *He was also easy on the eyes and made my heart skip a beat for no reason. Why wouldn't I want to work with him? How many times had I envisioned him as my prince charming coming to rescue me in my dreams?*

Before I knew it, my things were in a box being carried by Luke, and we were in the elevator. I'd never been above the fifth floor, but I was now headed up to the top of the building, the fifteenth floor, to the office overlooking all of Orlando.

The doors opened and my mouth just about dropped to the floor. The waiting area was extremely modern yet soothing in nature with lots of blues, whites, blacks, and silvers, along with some tropical plants and a small water feature in the corner. I still didn't know what I was doing here in this area, but I was about to find out.

I followed Luke off the elevator and through the open doors of Mr. Meyers's office. "Hey, Kaelin. Thank goodness you're here."

I looked toward the area the voice came from and found Van at the conference table with papers everywhere. His jacket was hanging on a nearby chair, his long sleeves were rolled up to his elbows, his tie had been removed, and the top two buttons of his shirt were undone, exposing a slight sprinkling of hair on his tanned, strong chest. You could tell he'd been frustrated with his work, since his normally groomed dark golden hair was mussed, but he was smiling ear to ear and seemed to breathe a sigh of relief that I'd come to help him with his assignment.

Luke placed my box on a chair at the end of the conference table. "Have either of you had lunch yet?" he asked politely.

I shook my head and explained, "I thought I'd be joining the department at Gina's luncheon today, so I didn't bring anything."

Van looked a bit puzzled before looking over at the clock. "It's that time already?"

Without missing a beat, Luke cited, "Mr. Meyers has said to offer up anything you need to help get this project done. What can I get you both so you can eat and work?"

Van looked over at me then suggested, "I don't know what you'd prefer, Kaelin, but I sure could go for a turkey and avocado wrap with some fresh fruit and an iced tea on the side."

Geez, that's strange. He seemed to somehow know my favorite lunch to bring from home. I ate this at least two or three times a week. Feeling a little uncertain as to how he knew my preferences, I finally offered up, "Sure. Sounds great."

Luke dismissed himself to get the food for us while Van began explaining what he was doing. "Mr. Meyers is trying to figure out why the former CEO made so many acquisitions of companies that should've been torn apart and sold for scrap or never purchased at all."

Answering my next question before I had a moment to ask, Van motioned toward the boxes upon boxes of paperwork. "Mr. Meyers is fearful someone's been tampering with the electronic copies of data and, pending the situation at hand, making things look better or worse than they actually are. He's pulled all the hard-copy financials from the past five years out of the warehouse to review and see if he can get any answers.

"We've already gone through last year's data but haven't found much other than a few questionable withdrawals from the company that no one can account for." Van looked up at me and motioned for me to have a seat next to him. He pulled a stack of papers over and flipped through to a specific page showing an example of what he meant. "See how this figure seems excessive for a deduction of depreciable goods?"

I nodded.

"These items, along with any others that might be suspicious, are to be highlighted, and we're to compile a report on any and all issues we find."

He sounded defeated as he leaned over to admit, "There hasn't been much luck with this year's or last year's financial data; they revealed only a few items in question. With the CEO frequently on business trips, I've put in so many hours over the last six weeks that I feel like my eyes are about ready to go crossed. It's time for a fresh set of eyes to look over this paperwork and, hopefully, pick up the things I've missed. With your goal aimed as forensic accounting, I asked Mr. Meyers's permission to pull you on board to help me out."

I was more than happy to help where possible. "Just show me what stack you'd like me to start on and let's get moving."

Van stood and walked over to one of the boxes holding the previous year's information to what he was working on. "Why don't we start with this one. We can go through it together and make comparisons of the changes from one year to the next to see if something jumps out at us."

His suggestion made sense. Comparing two years worth of financials side by side should force any idiosyncrasies in the data to pop out at us. As Van and I started to work in close proximity, we nearly bumped heads a few times trying to scan over each other's financials.

We continued on like that until Luke brought lunch in and we paused to say thank you. I didn't want to take a break though, so I very carefully ate, taking bites here and there while I hastily continued moving my chair between the two piles.

We agreed, given the pace I was setting, that I should mark any suspicious discrepancies between the years, and then Van would recheck them and compare them to the information listed on the computer. We discovered several unauthorized withdrawals of money—written off as various expenses or depreciations—wired to offshore accounts. It wouldn't have raised a red flag under normal circumstances, but the frequency of those happenings continued to increase up until the time of the former CEO's death. A couple of transactions had gone through recently, but Mr. Walters brought it to the attention of Mr. Meyers, and he shut it down, or so it appeared.

Several hours later, I hit pay dirt. I had to go back three to four years, but the discrepancies on a couple of acquisitions at that time were huge. Meyers Corporation was a company handling investments, acquisitions, and mergers. They invested in new ideas that had the potential to draw in a profit, they acquired companies who lost their way and helped them restructure so they could once again flourish, and they often absorbed companies through mergers, expanding their current abilities. At least, that's what Luke had told our class when he came to talk to us and was what psyched me up to go for the internship. There isn't much call for a forensic accountant in the real world, but in this style of business, the company would want to know if they would be at risk taking on various ventures.

The mergers, investments, and acquisitions as of late, with the new CEO, were turned down, because the companies seeking assistance were too far gone. And the ones that were acquired were well thought out, with every inch of their financials accounted for; however, the ones I just discovered for companies called Freidmont Pharmaceuticals and Hollings Shipping Industries should've been passed over. They were operating in the red, had been for years, and didn't have any hope of recovery. Their names seemed familiar, but for the life of me, I couldn't place them.

As I picked up my cell, I asked Van if he minded me googling the two companies in question. He said I didn't need to; he knew their stories. I got distracted for a minute, noticing the time was well after five o'clock, and I still hadn't heard from my roommate, Trent, which was so unlike him. Mr. Meyers's office didn't have the best reception, so I chalked it up to that.

Van moved to hover over my shoulder as I pointed out the issues I found. I was a little unnerved at how close he'd gotten; his deep woodsy scent was wafting over me, making my heart beat a little faster. He smelled familiar, much like the cologne my roommate wore. *What were the odds?* I noticed he breathed in deeply. Did he just smell my hair and neck? *I didn't know whether to be freaked out or flattered. Dad had never permitted me to date, only wanting to pass me off as a piece of property for someone to marry, so I didn't know how to act around guys. Trent didn't count. He was my very handsome roommate and friend for life.*

I inched forward a bit in my seat, while Van backed off somewhat. "The pharmaceutical company has been in headlines across every avenue of the news. Making some of the best medications on the market, they were in high demand until someone got the bright idea of substituting the real drugs with placebos and selling the actual medicine on the black market for profit. The employee was in management and was both fired and incarcerated for his fraud. His actions hurt the company's name severely, and they never recovered from it. What did you find on them?"

I pointed to the papers showing the initial financials of the pharmaceutical company, the ones they had turned over to our former CEO to show they were failing miserably. Attached was a hard copy of the business prospectus created with favorable figures for the board of directors to pass, portraying the company in a positive light. "See? Here they're over twenty million dollars in debt, whereas the computer presentation put together for the board shows them only one million in debt. The company was delivered as a profitable risk with some potential rebranding solutions to bring back their income, along with a positive turnaround within a six-month time frame."

Van shook his head. His eyes were full of question when I overheard him mumble to himself, "Why would that bastard take such a risk? He had to know someone would figure it out eventually."

I didn't want to interrupt his train of thought, but I needed to point out something else I discovered—a bit of information someone meant to keep hidden. "There's more." I flipped the original financials over to reveal a few handwritten words on the back of each page. It was clearly intended for the former CEO, because it read:

Push this merger through and you'll
have my silence. If it fails, all your
little secrets will be exposed to every-
one. – R. F.

I didn't know what the note meant, but apparently Van had more knowledge of the company than I did, especially since he worked for the new CEO. He balled up one of his fists against the arm of my chair, so I looked back and saw fury spread across his face.

He must've realized he was scaring me, because he grabbed the chair next to me, took a seat, and counted to ten, before laying a hand on my forearm and giving it a squeeze. *Why is it that every time this man touches my skin, I feel like I'm getting static shock? And why does my heart rate and breathing increase?* I couldn't understand it, except it was similar to the feeling I got when I was in the heat of the moment of getting off, only minus the shock. *You're falling for him.* That's what my mind was telling me, but my heart was still unwilling to trust.

"I'm sorry if I scared you. It just ticks me off that some companies, for their own selfish reasons, use tactics to screw over the consumers and board members. The new CEO suspected something like this was going on, but in order to nullify the acquisition and separate from the pharmaceutical company, he needs proof for the board."

I was a bit confused. How did Van know all this? I'd been working in the accounting department for the same length of time he'd been working with Luke and the CEO, and I didn't know everything that went on within the business. Instinct was telling me there was more going on than I realized.

I was ready to ask him what gives, when he moved our conversation on to the shipping industry. "Hollings Shipping made the news, thanks to their CEO's philandering son, Colton. He had a reputation as a ladies' man, multiple at a time, sometimes including men. He often used drugs and even managed to get some cocaine hidden in one of the shipments from overseas. For some reason he felt he was beyond reproach, maybe because his dad had enough money to get him out of any tight situation."

Van shook his head and laughed. "Mr. Hollings once had to pay a pretty penny to get his son out of doing time in the state penitentiary, and before the judge would release Colton, he had to agree to complete a drug rehab program and stay on the straight and narrow. The judge then suggested Colton might settle down with a steady girlfriend or wife. Sadly, our former CEO's daughter was forced to marry Colton to help his image. Their shipping business continued to suffer for a while but is slowly bouncing back if I remember correctly."

He looked over to me to verify, so I nodded. "Yes. The original financials weren't as bad as the pharmaceutical company's, but Hollings Shipping was in debt by several million dollars, and it, too, was presented as making money rather than losing it. Also, a note similar to the other was found within the original financial paperwork."

We were both quietly looking over the paperwork for a moment, when I couldn't help but ask, "Why would a father force his child to marry someone they didn't love? Of course, I'm assuming this was part of the business deal and no love was involved. Correct?"

He looked at me with questionable eyes. I guess he could hear how angry I was when I asked my question, knowing all too well how close I'd come to that very situation. "You're correct, Kaelin. Our current CEO fought hard to prevent his sister from being married off. He knew she wouldn't be cared for properly and that the marriage would be a front to protect Colton's wild ways." He leaned forward and whispered, "While Colton Hollings appeared to be the ladies' man, he was actually bi-sexual, leaning more toward men. If that ever got out to the press, their family name and possibly their business would be ruined, or so they believed."

I couldn't understand it. "Does the 'family name' mean that much? I'm not sure I follow."

He nodded. "It used to, not so much anymore. The elite used to have arranged marriages between their children, merging their companies together in the process. Love was not even thought of at that time, only what kind of deal they could force with their offspring's lives at stake. Most of the families are still operating on old-school ideals"—Van shook his head—"believing it should be a man and a woman, nothing more. But times change, and we all need to learn to adapt and accept the changes in the world around us."

"That's horrible. It should be outlawed." I kind of shouted it, not meaning to. I placed my hand over my mouth in shame for my outburst, offering up, "I'm sorry. I was out of line." *I was still reeling from the idea that my dad had tried to sell me off to marriage. Sadly, I could relate all too well to the story Van was painting for me.*

He threw me a half-quirky smile, one that I seemed to remember seeing years ago when I worked at the coffee shop, but at the same time, I guess it was just wishful thinking. That guy had slicked back hair and was dressed to the nines in Armani-style suits similar to the ones my dad wore when he could afford them. "Don't be sorry. I feel the same way you do. Did you know the former CEO, before he died, was trying to force his son into doing the same thing?"

Van reached out, running his knuckles over the side of my face.

The action caught me off guard, but I soon leaned into him. I don't know why, but he felt comforting.

"Do you know how amazing you are, Kaelin?"

He leaned forward, sliding the back of his hand down the side of my neck and around to my nape, before pulling me closer as he talked softly. "The CEO has had numerous accounting firms in here auditing the books over the course of the past two months. They only found a handful of the fraudulent withdrawals. You found more information in half a day than all the firms combined."

I started to freak out when he ran his other hand up the side of my arm, pulled me up to stand with him, and drew my body against his. My heart rate and breathing accelerated...but the warmth of being next to him...it did something to me. I felt comforted rather than wanting to run like I did when any other guy showed me the slightest bit of affection.

His hands came up to cradle my face, and he ran his thumb across my lower lip. Van leaned in to place a tentative kiss on my lips, before pulling back to check my reaction. I didn't pull away, not that I couldn't, but I didn't want to. That small kiss had me breathing heavy and wanting more.

"Van?" I questioned, wondering why he was just staring at me. I guess he got the response he was looking for, because his lips encased mine. He started out kissing me softly, but as the fire started to burn deep within me, my hands found their way up, encircling his neck and holding him closer as he began seeking purchase for me to open my mouth for him to plunder.

I felt his hand slide up into my hair while the other slid down to my ass to pull me into him, causing me to feel his hardness hitting my lower belly. He was turned on by me! But was it my body, my mind, or did he just try to get any girl into bed?

With our breath totally spent, we pulled away long enough for him to admit, "Kaelin, I've been enamored with you for a while now, wanting to ask you out but not knowing how to approach you for a date or if you'd even go out with me. I watched your lips as you gave your presentations and arguments for cases in class, and it's taken everything in me to sit next to you this long and not reach out to touch you." He leaned in to my neck and took a deep breath. "Your floral scent is intoxicating." He quickly pulled back to look me in the eyes. "But let me be clear, Kaelin, your beauty attracted me to you, but it's your mind that has me going crazy."

His words were like Cupid's arrow shooting straight into my heart. Guys who had approached me prior to him had only been interested in one thing: getting me into the sack. They even admitted it! That's one of the reasons I hadn't dated, besides my father prohibiting it while I was under his roof. He once caught me kissing a guy and went ballistic, throwing the guy out and grounding me for a month—just over a freaking kiss.

While I was lost in thought yet smiling from ear to ear, Van backed me against the wall and rocked into me, showing me the evidence of his arousal and bringing me back to reality. "I want you Kaelin, but I have a feeling you've never been with anyone before."

I could feel my eyebrows scrunch up in confusion. "How would you know that?"

He smirked. "Just by the way you're hesitant to let go and let me take the lead on things."

I started to panic, placing my hands against his chest to move him, but he didn't budge. Instead, he placed both his hands beside my head to cage me against the wall and alternated rubbing his nose against mine and kissing my forehead for reassurance.

"I won't go any further with you, not until you tell me to. I'll be the perfect gentleman." He held up three fingers, offering, "Scout's honor. But I do want to get to know you better, not just as a classmate and coworker."

I felt the walls closing in around me. No one had ever wanted to know the real me; they only saw me as a brainy geek or a beautiful body. Most importantly though, how would I keep him from knowing what I did on the side to help pay for school?

My mind panicked, and I shook my head. "I'm sorry, Van. No one can know the real me. I just want to remain a mystery for now."

Van leaned forward and planted small kisses along the side of my face. "There's no need to be afraid. We don't have to have any secrets between us. We know each other better than you think, Kaelin...or should I say Mystique?"

My body began shaking as he pulled me into a hug. "There's no need to fear me. As I've said here and online, I'll remain a perfect gentleman with you, only taking you as far as your limits will allow you to go, my sweet angel."

His touch started to relax me, but realization hit me and hard. I turned my eyes up toward his, my voice shaking as I asked, "You're not Eagle Eyes, are you?"

Van shook his head. "No, but I'd like to find that bastard. He's destroyed seven of my laptops with viruses just to keep me from talking with you online." His voice sounded pissed for a moment, but a salacious grin spread across his lips as he looked into my eyes. "It took me forever to figure out who you were. I thought I was going mad wondering how I could be drawn to both you and Mystique at the same time. No other woman has ever appealed to me as much as you do."

My mind was trying to catch up to all this new information and figure out if I could trust that he wasn't my stalker, when he said, "If you'd like, you can call me Master of your deepest desires."

"DaLuvMaster?" I figured he'd nod to this, but he only held my chin as he brought his lips to mine. The words, his actions, they were the same as what we'd played out online in fantasy.

I let the kiss linger. I always wondered why I felt drawn to Van but also DaLuvMaster. I couldn't understand how I could have the same feelings for two different people. I didn't know whether it was love or lust, but now he was starting to make me see it was both. At least, I think it was. I'm walking into uncharted territory, and I'm not quite sure I can trust him.

I wanted to pull back and ask him how he figured it out, since no one ever heard my voice, and I looked nothing like my online persona, but he continued to hold me tight, as though he feared I might run away if he released me. The kisses were intoxicating, making it harder for me to think, when I heard someone knocking on the office door.

Van leaned back and yelled, "Go away, Luke. I'm busy." The knocking persisted, but Van ignored it, pulling me tighter and continuing the kisses.

Finally I heard Luke yell out Van's name. When he didn't respond, Luke opened the door and came in, causing our lips to pull away from each other, but Van still held me against him.

"I told you not to disturb us, Luke." His voice was less than pleased, and I know I was turning all shades of red from being caught kissing Van instead of working.

"I have the hospital on the line, sir."

Van dismissively waved his hand at Luke. "Give them whatever donation we normally do and be done with it."

Luke shook his head, his eyes full of dread. Something was definitely off. "It's your brother, sir. He was attacked outside his condo, and they're having trouble locating your mother. They're requesting to speak with Donovan Meyers."

Luke then pressed the mobile handset into Van's hand. He immediately began asking the person on the other end questions left and right. "You have my permission to do whatever you need to do to stabilize him. We'll be there as quickly as we can."

My mind felt numb. I was trying to process the information. Van was the guy I'd been enamored with online—DaLuvMaster—and also the new CEO—Donovan Lane Meyers—not Van Ellings? *What the hell? And how did he know who I was?*

Van handed the phone back to Luke. "Get the car and bring it around to the private elevator in the garage. We'll be down momentarily."

Luke ran off in a hurry while Van locked the door to his office and grabbed my bag while still holding on to my hand and, therefore, dragging me with him. He walked me over to what looked like a bookcase, pulled down a book to expose a panel he depressed, which forced the case to slide open and reveal an elevator. He pulled me in behind him. My body followed his direction, but my mind was still working on overload trying to process all the new information. When the elevator began to move, I finally managed to find my words. "You're the new CEO?"

He nodded. "Yes. I didn't want you to find out this way. I was planning on telling you in a couple of days' time."

I was mad at him for lying to me, but was more concerned for his brother right now. "I'm sorry to hear of your brother. You can just drop me in the garage, and I'll get an uber or someone to drive me home." *I didn't want to let him know I was scared to go home, afraid of the stalker. And why hadn't I heard from Trent?*

He shook his head as he slipped an arm around my waist and pulled me against his side. "I'm sorry, Kaelin, but I can't allow that. I won't let you out of my sight from now on." His free hand punched the wall of the elevator, frightening me a bit. "I can't believe he didn't take these threats more seriously. Why he thought he wasn't at risk?"

"What are you talking about? Why am I here? Why won't you let me go home? You're frightening me." My body started to shake on its own. I was beginning to wonder if I had mistaken Van for the wrong person, that he was in fact my stalker. "I demand to know right now!" I yelled and stomped my foot on the floor to let him know just how pissed and fearful I was getting.

Van's face became serious as he looked directly into my eyes. "Because my brother is Trent, your roommate. That stalker of yours, EagleEyes4U, jumped him from behind and beat him to within inches of his life. Had Marcus not been making his rounds, Trent might've died. To think, your stalker was right outside of your apartment; he could've taken you, hurt you." He reached up to push a piece of my hair behind my ear and then cradled my face. His voice was pained and filled with worry, and I could barely make out his whisper. "I can't do without either of you in my life."

Van was definitely freaked out. I still couldn't believe they were brothers. Now that I was this close to him and tried to imagine my roommate, Trent, standing beside him, I could see their similarities. They were subtle but definitely there. The nose, the forehead, the chin—all looking like they'd been carved by the Greek gods themselves—were alike, but the shape of their faces and their hair and eye color differed. All the sudden, everything clicked, and I felt all the air leave my lungs...my BFF had been hurt, and Eagle Eyes had indeed kept his promise to come for me. Darkness started to spread across my field of vision as my legs began to feel like rubber, no longer supporting me. I hoarsely called out, "Van," but everything went dark.

Chapter 3

Van

THIS DAY HAD BEEN planned out down to the most infinitesimal detail, yet it went to hell in a handbasket the moment the deliveries were made this morning from that psychotic fiend Eagle Eyes. A few hours ago, my only fear was whether Kaelin would accept the position of helping me figure out the finances, because my strong suit was in the management and general financials of the business, not in accounting. I needed her mind, and I'll admit that I needed her as much as the air I breathe. Something about her grounded me and gave me comfort.

Looking up at the elevator's display to watch the floors countdown as we descended, I kept hoping it would hurry up so I could get to my brother and to see what caused Kaelin to pass out on me.

One minute she was demanding to know what was going on, and the next her eyes started rolling back into her head, and she nearly collapsed onto the floor of the elevator. Thankfully, I caught her before she fell. Feeling my heart racing with worry, I leaned back against the back wall of the elevator for support. This day kept getting progressively worse.

All the plans that had been carefully laid out, with both Luke's and Trent's assistance, to try and protect Kaelin from her stalker had just turned into a smoldering pile of shit. I knew Eagle Eyes, the fucking bastard, was territorial, since he pushed me out of both the public and private sessions with Mystique, a.k.a. Kaelin. He sent me several instant messages warning me off seeing her, even threatening violence against me and claiming to know who I was and how to find me.

I had Luke investigating since Eagle Ass, as I like to call him, blew up the first laptop. We came close several times to finding the bastard's IP address but then would get directed elsewhere. We deduced that this Eagle guy was tech savvy, definitely knew his way around a computer system and was able to block access to his system.

The threats were increasing, he found where she lives, and hell, he might even know who I really am and the company my family owns. Who knows? I didn't want to take any more chances. Look where that got us: my brother beat up, my mom and sister nowhere to be found, the love of my life passed out in my arms, a stalker determined to have her for himself, and all of our plans to protect Kaelin up in smoke. What am I supposed to do now?

Just as the thought crossed my mind, the elevator doors opened, and I saw the town car waiting for us. I yelled to Luke. "We need help!"

He jumped out of the car and rushed around to grab Kaelin from me. "What the fuck happened?"

Wanting to keep her to myself, I pulled her away from his outstretched arms. "She passed out. I think she might be in shock. Hell if I know."

Luke put his hands up in a sign of surrender. "Van, let me have Kaelin. There's no way you can get into the backseat while holding her. You get in and I will place her on your lap so you can hold tight to her while we head to the hospital."

Damn it, his words made sense, so I surrendered her over to his arms and climbed into the backseat.

Luke gently lowered her into the car and across my lap, with her head rested against my shoulder. Speaking in a calm voice, he offered some reassurances. "I think Kaelin's a bit overwhelmed with everything. You have to admit, you've both had quite the day."

I nodded in agreement.

"Her pulse seems to be elevated, but her breathing seems to be normal. I think she's going to be okay, but as a precaution, we could have a doctor check her out to reassure you."

My mind was running a mile a minute, trying to process everything. Before I even realized it, Luke had already returned to the driver's seat and had us on the road to the hospital. "Any updates to report?"

He nodded and looked back into the rearview mirror. "Finally, the Van I know is back. I was beginning to wonder if you'd end up in shock, too." Returning his eyes to the road, he informed me that Trent sustained some fractures but wasn't as bad off as he first appeared; he'd just been covered in a lot of blood. My mother and sister were unreachable because they'd just taken off from Paris in the family's private jet. They'd spent the week over there working with some charitable causes and doing a little shopping on the side. "We've called the plane and talked with your mom. She's making preparations to take care of Trent once he's released from the hospital. She and Alyssa are beside themselves with worry."

"Was there any video footage of the culprit entering or leaving Trent's building?" The building had video feeds all over the place to keep their residents safe.

Luke hesitated at first, causing me to ask, "What aren't you telling me?"

"The condo was broken into. The culprit used a sharp knife to carve 'She's Mine' into the kitchen cabinetry. He used some blood to smear the same message onto the mirror in Trent's bathroom and also ransacked his bedroom..." Luke's voice trailed off, making my eyes grow big with worry, knowing the next pieces of information were items that would probably enrage me.

I took a deep breath in and asked as calmly as possible, "And?"

"The perpetrator went through Kaelin's closet and dresser. We aren't certain but it appears some pieces of lingerie are missing. One piece I'm guessing she used as Mystique had been placed on her bed and he..." His words drifted off again.

I tried to remain calm, not wanting to cause any alarm to Kaelin. "He what? Tell me, damn it."

Luke gulped audibly. "He ejaculated all over it and the bed and left a note stating next time he'd be coming inside her."

My instant response was to hold her closer and kiss her forehead, whispering, "You have my word that I'll protect you with my life, Kaelin. I won't let this psychopath anywhere near you."

From the front seat, I heard my words reiterated. "We won't let that happen, sir. The police have been called and, along with our guys, are doing a thorough sweep of the place. So far, there aren't any prints. We're also reviewing the past few days of footage to find out how Eagle Eyes managed to get into the building and apartment. We've confirmed the alarm system had been deactivated, but we're trying to find out if it was prior to Trent getting home or after. We'll get this bastard, but I may need to call in some added assistance to get him faster."

My voice was stone cold as I uttered the words, "Do whatever is necessary to catch this monster and settle this immediately. The price doesn't matter. I want an end to her looking over her shoulder all the time. She's already been through enough. In fact, get Titan Security on the line. I believe this now qualifies for his team to start investigating."

"Consider it done." The words had just left Luke's mouth when we pulled up to the emergency entrance of the hospital.

Members of the ER staff came rushing out of the hospital with a gurney in hand for Kaelin. I placed her carefully on the stretcher and explained why we were there. The doctor checked her over quickly in an exam room, deducing her mind was in overload and she just needed time to wake up on her own. Thankfully, he'd also worked on Trent and led us to his room while giving me the details of his condition. Before rushing off, the doctor let us know he'd be back in to check on Kaelin and Trent shortly.

Trent was awake but looked a mess in the hospital bed. His face was swollen, one eye nearly shut; his leg was covered in black and blue marks, and more continued to rise to the surface; he had a splint on one arm, which they would cast once the swelling went down; there was tape around his ribs to help him breathe a little easier; and he had a bruised kidney. One whole side of his body looked like it took the brunt of the attack. The sight of him made me hurt, wishing like hell he'd taken my warnings that he needed a bodyguard seriously.

He caught sight of Kaelin still passed out on the gurney, my hand still wrapped around hers. "Is she all right? Was she attacked, too? Why is she unconscious?" His voice was filled with alarm.

Before I could answer, Luke touched me on my shoulder. "I'll have two armed guards standing watch on the room at all times. We requested a clean-up crew to handle things at the condo once the police are done, and I've placed the call to Rick with Titan Security, per your request, and explained how the stalker has upped his game. They're sending over one of their top computer hackers to figure out how this guy managed to get into everyone's computers. He'll also send a team of people to investigate how to find this guy."

I nodded. "Good. Get this bastard with everything you have as quickly as you can. No further harm can come to anyone I care about. Since the condo is a mess, get some of Kaelin's things and bring them to the first safety point." I didn't want to say things aloud in case there were ears. The closer this stalker got, the more refined our plans between Luke, Trent, and myself had become to ensure Kaelin's safety.

He nodded. "I'll be out in the hallway if you need anything further, placing a few phone calls and arranging for a departure from here."

Trent reached out his good arm and motioned for Kaelin to be placed beside him in his hospital bed. They'd given him a huge bed, since he was six feet five inches tall—I'm only a few inches shorter than him. "I know you want to hold her and protect her, Van, but I need to hold her right now to know she's fine." Full of worry, he looked up at me with his good eye. "Is she okay?"

I nodded as I picked her up and placed her gently against Trent's uninjured side. It looked like the stalker dropped Trent to the ground and just kept kicking one side of his body. The other side seemed unharmed. She rolled into him and sighed the moment her head hit his chest. I didn't realize just how close and comfortable they were with one another. "The doctor states she's in shock, with her mind overloaded with too much information at one time. She found out you and I are brothers, and then realized you were the one hurt when the hospital called."

I was hesitant to step back and take a seat, when Trent assured me, "I'm still dating Mark, but I care for Kaelin like a sister. When her nightmares flare up, we often snuggle on the sofa or in bed and watch television until she feels safe again. This is our normal, brother."

I took a seat by the bed so I could talk in a whisper as to not wake Kaelin. "What happened? Do you remember?"

Trent nodded, his face full of contempt for his attacker. "I was in the hallway about to open the door, when I got hit in the back of the head with something. I fell onto the ground, and he began kicking me. I tried curling into a ball to protect myself." Filled with apprehension, Trent looked deep into my eyes. "Whoever this guy is, he's relentless in his pursuits of her. He told me to back away from her, to set her free for him to care for, or else I'd pay with my life next time."

I couldn't understand it. "Doesn't he know who you are and that you're dating Mark? Hell, it was plastered all over the tabloids after Dad's death when you came out. Why would he feel threatened by you?"

He tried to shrug his shoulders but moaned in pain. "I don't know, man. I love her. She's family to me." I guess he didn't want to continue talking about things, because he changed the subject. "How'd today go?"

I waved my hand around the room. "How do you think?" Then I realized I was just being a dick. "She took the car you ordered for her. They found no fingerprints on the first delivery, but she managed to get a card off the flower delivery and stuff it in her purse before giving the flowers to Anthony to give to his wife. Marcus was none too pleased. We have no idea whether she still has the card or not or what it said, only that it spooked her."

I twiddled my thumbs for a moment, and then looked up to my older brother. I hated to see him like this. Even when he was at his worst out on the streets, he didn't look like this. Hopefully, this wouldn't affect his career as a model; then again...I could use him back at the company.

"What are you thinking so hard about, bro?"

"How long will it take for you to heal? Will this affect your career as a model, or will you decide to come back to work for the company? When will we catch this asshole? How are we going to protect her?" There was too much going on in my mind right now.

"Our priority is Kaelin—"

His words were interrupted by a moan and slight movement on her part.

We both managed to speak her name softly. "Kaelin?"

Trent ran his good hand up and down her arm and placed a tender kiss on her forehead. "Hey, sleepyhead, are you ready to rejoin the living?"

She didn't open her eyes, only curled into Trent's side more, causing me to be jealous, wishing I was the one she sought comfort from. "Oh, thank goodness. It was all a dream, just another one of my horrific nightmares."

"What was your dream about, sweetie bear?" Trent questioned, looking at me like he wasn't sure what to do. I just shrugged my shoulders and moved my hands in a motion to encourage him to talk. "Come on, tell us."

She took in a deep breath. "You smell off, T-man."

"I've had a rough day and workout," he tried to explain in a round-a-bout way.

That was good enough, apparently, because Kaelin moved on to explain her dream. "It started off with my dad trying to sell me off to one of his associates' sons, then shifted to talking with my favorite client on the webcast and feeling myself get all worked up, and ended with Eagle Eyes threatening me again. I dreamed he found where I lived. At one point while I got dressed, I noticed my camera was on despite knowing I'd turned it off a couple nights ago, and then you'd texted me you'd be late coming back from a photo shoot and to use the driver they hired for you. I was halfway to the car when I was told of a flower delivery, which I imagined was from you, only to discover they were from *him*."

Her body tensed as she explained her "dream."

"Did the flowers have a card? What did it say, sweetie?" Trying to reassure her, Trent held her closer.

She started to shake and her eyes flew open, taking in the surroundings before looking into Trent's face. A shocked gasp escaped her lips. Subconsciously realizing Trent might feel the movement, causing him more pain, she didn't pull away from him. Instead, she looked him over. "Oh my god, what happened? Were you in an accident?" She looked around the room, until her eyes landed on mine, and she looked again at Trent for some kind of explanation. "Where am I?" Then realization struck her, remembering what I told her in the elevator.

Trent and I didn't know what to tell her, how to explain things.

Kaelin began crying. "You getting hurt was all my fault. It was him, Eagle Eyes, wasn't it? This wasn't a dream."

Needing to touch her and comfort her, I started to move toward the bed, but she jumped slightly, so Trent leaned in to her ear and whispered sweet nothings to reassure her.

He spoke just loudly enough so I could make out what he was telling her. "This is not your fault, Kaelin. You can't be responsible for some enamored fool on the internet. He's definitely become an issue, and we should have taken more precautions against him. He's been getting closer to where you live and work over the past week. We realized the potential for a threat and put up some safety measures, but didn't take into account his level of obsession."

Her face was definitely confused as she looked between the two of us. "What do you mean by 'we' and 'taking precautions?' He sent other threats?"

At that moment, the doctor entered, scowling when he saw Kaelin in bed with Trent. I threw the doctor a pleading glance to just overlook it and mouthed the words "Please let it be."

He nodded and then smiled over at the two patients. "How are you feeling, Ms. Richards and Mr. Meyers?" the doctor asked with a smirk on his face.

Kaelin spoke first. "Fine, a little confused though. What happened?"

"You went into shock for a bit. Your mind was overwhelmed by too much going on." He pointed to me. "Mr. Meyers brought you into the hospital and explained that his brother is your roommate and that you'd just learned of him being hurt before passing out."

She nodded in agreement. "Yes, that's right." Then a small blush worked its way up her chest and through her face. "I'm sorry if I worried anyone. That's never happened to me before."

The doctor held up his hand to stop her apologies. "The body can only take so much stress and upheaval at a time. When we've had too much, it happens."

He moved closer to Trent to check his eyes with a penlight and ask him to follow his finger. "How's your head feeling? And the rest of your body? The x-rays didn't show signs of a concussion, but we're not going to rule it out. Your eyes aren't responding to the light like they should, so we'll be checking in on you every hour or so to make sure you're doing fine."

"I'm quite sore and starting to hurt, my arm and ribs especially," Trent admitted sheepishly. He wasn't one to complain about anything; he dealt with things and moved on.

"I'll have the nurse bring in some pain meds to help with the discomfort, along with ice packs for your face, leg, and arm. We need to try and get the swelling to slow down and subside. You're lucky the guy didn't manage to break more than your arm and fracture a couple of ribs. You'll feel some discomfort when you breathe too deeply or try to move too suddenly, so take it easy. Don't hesitate to use the call button for the nurses to help. I know several of them are vying for the chance to help you with anything you need." The doctor smiled amusingly. "They recognize you as the model from that underwear advertisement."

"Please let them know I'm taken." His voice was short and to the point. He hated lots of attention, but I'd always told him to get used to it if he's going to be a model. "So how long do I have to be here?"

The doctor wrote some stuff on his electric tablet. "You'll be here a few days minimum. We want to be able to cast the arm before you leave and make sure your breathing is okay and your pupils are responding appropriately. You will need someone to help care for you when you leave, and you're looking at at least a couple months of recovery." He looked up to Trent and stated pointedly, "The cops want to talk to you. Should I tell them to come back tomorrow for a statement?"

I interjected for a moment. "Our mother and sister will be caring for him once he's discharged. We have a physical therapist and nurse at the ready to help care for any needs he might have."

Trent spoke up. "Give us a few minutes alone, and then the cops can come in to take my statement. I want my brother and roommate here for moral support."

"Okay. I'll let them know and will go ahead and order your meds. I'll have a nurse bring them in after you give your statement." The doctor headed for the door before adding, "I'll be back to check on you in a few hours."

Trent and I uttered our thanks but turned our attention toward Kaelin. He beat me to the punch, asking, "Where's the note from the flowers?"

She was hesitant but looked around, finding her purse on the floor beside my chair and pointing to it.

I picked it up, asking, "May I?"

Her demeanor had become subdued as she nodded.

I opened the bag and found the card crumpled up in some tissue paper.

Trent rubbed his hand up and down her arm as she laid her head on his chest and wept softly. "It's okay, sweetie."

She mumbled something that sounded like "sorry" as I pulled the card out of the envelope. Red immediately clouded my vision.

Trent picked up on my fury and asked for me to read it aloud.

> *I'm coming for you my Mystique –*
> *my Kaelin. You are Mine to claim,*
> *Mine to conquer, Mine to break. I*
> *WILL OWN YOU! I'm always*
> *watching you, my precious slut. – Ea-*
> *gleEyes4U*

Neither Trent nor I was happy about her keeping secret the flowers she'd received earlier that day. I couldn't let her know I'd known all along, thanks to Marcus, that she'd had a note, but I'd need to come clean to her as soon as we got out of here. She explained how she gave the flowers to the doorman to take home to his wife. At least she treated the note like evidence and wrapped it up in some tissue paper to keep any fingerprints intact. I'd hand it over to Luke for analysis later tonight.

This guy was definitely a nut case, and I'd move heaven and earth just to keep her safe. I couldn't explain it, but I cared for her that deeply. I knew we still had a lot to learn about each other, but what she didn't know was how Trent had given me a lot of details about her already. Everything I'd heard, from her kindness to her perseverance toward her degree, made me fall for her a little more. I knew her dad had been an ass toward her, but I didn't know the entire story. Trent would always say we had more in common with her than we realized. I knew my mom and sis loved her; they pretty much adopted her into the family when he took her there for dinner one night.

You need to come clean about everything you know about her, along with how. My subconscious was right, but how did I tell her without her freaking out and running? We definitely needed to talk, and the first place we were headed would provide us ample opportunity, since we'd be confined in close quarters for a while.

Chapter 4

Kaelin

I COULDN'T LOOK AT either of them. Trent was in here and in pain because of me. I hadn't texted him about the threat that came today. I should've said something, but I didn't. But then again...I looked up at him as tears still poured down my face. "You never did answer my questions about 'we' and 'precautions.'"

A tissue showed up in my line of sight. I looked over to see Van with a box of tissues at the ready and a look of apology and sadness etched on his face. I took the tissue from his hand and began drying my tears. Van spoke up first. "Trent asked for my help and thoughts in keeping you safe. The threats started coming a little over a week ago, though I know he's been threatening you a lot longer online. He's done the same with me, too, even blowing up my computers with viruses and demanding I stay away from you."

I was shocked to know my stalker had extended to him, too. Trent was about to speak—to tell me what, I didn't know—when the police knocked and entered.

There were two policemen asking Trent questions left and right. I became fearful when they asked why I had a stalker and why I hadn't reported it. Thankfully, my roomie had my back. "She's not sure who this guy is. We only know that he's become more and more obsessed with her and started sending threats first online and then to our condo complex. My brother's assistant has all the information you'll need regarding the threats."

When they were busy conferring with one another, Trent whispered in my ear, "Van and Luke will only let them have what's necessary to start an investigation. No one will know your other persona or what you do on the side. That's our little secret."

The police asked Trent quite a few questions. I shivered every time he recounted a kick or punch to his body and the statements that psychopath uttered, claiming I was his and that no one else could look at me or be near me; I was his property. *As if! I'm nobody's property. But now I was scared for my life and the people around me.*

The nurse came in to dismiss the police, who were wrapping up anyway. She pushed them out of the room while announcing Trent needed his rest and his pills. I looked up at Trent and watched him take his meds. Seeing the pain etched on his face and the continued swelling of his eye made me wince.

The nurse flirted with him for a bit, asking first if I was his girlfriend and smiling when I said I wasn't. She was quite friendly, leaving only when he was settled with several ice packs on him. "Just buzz me if you need anything else; otherwise, I'll check on you in an hour to see how your pupils are responding." Trent mumbled something incoherently at the idea, so she stated, "Doctor's orders."

She'd tried to push us out of the room, but he refused to let us go yet, citing he needed to tell us a few things first. Once she'd cleared the room, he pulled me closer with his good arm. "I don't know how long I have before these pills take effect, so I'll make this quick. I want you to go with Van. You can trust him with your life. He's been smitten with you for some time now. I kept your secret, though. He only knew I helped someone who had been down on their luck like I was when Dad kicked me out on the streets. Van knew my roommate was Mystique, but he never knew it was you, Kaelin. I didn't know he kept watching you online until recently, when you were threatened one day. He wanted to ensure you were safe, so he called me to check on you."

Trent yawned and started to draw out his words. The meds were definitely kicking in. "I trust my brother with my life, and I know I can trust him with yours. Go with him. You both need to have a good talk. He will fill in the gaps and answer all your questions." His arm started to loosen its hold on me, and his breathing started to level out, indicating he was close to sleep. His words were but a whisper. "He loves you. Trust him. Love you, sweetie bear..."

A soft snore escaped Trent's lips. It was good to see him breathing more easily and resting. He'd been talking but struggling a little between some words; I imagine from his ribs. Thankfully, they were only cracked and not broken. I started to try and move from the bed, when Van laid a hand on my shoulder. "Don't move, Kaelin. You might jostle the bed and cause him more pain than if I just lifted you out."

I nodded and felt his arms reach up under my legs and around my back. I placed my arms around his neck to help anchor myself to him as he lifted me up and away from Trent. He didn't put me down right away; instead, he gave me a squeeze and held me tightly to his chest before breathing in the scent of my hair. I still wasn't used to Van acting this way toward me. I'm a little spooked, I admit. We were friends in class and worked well together both on assignments and at work, but to one minute be looking over financials and the next be pushed up against the wall kissing like crazy—and boy could he kiss, taking my breath away and making me forget about my troubles for a moment—was uncharted territory, and I wasn't sure how to respond. I tensed a bit, causing his face to show concern.

"Do you want me to carry you, or do you feel you're steady enough to walk?"

I released my arms from around his neck. I couldn't find the right words to convey that I was unsure how to act and that the idea of spending time alone with him over the next days, or however long it took to find this fiend, scared the shit out of me. He must've read my mind, and I'm sure my face showed how uncomfortable I was, so he set me down but kept his hands close by to test my ability to stand on my own.

I managed to step back and lean over the bed slightly to place a small kiss on the unaffected side of Trent's face. "Love you back, T-man. I'll check up on you soon and do anything you ask. If you say I can trust him, I'll try, just for you."

I hated leaving Trent at the hospital. Every time I looked at his poor, battered face and the bruises on his arms and neck, I wished I could trade places with him.

I told him that earlier, but he reminded me I might not be alive had I been the one to come home first. The stalker had definitely stepped up his game on things and went from being a nuisance to a definite threat with violent tendencies.

It was agreed that I would go with Van, who had a secret location that only a handful of people knew about. He held on to my waist as he led me toward the door. After handing me my purse, he explained that the place we were headed to would be cramped, and I'd have to do most of my schoolwork via computer, which, thankfully, I'd completed most of the assignments already, with the exception of the finals and a couple of term papers. Apparently, he had connections at the campus and could arrange that for each of us.

You could imagine my surprise when we left Trent's room and I saw someone who could pass as my doppelganger. Luke held up both hands to try and calm me as he explained. "Your stalker thinks you're shaken up and that you'll probably avoid going home for a few days, especially since the police are still processing evidence. We hired Cat Anderson, of Titan Security, to run your routine for the next few days to see if we can expose a weakness. We'd like to try and avoid you going back online and doing further webcasts if possible. We'll discuss that option when and if necessary."

I must have blushed every possible shade of red in the hallway of the hospital. Van leaned in and whispered, "Only Trent knew for the longest time. I figured it out just recently, but I had to explain things to Luke in order to get his help in capturing this stalker. He's the only other one who knows, not even the police know the full story. Your secret is safe with us."

Luke, donning a cap and glasses to hide his red hair, led us to a side entrance of the hospital where he'd parked a different vehicle than we'd arrived in. The stress and anxiety of the day caught up to me as the rocking motion of the town car we were in lulled me to sleep. I woke up to the rub of Van's hand up and down my arm.

"Kaelin, honey, we're here."

I was disoriented, noting we were in some form of underground garage. "Where are we?" Had we traveled outside the city? Were we in a safe house of some sort? "What's going on?"

Van said nothing as Luke punched in a code to unlock a hidden panel to the side of what looked like a door. I was shocked to see the doors open to a private elevator, which needed another set of codes before the metal doors opened and the lights came on. *Was this the same elevator as we'd taken earlier? Were we going back to the office?*

Luke nodded to Van. "Text me to let me know you're secure and locked down for the evening. I'll have my boys working through the night, adding to the security of the building, and seeing what our contacts, along with Titan Security, can do to broaden the search."

I watched as Van took out a special key that activated the panel within the elevator. "Thanks for all your help today, buddy. Do whatever is necessary to ensure the safety of my family and Kaelin. No expense is to be spared. You have the ball on this one; run with it."

Luke disappeared into the shadows as Van closed the doors and punched in some digits to get the elevator moving. "This is a private elevator which only I have access to at this point, but I'll make sure a key and your own personal code are provided to you tomorrow. In the event of an emergency, this elevator also functions as a safe room. It can be deactivated from within and can't be restarted without a special authorization code."

The doors opened into a small one-bedroom apartment with an open floor plan. The place looked to be modernized with the latest stainless steel appliances, white cabinets, and dark marble countertops in the kitchen. There was a small table for eating, right next to a small gathering area with a couple of seats, a small sofa, a flat screen television, a couple of end tables, and a coffee table. All the tones were neutral grays, whites, blacks, with some subtle touches of blues and gold thrown in here and there. The opposite side of the room held a king-size bed up on a platform with nightstands next to it. Off to the side of the bed was an open door to a bathroom and a few closed doors beyond that—maybe a closet. The place was definitely a bachelor pad of sorts. The only things missing were windows, which was odd.

I looked over to Van after feeling his hand squeezing mine in reassurance. "Where are we?"

He walked to a large painting on the wall and pulled down a lever hidden in the frame. I watched in awe as the piece of artwork disappeared into the wall, revealing a wall of monitors and a few buttons. The monitors had views from all over the inside of the Meyers' building.

Van pressed a button, and the wall slid open just enough for him to slip through into another room. He poked his head back through. "Are you coming?"

He grabbed hold of my hand and pulled me through the opening of his private apartment and right into his office. The bookcases were open, exposing the elevator we'd taken down earlier in the evening.

I had to smile and laugh. "We always wondered why we never saw the new CEO enter or leave his office, and we never understood how you knew what was going on within the departments, but it all makes sense now."

"I couldn't let people know that Van Ellings and Donovan Meyers were one and the same. Not until I graduated from the master's program, anyhow. Always keeping me hidden from everyone, Dad never let me come up the regular elevators. I only had interaction with the board members and a few of the managers." He laughed a bit before adding, "Damn fool thought they'd run all over me if they knew who I was. He also insisted on me slicking my hair back and wearing overpriced suits, but as soon as he was gone, I took on my own style. I wanted to fit in, not stand out."

So he had daddy issues too. "Sadly, I can relate. I wasn't allowed to wear what I wanted either, always being dictated to. My sister was able to wear anything she wanted, while I got the consignment shop specials and purchases off discount racks. He didn't know mom and her parents slipped me clothing from time to time. I always had to convince him it came from a secondhand store."

He motioned for me to walk back into the apartment. I didn't pay much attention to my surroundings, instead wondering, "Where did this come from? How long have you been living here?"

Van leaned against the opposite side of the door, while I took the wall by the doorframe. "I didn't know this room and the separate elevator existed until after my father passed. I was redoing the office to make it more inviting to work in, because the former décor was rather morbid and depressing. I replaced some of the paintings and was in the process of removing the one with the lever, when I realized it wouldn't budge, it controls entry and exit into this room on each side of the wall. On further inspection, I found this place, but not in its current state."

He ended with that, forcing me to ask, "Okay, I'll bite. What was in here?"

"Have you ever heard of BDSM rooms or sex dungeons?" A small smile played on his lips.

He must be joking around with me and trying to lighten the mood. I nodded. "And?"

"I didn't know the old man was into such things. Some of the equipment he had in here scared the freaking shit out of me. I had to ask for help with getting the unwanted items out of here, and then anonymously donated it to a local sex club—The Shanty. They welcomed it, given they're growing so large, and have plans to open up a new club to appeal to people our age."

"You're serious. He actually had that junk in here?" I thought he was pulling my leg, but was he?

Van nodded. "I had been living at home with my family, because Dad wanted to keep a close eye on me, but after he died and I discovered this hidden gem, I rented a furnished place close to here while they completely gutted and redid this place. It offered me the opportunity to stay close to the campus for classes during the week and to just as easily be at the office to work. I often worked long hours into the night. My only stress relief was working out at the gym on the third floor...or watching you as Mystique."

My eyes started to droop, and my mind was definitely beginning to wander. He lifted me up into his arms and walked me over to the bed. I tried wiggling free. "I can walk on my own, Van."

He smirked before setting me on the side of the bed, which ran parallel to the bathroom. He sat down beside me and pointed everything out. "As you see, the bathroom is over there; you'll have a door for privacy. There are extra linens, and I had my men move your personal items into their respective locations within the bathroom.   Feel free to poke through the drawers to find whatever you need."

Van motioned toward a set of double doors to the right of the bathroom. "Good portions of your clothes and shoes have been placed into one side of the closet. Trent and I thought it wise to give the impression you were still living at his condo, so we didn't grab everything."

He hid his face and spoke contritely. "My brother and I have been trying to figure out this stalker of yours for a while now. Since he upped the ante, Trent gave me a list of your sizes, and I have a new selection of casual to dress attire waiting for your use. We hoped this day wouldn't come, where we needed to hide you, but it has. My apologies we couldn't figure this mess out and get it resolved sooner."

I moved my hand to rest atop his on the bed and gave it a squeeze, causing him to look up at me. "I still don't know how I didn't notice the slight resemblance between you and your brother. Regardless, I appreciate everything you're doing to keep me safe."

He leaned forward to give me a peck on the cheek. "Thanks, my sweet angel, that means a lot coming from you. Since you're my guest, you can have the bed, and I'll sleep over on the sofa."

I glanced over at the sofa and noticed how small and uncomfortable it would probably be. "Please tell me it's a pull-out sleeper."

He shook his head. "Sadly, no, but I promised I'd be every bit the gentleman. While I do admit I'm attracted to your body, I'm also fascinated in the way you think. I won't touch you inappropriately, only offering a shoulder the lean on or a hug for support. If you wish for anything more than that, you'll have to tell me what you desire."

I could feel my eyelids starting to droop again and was having a hard time holding my head up.

"I have a t-shirt and shorts waiting for you to change into if you'd like."

Feeling confused, I looked over and asked, "How did you...?" Realization dawned on me. "Trent must've told you my sleeping preferences."

He didn't say anything, just nodded. I got up and was about to close the door to change, when I questioned, "When exactly did you figure out that Mystique and I were one and the same?"

Van shook his head. "I've known for a bit but wasn't sure how to approach you to discuss things. I can guarantee that my brother never divulged your identity to me." He paused as I leaned further into the door, feeling like I could fall over at any moment. "Kaelin, you're about to fall over. Please get some sleep while my security guys go over some of the details so we get a clearer picture of what we're dealing with, and we can discuss everything else at that time. We've both had a traumatic day filled with ups and downs."

I started to argue, but he got up off the bed, walked over to me, and pinched my lips shut.

"Let's rest first. We can talk later, filling in all the gaps of our respective stories. I would say boss's or even your master's orders; however, I'm quite attached to my groin and don't think I'd like the taste of nuts this time at night."

He was right. I closed the door and nearly fell over removing my clothing and putting on my comfort sleepwear. Trent knew me well, and I knew he'd talked to his brother about me. I just never realized who his brother was or how comfortable my friendship with Van had become. Maybe he was more than a friend. Only time would tell.

When I finished up in the bathroom, I discovered Van in a t-shirt and boxers, and he had the sofa already made up with a pillow and blanket. I felt a bit insecure in my shorts and comfy t-shirt. I was used to being fully dressed around him and seeing him in regular clothes. *He's seen you naked as Mystique, get over it already. That's true, but I've never seen a man with this little clothing on—not one I had some sort of feelings for.*

"Everything okay, angel?" Van asked cautiously.

I could feel the blush spreading up my neck and face. Trying to hide it, I turned away from him, only to feel his warmth come up against my back as he moved my hair aside and kissed my neck.

"What's wrong? Why are you blushing?"

My voice was cracking with nerves as I admitted, "I've never seen a man, other than my dad and your brother, in their nightwear."

His arms encircled me, giving me a squeeze. "Really? Never?"

I shook my head. "No."

His lips pressed against my neck, just below my ear, as he whispered, "It's only me. You know I won't hurt you, right?"

I nodded.

He kept his arms around me as he walked me toward the bed, only releasing me to pull down the covers and tuck me in. He pressed a small kiss to my forehead. "Sweet dreams, my angel."

I watched him walk over to the kitchen and turn on the stove light.

"There are no windows in here, so it gets super dark. I'll leave this on for a little light. That way, if you need anything in the night, you'll know where to look. The bathroom has a nightlight that comes on when the lights go out, which will help as well."

I couldn't help but smile. He was going overboard to make sure I was okay and comfortable. I watched as he headed to the bathroom to brush his teeth. "In case I'm asleep when you get out of there, thank you. I don't know what I'd do without you and Trent in my life."

Van smiled at me. "Ditto, angel, ditto."

The moment I turned on my side, the day's weariness hit me like a two-ton wall. I was out cold.

Chapter 5

Kaelin

"*GET THE HELL OUT of my house and NEVER come back!*" My father yelled as I walked away. "*You're nothing to me, never have been, never will be.*"

The recollection switched from the hazy image of the night I left home to that of my coworker attacking me at work. "*Come on now, Kaelin, you know you want me. I can see the way you look at me. The way you come into my office every day when your work is completed.*"

I began feeling restless knowing what was coming next, how I'd stayed late at work to speak to the boss's son about an issue with my paycheck. One minute we were talking calmly, and the next, he was talking dirty to me and trying to force himself on me.

"*You want me. The way you look at my desk, this table; you want me to bend you over them and take you with everything I have.*" He trapped me against his desk with his hands as his leg tried to seek purchase between mine. "*I'm told you're a virgin. I can't wait to see if my source is right. I want to test the goods now, not wait until our deal is complete. I'd love a taste of your nice virgin center—so tight and ready to wrap around my hardened cock.*" He kept trying to kiss me, but I kept ducking to avoid him.

As he raised his arm toward me, I slipped underneath it and bolted for the door. He grabbed hold of my hair to pull me back, but I twisted away, only to be grabbed again. I made one attempt after another for the door. My clothes were torn in various places, but no way was I going to give up. The last attempt, he tripped but managed to grab my ankle and bring me down as well. He quickly straddled my body and forced a kiss on me. The only way to get out of this was to play to his advances, so I did...and that's when I left him howling on the floor, grabbing hold of his nuts that were hopefully lodged into his throat.

"You're nothing but a teasing whore. Don't expect to come back to work here tomorrow. You're fired! And tell your father the deal's off. I want my money back."

I ran and kept running. Not wanting to give him the satisfaction, I didn't reply, even though I wasn't sure what my dad had to do with all this. I needed shelter and reassurance from my mom, but I wouldn't find that, not immediately; instead, I found my father, who insisted I go back to that beast. How could he? But I choose to leave. I'd rather be on my own.

The murky image of my memory twisted to the voice of my stalker. *"You're mine. I own you, slut."*

I heard screaming in the background. Who was that and where was it coming from? I felt the Earth shaking around me, and then I realized I was being shaken. I was the one screaming.

"Wake up, Kaelin. You're having a nightmare."

My eyes popped open as my shaking body shot up straight in bed. Warm arms and a familiar scent encased me...Trent. But then my mind and the visual of my surroundings brought everything to light. I started to push away, when Van held me even tighter. "It's just me, angel. It's just Van. I've got you. You were having a bad dream. Trent told me you had these from time to time."

I shook my head. No, it wasn't a bad dream. It was memories of my life, things that happened to me. I don't know if any amount of happiness could eradicate them.

Van ran his hands over my back in a reassuring manner while rocking me back and forth—something my mom used to do when I had a frightening dream. After a while I calmed down, and he pulled back a bit, running his hand over my face to push away the hair and dry the tears. His voice was soft. "Do you want to talk about it? Trent told me sometimes that helps you fall back to sleep."

I'd been scared when I told Trent, but he had a similar issue with his father and, therefore, understood and offered sympathy. I had no idea how Van would take it. He did have to deal with the same beast as Trent, so maybe he'd understand, too. There was only one way to find out. If he truly wanted to get to know me, he needed to know my past.

Trying to ready myself and choose my words carefully, I took a deep breath. "My father told me, 'You have two options: Number one, you follow the career path I was forced to give up when you came along and give me half of whatever you earn in life, but if you decide to pick your own career path, I'll refuse to pay for it. Number two, you forget about school and accept the monetary deal I struck with Robert Chadwick to marry his son, Roger, and become subservient, doing everything you are ordered to do, being the perfect trophy wife—though why he finds you attractive I'll never know. There are no other options.'"

Taking a deep breath in and shuttering at the memories, I continued. "That's where he was wrong. I grabbed my purse and walked out into the streets with my tattered clothes, never to return to his house.

"I think I'd shocked the hell out of him with my audacity, as he yelled out, 'Your ATM card will no longer be effective in a few hours, thanks to me insisting you put me on your account, and your cell phone will be turned off immedia tely.'"

Van's face remained a mask, but I noticed his hands clenching the sheets so tightly his knuckles were becoming white. His voice was laced with fury as he asked as calmly as possible, "What led up to this ultimatum?"

I took a deep breath in, running the events of that day through my mind and wondering if I did anything to bring about Roger's actions at the office. I only ever told this to Trent and my mom, no one else until now. I tried to tell my sister, but she didn't believe me and called me a liar. As I opened up to Van, I felt him move to put his arm around me and pull me closer to his side, where I could cry on his shoulder as the events of that day unfolded through my words.

"I was tired of putting up with my father taking complete control of my life. He treated my sister, Bethany, like a queen, giving her everything she ever wanted. I was treated like the unwanted stepchild, yet I was his firstborn. Cinderella had a better deal than I did.

"Dad heaped all his mistakes in life on me and expected me to pay for them. He kept me from going back to school, because I received one B—the rest A's—and he forced me to work for his buddy's computer company, and then took the majority of my paycheck. I complained to Dad about it, but he insisted I pay for room and board while under his roof. I wanted to complain to my mother, since she was the only one to show me mercy, but I was threatened."

Van put his other arm around me to hold me close, but I felt him tense. "What. Did. He. Do?" The words were enunciated with just enough restraint not to scare me.

"I was to do as he said or he threatened to hurt my mother. I didn't ask for details, but I'd seen him get pissed off at other people before, even hitting them, myself included." After several hits, I soon learned never to question him again; although, this time I didn't care.

"My fury had the better of me, so I went to Roger; he had always been nice to me. We spent a lot of time together at work, even sharing lunch at times, and he was the boss's son. Not knowing about the deal our fathers had struck, I figured Roger could help me."

I started to shake in Van's arms, and then felt him lift me onto his lap and cradle me like a child while he rubbed soothing circles up and down my back. "Take your time, honey. We're safely hidden away from the world for as long as we need to be, to not only catch your stalker, but to help your mother bring your father to justice."

Van handed me a bottle of water from the nightstand and asked me to take a few sips. *I guess he put it there before going to bed in case I needed some during the night. Boy, this guy was thoughtful.*

A few minutes passed before I got up enough courage to continue. "I should've known Mr. Chadwick and his son, Roger, were part of my dad's crazy scheme. Roger told me my father made a tentative deal with them: if they could break my spirit and make me give up on the life I wanted, he could have me—for a price—because my father no longer wanted to claim me as his daughter and he'd amassed some substantial gambling debts, so I was being sold for a price."

I pulled back, looking into Van's eyes, only to see pity. I put my hand on his chest and could feel his heart racing. "Don't pity me, Van. Roger needed a trophy wife, and for some strange reason, he wanted me. He thought I'd given up when I found out about my paycheck going to an account my father set up without my mother's knowledge, providing me little to live off of. They all thought they'd break me, but they didn't." I smiled lasciviously. "I made the mistake of approaching him after work while we were alone in the office. Forcing me into a corner and ripping my top, he tried to dominate me. He didn't suspect I'd taken a class in self-defense my first year at college."

A small laugh bubbled up from Van's chest. "And?"

"I let him get close, led him to believe I was falling for his charms, and then I punched my knee up so hard into his groin, I'm sure he was tasting his own nutsack. I ran as quickly as I could as he called me every filthy name under the sun."

A smile spread across Van's face as he shook his head from side to side in disbelief. "I knew there was a reason I was drawn to you; it's your fire and spirit that captivate me, but your mind and body blow me away. I love feistiness in a person."

I eased back on his lap after realizing the compromising position we were in and feeling his arousal begin to stiffen under my backside. "Whoa there, buddy. I thought you promised your brother you'd be the perfect gentleman while watching out for me."

He held both hands up in surrender. "I'll admit, I've always been fascinated by you, Kaelin, but you've entranced me with just being you and with your performances as Mystique. I'm having a hard time coming to terms that you are one and the same." He looked down at his crotch. "Sorry, angel, but my other head sometimes has a mind of its own. I can't help that you arouse me in ways no other female has ever done."

I'd forgotten all about Van revealing how he'd figured out I was Mystique and how he'd been the one that had captured my heart with his titillating voice and dominant personality online as DaLuvMaster. I hated that he'd used his nickname and false last name to hide his identity from our fellow classmates at school; although, I could understand why. If everyone knew he was the head of a multibillion-dollar company, who invested money into smaller companies and helped market new ideas, every individual on campus with an idea would've hit Van up. Who would have thought that Van Ellings was actually Donovan Lane Meyers, the new CEO of Meyers Corporation? *OMG...He had his initials right in his onscreen name the whole time.*

I wanted to change the subject, when my stomach started to rumble. I found an electric clock by the side of the bed showing it was 2 a.m. I don't recall eating anything for breakfast, only having the lunch Luke got for us in Van's office, and then racing off to the hospital.

"Are you hungry? I know I am. I woke up about half an hour ago feeling hungry, wanting to get something to eat but not wanting to make noise and wake you, so I laid there for a few minutes until I heard you start to roll around in bed," Van offered.

I nodded and moved off his lap, his arms reluctant to let me go. "Show me the kitchen, and I can fix us a little something to eat."

He grabbed hold of my hand and turned a couple lights on as we headed to see what was available to eat. He pulled out a barstool and surprised me by picking me up and putting me on the seat. Before I could argue, his finger was over my lip. "This is my place, and you're my guest, so let me serve you. You're time of catering to others' needs is going to end. It's on your terms, not everyone else's, from now on, understood?"

I didn't know what to say. I was so used to serving other people in life and in work that this felt odd to me. "But..."

He put his hands on his hips, bringing to my attention the evidence of his arousal slowly starting to wane. "No buts, Kaelin." His face began to blush a bit. "Well, there is only one butt I'll consider, and that's yours, angel."

The flirt. I let my eyes carry over his body from top to bottom before looking him in the eyes and shrugging. "Only time will tell, Van." I tried to act indifferent, but I think he knew the attraction was mutual.

Van opened the fridge and freezer areas to scan the shelves. "I have the makings for grilled cheese sandwiches and tomato soup."

I couldn't help myself when I blurted out, "Yum." Then I wondered aloud, "You eat everyday food? I know Trent eats it on occasion, but it's rare with his photo shoots and all. We mainly stick to tons of veggies and lean proteins at our place."

He laughed and smiled at me as he dug the ingredients out of the fridge and cupboards. "Just because our family is well-off, doesn't mean we don't enjoy the simple pleasures in life. Besides, one grows tired of fancy foods after a while. Just ask my mother; she hates anything to do with *high society* anymore and detests luxurious dinners except on special occasion."

Thinking back on meeting Trent and Van's mom, I smiled for the first time that day. She was very welcoming and someone a complete one hundred and eighty degrees from what I'd expected.

"I knew you had a smile in there somewhere. What was the pleasant memory you just had?" he asked inquisitively.

I wasn't quite sure how to start, but the moment my mouth opened, the words began pouring out. "I'd had a rough day, thanks to my maniac stalker. Trent came home in a panic to check on me, and then talked me into going to his mom's for dinner. Apparently, they were celebrating your sister's divorce. He'd called his brother..." I looked at Van for a moment, and I revised it. "I guess I should say, he called *you* to verify you weren't coming to dinner." I laughed for a minute when realization dawned on me. "So that's why he never wanted the two of us to meet."

Van just nodded and continued preparing our late-night snack. I was mesmerized by the musculature that lay underneath his t-shirt. Every twist and turn of his body highlighted a different muscle group, showing just how ripped he was. Trent was tall and lean, like a swimmer's body structure, while Van...he must've been an athlete at some point; his muscles were ripped. I could only imagine what was underneath on the front. Did he have a six- or an eight-pack? And why the hell was I thinking this. *You like him. Deal with it.*

He was standing there smiling at me. "See something you like?"

I felt the blush starting before he even chuckled. "Sorry, just noticing the differences between you and Trent. You have more definition in your muscles."

I shook my head to counter the draw his body had on me. "I got off subject about dinner with your mom. I guess you'd had a dinner meeting here in town, so Trent drove us to your mother's. She was happy as a lark and three sheets to the wind with drink.

"I'd been so nervous about meeting her and your sister but found them very down-to-earth. I thought we'd be dining on something extravagant that I might not like to eat and instead was surprised to see roast beef with all the trimmings."

Van finished up at the stove and then placed two bowls of soup and two grilled cheese sandwiches on the bar area in front of our seats. "I have some soda, tea, and water. What's your preference?" Before I could answer, he grabbed two glasses that were already filled with unsweetened iced tea.

"How did you...?" Then realization dawned on me. He'd known at lunch, too. He'd either been paying very close attention to everything I'd done, or Trent had told him. "Trent?" I asked curiously.

Van shook his head. "Every time we worked on assignments together after class, you were sipping either a café mocha or an unsweetened iced tea. See, I told you I paid attention to you."

I laughed as he took the seat beside me while caressing my arm and sending shivers up and down my spine. He motioned for me to dig in before adding, rather boldly, "I'd like to hear the rest of your story, because I know I can fill in some gaps with it."

"Your family was so nice. I expected, no offense, snooty and conceited. My dad, his siblings, and their friends were all that way." Realizing how rude I sounded, I put my hand over my mouth in horror. I regretted saying the pretentious comment the moment it slipped from my lips.

"My father was showy. Whenever he was away for business or spent the night in town for 'work'" —he made air quotes with his hands, insinuating that it was something other than work—"we had simpler foods like grilled cheese sandwiches, mac and cheese, and even burgers, which were strictly forbidden with my father around. I guess you could say my mom beats to a different drum, like the rest of us. We all seem to have her spirit rather than father's domineering persona. She's been showing more and more of her true nature since our father died. It's brought our family back to life."

I nodded in agreement. "Your mother was singing the praises of being a free woman and so was your sister. I relayed the story of my father trying to force my hand in marriage—leaving out the part of me being sold—and how he'd managed to have my mother thrown from her own home and her bank accounts temporarily frozen while he drained most of them. She was spending a fortune trying to request a divorce and getting nowhere. Your mom offered assistance to find dirt on the..." I had to think for a moment on the exact words she used that night.

Having just taken a sip of his tea, Van spoke up. "The pompous ass of magnanimous proportions?"

The way he said it was so comical I laughed. Wait a minute. "How did you know what she said? You weren't even there."

"I wasn't supposed to be there, angel, but my dinner meeting was rescheduled at the last minute, so I figured I'd join you. I was hoping, since Trent said he was taking his roommate, I'd finally get a sneak peek of the elusive Mystique."

My head was feeling a bit fuzzy, when Van reached for my sandwich and held it for me. "Take a bite, love. Our energy's depleted from missing dinner and having everything to deal with today."

I did as he suggested. Maybe I was off because of the events of the day or maybe... "Is that how you figured out who I was?"

He nodded. "We'd had a session earlier that day resulting in Eagle Eyes trashing the first laptop. He'd stepped up his game, because up until that day, he'd just pushed me out of the session. I'd been able to get back in the room within minutes to check on you to make sure you were okay, but this time I couldn't, not until I had another computer, and by that time, you weren't there, so I panicked and called Trent to check on you. That's when he found out I was still watching you."

I took a few spoonfuls of soup, before wondering, "Was Trent mad that you were watching me? He seemed upset that day when he came home and found me crying in the bathtub and trying to soak off the fake tattoos."

He shook his head. "I have to confess something to you, and I'm not sure you're going to like it."

I hadn't a clue what he was talking about. "I'll try to keep an open mind. Just know I value trust and honesty above all else. I don't like things going on behind my back or someone planning my life for me, controlling me." I looked him in the eyes. "It's hard enough for me to be here when I know Trent is hurt. I'm giving you my trust because you've always been kind to me, and your brother said I would be safe with you."

He brushed the back of his knuckles against the side of my face. "I'm the same way, angel. Trust is hard for me, too, especially after dealing with my father. I'm sure Trent filled you in on some things, but not all. Father was pure evil.

"I guess that's why I'm so drawn to you, Kaelin. We share more in common than you'd believe."

I reached up turning his hand around so he could cradle my face. "Sounds like our dads were cut from the same cloth, so to speak. Now what were you about to tell me that had you running off on a tangent?"

He swallowed hard, not wanting to let go of my face. "You know how Trent turned to someone he knew for advice on setting up your webcast?"

I nodded, not liking where this was headed.

"It was me. I hate to admit it, but he knew I watched a lot of porn to de-stress and find some relief. I'm not proud of watching it, but father wouldn't let me date anyone I wanted to, only those he approved. As a result of my viewing tendencies, I knew the way to phrase what you wanted to offer to your clients, what your hard and soft limits were—one of which was keeping your virtue intact—and what to charge. We used one of the computer services we reserved for special projects to help make your IPA address untraceable and your signal bounce all over creation so no one could track it." He stopped to lift his glass of tea. I noticed his hand was shaking with nervous energy, almost sloshing the tea onto the counter.

He was avoiding finishing the story, so I finally asked, "Is there more? So far I'm okay with what you've told me. Truthfully, I'm relieved to know Trent kept it close to home, so to speak, without everyone knowing my business."

Van cleared his throat. "Trent came up with the faux persona, while I suggested various background and set changes to make it look like you were all over the U.S. and the world. I also suggested keeping your voice disguised by using a talk-to-text program, where you could hear them, but they couldn't hear you, only read your responses.

"You started your webcast, but there wasn't much profit at first, so my brother asked me to create a screen name so I could log in to your site and make suggestions on how you could better your performances and draw in more crowds."

My mind started running through the list of names I'd seen pop up in the beginning. Eagle Eyes came online within the first month, but there was one or two that came, stayed for several weeks, and then suddenly disappeared. I looked over at Van. My eyes grew as wide as saucers when I honed in on a name. "Lustful Intent? That was you?"

Flushing a little, he nodded but didn't say anything. *He's handsome already; does he have to look sexier when he blushes?*

"I always wondered what happened to him. I enjoyed our talks." Okay, now I felt confused. "Why did you leave?"

"I noticed your webcast was doing well and had promised Trent I'd leave when you no longer needed my suggestions." He let his hand slip from my face and onto his lap. With his face looking down at the counter, he continued explaining. "I couldn't stay away from you. Every night in my dreams, there you were as Mystique, but also as Kaelin. I guess my subconscious knew, but I wasn't sure why I was drawn to both of you, so I came back as DaLuvMaster." Van glanced up for a brief moment. "I guess I wanted you to know it was me, because I put my initials right into my name. It was a long shot, though, since you only knew me as Van Ellings. I rarely drink alcohol, I don't smoke or do drugs, and I've never had an addiction...until I met you." His eyes lifted until they met mine.

I hadn't realized the intensity of his blue eyes before now. They were like two clear pools of water, crystal clear in the center and darkened around the edges with burning desire. I could easily get lost in his eyes. Heck, I could get lost in his whole body.

Van inherited his coloring from his mother. His hair was dark brown with deep-golden highlights. He was a cross between my favorite actors Paul Wesley and Chris Pine. Favoring his father, however, was Trent, with his emerald green eyes and really dark hair. He was drop-dead gorgeous and easily becoming a big-time model.

No one affected me the way Van did. His caring personality and sensual voice made my body smolder to the point of need, and no one's ever made me come with his words, until Van.

His hand touched my shoulder gently. "Kaelin?"

I'd gotten lost in my fantasies again. I took a sip of tea, trying to cool the heat that built in my belly every time he touched me. "An addiction?" I shrugged my shoulders, not quite comprehending what he was saying.

His face inched closer to mine, causing my heart rate to speed up. His eyes were serious, and then he began talking in that voice—the one he used as DaLuvMaster—that affects me deep in my core. "I crave you. I had to see you in class during the day to be close to you, Kaelin, and I would frequent the coffee shop during the hours you worked. Then in the afternoon, if things got hard to deal with, I'd take a break to watch some of your earlier timed webcasts, but at night I couldn't sleep until I'd wished Mystique a goodnight." He placed a gentle kiss on each side of my lips. When I didn't fight him, he whispered, "I only feel settled when I'm around you. You're my air, my breath, my very soul. I know I must sound mad, but I care so deeply for you that I can't stay away."

I opened my mouth to respond but nothing came out. His confession managed to leave me speechless. Van saw this as an opportunity; he slowly and gently placed his lips on mine, building the passion with each touch of his mouth. I let him inside, allowing our tongues to caress one another. I was lost in the moment, letting my mind relax for the first time in years, when he pulled away. "I'm sorry. I shouldn't have."

I grabbed hold of his face with both hands. "We both seem to be on uncharted grounds when it comes to dating. I'm not quite sure how to respond to your admission. Apparently, you know a lot more about me than I do about you. I have several questions and would like to get to know you better. Did you have any clue I was Mystique prior to that night at your mom's house? And why didn't I see you there?"

"You'd dropped your pencil in class a couple times and bent to pick it up, which revealed bits and pieces of something on your skin. I kept trying to picture what it was and finally concluded it was from a fake tattoo you'd tried to wash off. So I had my suspicions, but that night at my mom's confirmed it."

He sat back in his seat and grabbed my hands. "I listened in on the story about your dad and how your mom was trying to fight to get her money and items back. I was worried Trent would be upset with me for showing up, and I knew you'd already had a bad day with Eagle Eyes and didn't need any more stress, so I left." Van jumped in his seat and his face lit up. "I almost forgot. My mom's private investigator compiled quite the list against your dad, including him cheating, some criminal activity, and gambling. He's been quite naughty. The PI's about ready to anonymously hand it over to your mom, along with some cash from my mother to help her fight for her freedom."

My heart was overjoyed to hear that my mom was going to be able to rid herself of my father. I knew my sister would stick beside him no matter what, since she's a "daddy's girl." I just wish he'd never married my mom in the first place. Life might have turned out better for us, but then again, it wouldn't have led me to Trent, Van, or the Meyers family.

I began to yawn while Van carried on with words of promise and hope that we'd finally be rid of my father, find the stalker, and get our lives back in order. I was half listening to what he was saying, when I began floating through the room in his arms, with my head perched against his shoulder as he carried me over to bed and placed me under the covers.

He kissed my forehead goodnight and turned to leave.

"Don't go," I begged. "Trent usually curls up in bed with me or on the sofa so I don't have to face the nightmares alone. Please, stay."

The expression on his face was that of a child's on Christmas morning, except I was the present. I knew I would be safe in his arms, because he hadn't tried anything more than kissing me. He held up his finger. "Just a moment, let me put the dishes in the sink to soak and turn off some of the lights."

I turned to my side and my mind started to drift in and out of consciousness. I felt the bed dip behind me as a warm body pressed up against my back.

Van wrapped his arms around me, holding me, protecting me while I began to fall asleep. "Is this okay, Kaelin?"

I was too far gone to talk, only managing, "Mmhmm," and nodding.

He placed a tender kiss against the back of my neck. "Sleep well, my angel. I'll drive off any threat of evil dreams. Let me be your white knight, your hero who'll slay the dragons and rid you of these horrible visions."

I managed a laugh as we both settled into a synchronized breathing pattern and soon drifted off.

I'm not sure if I heard him correctly, as my mind was surrendering to slumber, but I thought I heard him say, "Please be mine, Kaelin, my love."

Chapter 6

Van

I LOOKED AT THE clock through bleary eyes, noting it was only 9 a.m. Kaelin moved slightly, and my eyes became transfixed by her face, finally peaceful during her slumber. I slept well lying next to her. I only awoke because her body kept pushing back against mine, causing me to groan. Her backside kept rubbing up against my morning wood, eliciting a severe case of blue balls. I knew what lay beneath those clothes. I saw her naked enough times to memorize every curve of her body.

My heart was soaring as I held her warm body against mine. I noted how perfectly we fit together. Her head came just under my chin, and she fit every inch of my body, which confirmed my theory that we were made for one another.

While my family might be more affluent, I noted the similarities in our career paths, difficult fathers, and desire to help others. Trent sung her praises more than once. I envied him the moment I realized he had Kaelin living with him. I wanted to come over, sweep her off her feet, and bring her back to my place.

Yes, I wanted her, but I wouldn't act on my impulses, because she wasn't ready, not yet anyway. Her stalker's threats and Roger's attack on her at her former workplace were enough to make her distrustful of men. Hell, my father had me distrustful of women with the stunts he pulled on my brother and me. I couldn't tell if someone wanted me for my money, name recognition, or both. All I wanted was to marry for love, something my parents were denied, and I saw what that did to each of them.

I thought about getting up and going into the bathroom to take an ice cold shower and rub out some frustration, letting myself come a few times. Yes, it would take a few times getting myself off to feel satiated for the rest of the day. I did it every morning I knew I'd be around her so she wouldn't see me sporting a hard-on.

My phone vibrated softly. I reached back to grab it quickly to quiet it. Luke was wondering where I was. He had coffee ready for both of us, along with a quick snack from a bakery.

I texted back and told him to come through the office to the hidden apartment, but to be quiet since Kaelin had a rough night.

I watched her closely, hoping she wouldn't wake with the sounds of the wall and painting pulling away to reveal this room, which like the apartment's elevator, doubled as a safe room. When Luke managed to get into the apartment, he looked at me and held up the goodies—his way of silently asking where to put them. I motioned him over with my free hand, still having one wrapped around Kaelin to comfort her.

I should've known that the moment the mocha smell permeated the area Kaelin would start to wake. She groaned and stretched before rolling my direction—freeing my arm in the process and allowing me to move up the bed a bit—and resting her head on my chest and sighing. *God I could get used to having this every day of my life. Those little groans and movements were turning me on something fierce.* I grabbed at the extra pillow I'd placed against the nightstand and quickly covered my lower parts. I didn't need Luke or Kaelin seeing me tent the bedsheets. With her right next to me, I couldn't help having wood twenty-four seven.

I reached for a coffee and motioned for Luke to take the other one out of the holder and place it on my nightstand, along with the treats. He tipped his head. "Good morning, Ms. Richards."

Kaelin jumped, causing me to nearly spill the hot mocha in my hand. Thankfully, Luke was quick to grab it before any damage could be done. Blushing every shade of red imaginable, she pulled the sheets up to her chin. "Why are you here? What time is it?"

I pulled her back onto my chest and rubbed my hands up and down her arms and back in reassurance. "It's a little after nine in the morning. Luke brought us some café mochas and a little breakfast to nibble on."

"Oh my gosh!" She looked up to me in horror. "I'm late for class."

She started to move out of bed, but then realized Luke was still present.

I grabbed on to her, holding her close to me as I turned her head back to mine so I could look deep into her eyes. "Remember last night?"

She nodded.

"I explained that we'd be sticking right here for a while. I have already contacted a high official at the school. The sessions are taped, so we can watch the classes we miss and turn in our assignments via computer."

Kaelin started to relax. "What about work?"

"We'll work from here or inside the office. No one really needs to see me in the office. The only people who know who I really am are the board of directors, headed up by my mother, and a couple of managers, that's all."

"We can't go anywhere?" she asked with alarm in her voice.

I shook my head. "Do you remember seeing what the stalker did to my brother, your best friend?"

She nodded.

"I don't want to risk you getting taken by that monster. We're in a holding pattern until we draw him out or figure out how he knew where to find you. Speaking of which," I looked up to Luke, "any findings to report?"

I moved my legs and made a motion for Luke to sit on the edge of the bed. His eyebrows rose in question, which meant he was wondering if he was free to talk in front of Kaelin.

"You can speak freely. This concerns her just as much as it concerns my brother. For all I know, this guy may have figured out who I am and might be coming for me next. He has made threat of that." Whoops, I didn't mean to admit that.

My sweet angel began to shake in my arms as Luke proceeded. "So far we don't believe he knows who you are. We see no evidence of him tracing back to your laptops, but we can't be certain. We have acquired the services of a high-level computer expert and hacker who works for both Prescott International and Titan Security here in the Orlando area. In talking with Ethan, we discovered he works closely with a forensic accountant named Nate. Apparently, both he and Nate have some high-level software they've developed that might be able to more quickly sort through the mess you and Ms. Richards are sifting through." Luke gestured toward me with his hand. "I thought I'd better ask you first before accepting that offer."

Kaelin spoke up. "I hope I'm not interrupting, but there have been quite a few quirks going on with the accounting system. I know you were testing me to see if I'd find the mistakes you planted, but my coworkers are constantly complaining that the figures keep changing in their work, without their permission, and they are continually being slowed down trying to correct the mistakes. Also, Mr. Walters found evidence of unauthorized withdrawals in small amounts and has shut it down numerous times with the bank, setting up a system he thought was full-proof but keeps getting usurped."

I gave her a gentle kiss on the cheek. "Thank you, love. I had no clue there were so many issues going on in accounting." I turned to Luke. "Were you aware of this?"

"Yes. Mr. Walters was hoping to find the source first; however, he has made an appointment to discuss this issue in detail with you tomorrow afternoon. That's why I was asking about accounting software and hiring the two experts to try and figure out what's going on. It was actually Ms. Richards who'd suggested the idea of the software. She read up about it and found the creators here in the area." Luke looked over to Kaelin, who was blushing a bit. "Sorry, ma'am, I accidently overhead your conversation with Mr. Walters one day while passing through the department."

I nodded in agreement. "Move the appointment up to this afternoon. I want to go ahead and get this out of the way. Hire both people and get a resolution on all this mess. We can't afford to have any further unauthorized transactions. They need to be stopped before they quickly eat away at the company profits."

Feeling a headache coming on, I pinched the bridge of my nose with my forefingers. "What about Trent? How's he doing? Have my mother and sister seen him? And what's the update on the attack?"

"The police have finished combing through the condo and collecting evidence, what little they could find. The item on the mirror," he was, thankfully, being careful not to let Kaelin know it was blood, "was not your brother's. We're trying to see if we can get a DNA match from that and cross reference the other fluids found in the apartment with any offenders who might be in the criminal files online.

"I talked one on one with Rick Caldwell, the new CEO of Titan Security. They seem to be tied up with multiple cases. They loaned us Cat to portray Kaelin for the foreseeable future, or until such time she's no longer needed. However, he doesn't have any other available agents, so he's offered us several individuals who plan to join Titan once their contracts end in the military. They're Navy SEALs currently on leave, so they've worked covert operations before. I actually grew up with one of them. You might remember Peter Daniels."

I couldn't help but smile. Peter and Luke were always getting into trouble; Peter being the cause of it all. Surprising how he ended up as a SEAL and wanting to work in security. "I do remember him. If Titan Security gave Peter and his team high regards, then hire them and catch them up on what our staff knows. Maybe we can work together to put an end to this sooner rather than later." I waved my hand around at what would now feel like our prison for who knew how long. "These are not exactly ideal accommodations for the long term, but I can't take this fight to my mom's house. I can't risk my family any further."

"I agree, Van. We set an authorized visitors list in the reception area of the hospital. No one's supposed to reach the elevators unless they're on the list. The guards at Trent's door have the same list and won't let any unauthorized staff in, including hospital staff, unless they've checked in at the nurse's station and someone can verify they know the employee. I hate to be so strict, but I'd rather err on the side of caution.

"As for the other information regarding deliveries and surveillance cameras, we did get something." Luke looked optimistically at me.

"Well?" I needed to know now.

"The camera showing Trent's hallway was deactivated moments before the attack. That's what propelled Marcus to check things out. He could see Trent was hurt and focused more on him than chasing after the perpetrator. Marcus called for backup, but by the time they figured out what was going on, the guy was gone.

"We did note that an employee from the camera company came a few days ago to perform the annual check of the equipment. We looked through the records and discovered it had already been completed three months ago, and everything was in working order. We were able to get a side shot of the guy's face before he took down several cameras and brought them back up again. The company has no record of the employee working for them; although, they admit that he was wearing a coverall from their place. Turns out, about a week ago one of their employees had their company van broken into, and a pair of coveralls and some equipment were stolen. The same thing happened with your brother's security system. While everyone was out of the apartment, someone came by needing to check the system, claiming it was giving off alarm signals. Not thinking anything of it, Anthony let him inside and disarmed the system but stood there watching him, and then rearmed the system when the guy was done. So that explains how our perpetrator knew the code to disarm it prior to Trent opening the door. The guy was there waiting for Kaelin but got Trent instead."

I lifted my free hand and punched the bed, causing it to bounce a bit. What I wouldn't give to have the little fucker right in front of me and use his face and body as a punching bag, giving him a taste of his own medicine.

Kaelin began shaking in my arms. Her eyes were wide and full of fear, and her voice was barely a whisper. "He knew where I lived for over a week?"

I pulled her even closer and gave her a long hug while running my hand in circles on her back. "It looks that way, angel. He might've known even longer." I shrugged my shoulders. "We just don't know."

Luke's phone beeped with an incoming message. He took it out of his pocket and scanned it before standing up. "The extra security team will be arriving after hours tonight. They're wondering whether to bring the hacker and accounting expert with them or if you'd like to see them sooner."

"After hours is fine. We've had quite the night, not able to sleep right away, so I'm moving slowly this morning. Please cancel anything on the calendar for today with exception of Walters. I'll see him this afternoon around four. Have the others come in after everyone else has left the building. Can you and Marcus make yourselves available at that time?"

Luke nodded. "Consider it done." He started to walk away. "Just text me if you need anything. I'll be at my desk, running interference for anyone wanting to see you today."

"Thanks, man. I owe you one."

Kaelin stayed glued to me while we watched Luke walk out and close us into our own little existence. The moment the door was sealed shut she seemed to breathe a little easier.

I slipped my hand underneath her chin and lifted it so our eyes met. "Are you ready to have some caffeine and a little food?"

She smiled as she reached her hand out for the coffee. "Just give me the coffee and no one will get hurt."

Hmm, she had a sense of humor. I enjoyed someone who could laugh in the face of adversity. We were so much alike, and I loved it!

Before handing her the café mocha, I held my hand to my heart and smiled at her. "You are a woman after my own heart."

I watched as she sat up in bed, held the coffee carefully to her lips, and took a tentative sip. I was mesmerized with her mouth forming a tight little "o" and imagined her lips making that same shape over my cock as she sucked me off. *Damn it, man! Get your head out of the gutter. If you keep thinking that way, you're going to scare her off before you even have the chance to know her.* My subconscious was right, though my other head was getting harder and harder, which lifted the pillow covering my junk up a little higher.

She looked at me confused, and then down at the pillow. "Why do you have a..."

I placed my hands over it so she couldn't move my hiding place. I guess she realized what was going on when she said a soft "Oh" before turning her face and blushing.

"Sorry, love. You were grinding your backside on me in your sleep and got his attention," I admitted with a smirk.

"You mean I caused that?" Her hand pointed down toward my crotch.

I nodded. "I usually wake up with a hard-on from dreaming about you as both Kaelin and Mystique. But today with your every touch"—I pointed to my jewels—"you have him worked up, literally."

A small laugh escaped her lips.

I was a little upset, citing, "It's no laughing matter, Kaelin. I've got a serious case of blue balls. I can't help it. I've been hard every time we've been near one another, more so since we were shoved together yesterday through all this chaos."

She put her hand to her lips to stifle her laugh. "I'm sorry. Blue balls, do they really turn blue? Do they hurt?"

My sweet angel, my Mystique, she was so innocent and naïve despite her webcasts. I couldn't help but laugh a little at her question. "No, they're not really blue. It's a figure of speech meaning they hurt, but not in an 'I stubbed my toe' kind of way." I thought for a minute about how to describe things, when it hit me. "When you were Mystique and I'd get you worked up but deny you the ability to come right away because I'd ask you to hold it in until I gave you permission?"

Her eyes were as wide as saucers, and her bottom was moving against the sheets, which told me she was thinking back on those times and getting worked up over the memory. She pressed her thighs together to stifle her need. I pointed down to what she was doing, and she stopped.

"Now you know how I feel."

She looked almost ready to cry. I held my hand up, caressing the side of her face. "Don't cry, love. Neither of us can help how we feel toward one another.

I promised to be the perfect gentleman, and I will be. But I will offer: if you need my voice to help you get off later, or any other part of me, I'll be more than happy to oblige. You have to be the one to ask, though. I won't pursue anything more than a kiss or a simple touch without your permission. If you tell me to stop, if I've made you uncomfortable, I will cease what I'm doing."

Kaelin reached up and ran her hand over the scruff on my face. "I know I can trust you. I don't know how I know that, but I do." She smiled for a moment. "You're cute with the scruff and bed hair in the morning."

Okay, now she had me blushing. I decided to tease her by leaning over and running my scruff against her face.

She squealed immediately. "Okay, I give. It's cute, but scratchy."

I picked up my mocha and began to drink, relishing in the intense flavor and the extra shot of espresso Luke put in to help me perk up a little quicker. I reached into the bag to discover a selection of muffins and croissants along with a container of scrambled eggs and two forks. I put the bag between us, opened the container, and offered her a fork. We both dug in, moaning our appreciation for hot food and caffeine.

"We'll need to take showers and get dressed. We still have a lot of paperwork to go through regarding the finances so we can discuss things with the accounting expert tonight. I'll need you to be there with me to explain what you've seen, heard, and discussed with Mr. Walters. I also want you close to me all day so I know where you're at." I just realized I sounded like I was trying to dictate what she did, so I added, "I'm not trying to control you, just politely requesting, given the threat we have coming after you and possibly me, too."

She nodded. "Thank you for adding that last part."

I watched as she chewed on a piece of croissant and swallowed, only I was imagining her swallowing other things. *Stop thinking with your dick.*

She turned her body toward me. "Can I ask what threat Eagle Eyes made toward you?"

It was only a matter of time before it came out. I didn't hesitate to answer. "He warned me off watching you. He hated that I suggested private-room sessions with only one client and then bought all of them in advance, leaving him nothing. That's when he started escalating the threats against me, starting with blowing up the first laptop."

She nodded. "He blew up seven, right?"

"Yes. What I don't understand is how, because I was operating on a wireless system in my office and not directly linked to anything." The moment I said the words, I realized a solution. He embedded it into the private session. If he had the ability to interrupt our sessions by kicking me off, he also had the ability to send the virus directly to me just by me going into the webcast room. Unless he was hitting through my Wi-Fi here at the office. But what were the chances he knew where I worked?

I grabbed my phone to text Luke, as Kaelin added, "I had the same thoughts. He's been able to force a lot of things. Speaking of which, now I wonder if that's why my webcam was on when I woke up yesterday. I know for a fact I turned it off a couple nights ago after the last session, but I noticed the light was on as if it was broadcasting prior to me coming to work."

"I'll let Luke know it needs to be taken out of the apartment and looked at carefully. In order for our stalker to get away with everything he's done, he was definitely tech savvy and possibly had a degree in computers."

I noticed Kaelin was a bit shaken by the revelation that this guy had been watching her outside her webcasts. For how long? We didn't know. Why? We were clueless, but going to find out. He definitely had an unhealthy obsession with her; one I'd like to put a permanent end to.

I took our coffees and set them on top of my nightstand, along with the bag of pastries and the empty egg container. I scooted closer to her, drawing her against my chest and ensconcing her in my arms. She seemed to settle against me. I bent my head to kiss her hair and noticed for the first time how amazing she smelled. She carried a hint of natural musk mixed with a light vanilla cookie smell. "I hate this just as much as you. I never wanted this to happen—being thrown into this situation. I wanted to have a chance to get to talk to you more, maybe ask you out on a date, and then progress things along."

She looked back at me. "I know. I've declined dates before. You've overhead me tell other guys I couldn't, but for the record, I would've said yes to you. It doesn't mean we can't take this chance to get to know more about each other. Although, I feel at a disadvantage, because you know more about me then I do about you. I only know what I've experienced and what little your brother told me."

I wanted to take hold of her chin and draw it up toward my lips. The need to kiss her was overwhelming. The need to make her mine and drive off this threat, marking her as my territory, was intense. But I'd move on her terms, at her pace. So I offered up, "Ask me anything you want to know. My life is an open book to you."

Chapter 7

Kaelin

I WAS TAKEN ABACK by Van's need to make me happy. Other than my mom and her parents, no one ever cared about making me happy.

Then Van added, "Actually, angel, let's make this a twenty-question game. I still have a few more I'd like to ask, too. For every two or three inquiries you ask, I get to ask one. Sound fair?"

I could agree to that. "Okay. Why do you call me 'angel?'"

His smile was mesmerizing. "Because you are my angel, my saving grace. My father was coming down on me hard, not allowing me to date anyone, because I was to be wed to a woman named Heather Thresher."

He looked over apologetically. "I guess I need to go off topic and fill in that gap for you to understand what I mean. Her father owns several restaurants and nightclubs in the area. They aren't doing horrible, but customers are dwindling. Heather would like to get a chance to run it. She has some promising ideas to change the way they do business and draw in new clientele. Unfortunately, her dad is of the mindset that women belong at home and pregnant, not at work. She's in love with a manager at one of the restaurants they own, and I am smitten with you. When Dad died, it freed us from having to marry one another and nullified the agreement my father had tentatively made, since we refused to honor it once he was gone.

"I have wanted to be with you longer than I let on. The moment I saw you in the coffee shop—the day you were training with Mark—I knew you were for me. Don't ask me how I knew. I just felt, for the first time, I could breathe. My father quickly shot it down, citing my impending marriage, but he couldn't change that you and I were in some of the same classes at the university. He couldn't prevent me from getting assigned to work with you on various group tasks." Van kissed my cheek lightly, his scruff tickling a little. "Does that answer it for you?"

I nodded. "Yes." *That was him. I can't believe it. Somehow my heart knew.*

"Okay, hit me with your next question." He smiled.

I twiddled my thumbs as I tried to figure out how to ask it.

He seemed to sense my hesitance. "You won't offend me with whatever you ask, Kaelin."

My hand gestured toward the room. "You said your father had a den of debauchery in here, one designed for a BDSM lifestyle. Do you have similar tastes?"

He let out the breath he'd been holding, looking relieved by what I'd asked. "Hell no! My father was into things none of us had guessed." A smirk spread across his face. "He was so judgmental and narrow-minded against Trent being gay, when Dad should have been trying to clean up his own act."

I didn't know where he was going with this. "What are you talking about, Van?"

"My father ostracized my brother for his sexual preferences, when his own were more shameful. He bent toward the darker side of sexual relations. He was into having orgies with multiple women and men. The equipment he had in here was downright scary, like nothing you'd ever find in romance novels. It was hardcore stuff." He shivered at the thought. "I'm not against anyone's predilections in the sexual world; everyone has their own preferences. I just always hated how Dad treated Trent. Essentially, my father was throwing stones at glass houses, when his own foundation and glass were shattering all around him."

I looked around the room with new eyes and shuttered at the idea of multiple people having sex together. That was far worse than me getting myself off while others viewed.

Van must be a mind reader, because I was going to ask about his preferences toward sex, besides liking to watch porn and why he watched it, when he said, "Since I couldn't date much, I turned to porn to get off. I'm not a virgin, though I haven't been with many women, and I'm not into the hardcore stuff." A smile played across his lips, and a twinkle was in his eyes. "Just watching you as Mystique was enough to get me to come.

"I'm not sure I would qualify as a dominant in terms of the BDSM aspect. I have to be in charge because of the company I run—one I wish Trent would come back too, because he handles the business much better than I do—but I hate being in control of so many things at once that I feel overwhelmed as a result. That's why I like to have a level of power in the bedroom, because it's a place where I can have total control. The tone I used with you, the way you let me guide you through what I wanted to see, the toys you bought at my request and used at my discretion and no one else's, that's who I am, what I want." His hand came up to caress my face before slipping down my neck and around to the nape, where he drew me closer to him. He took my lower lip between his teeth and bit lightly, taking control of my mouth. The kiss was more intense than anything he'd done to date.

I was lost to him. He had command over me as he guided me down onto the bed and climbed up over me, hovering, not letting go of the kiss. I nearly fainted from the lack of oxygen, so I was thankful when he finally pulled back, letting me breath.

"I might want to deny you an orgasm, maybe tie your hands to the bed, use a toy we agree on to spice it up, and I prefer to be in the lead most of the time, but this is as intense as it gets with me." He supported his weight above me by leaning to one side on his elbow and legs while his hand stroked my hair. Worry filled his eyes. "The idea of hurting you would wound me, tear my heart in two."

He knew all the right words to say to put my mind at ease. "How is it that I lucked out with Trent coming into my life and saving me, and then meeting you? Was it coincidence...or design?" I needed to know. He's known about me for a while, which made me wonder if Trent knew about me before we met.

Van stopped hovering over me; instead, he lay down beside me and guided me to roll over on my side as he encircled me with his arms and drew me into his body to spoon. I had to admit that we did fit together perfectly, and I felt comfort in his arms, whereas I'd never felt comfort in another man who was interested in me beyond friendship.

Pushing my hair aside, he nibbled on the side of my neck as he answered, while the warmth of his breath and the gentleness in which he nipped me warmed me with desire, making me feel cherished for the first time ever. "It was a little of both. When you and I first met at the coffee shop, I was with my father. Mark couldn't acknowledge who I was or that he'd met me before, because Dad was checking up to see that Mark had kicked my brother to the curb."

I looked back at him. "What do you mean?"

He shrugged and continued nibbling down to my shoulder. "Mark's coffee shop had been one of Trent's investments. They hit it off and secretly dated through high school and college, but lost touch with one another until this investment opportunity brought them back together. That is until my dad found out. That's when he renounced Trent as his son, and similar to how your father forced you to leave, ours actually kicked him out without anything to his name. Trent had only the cash in his wallet—his credit cards deactivated—the clothes on his back, no car, no nothing. He turned to Mark for room and board in exchange for working there. Mark would have taken him to his place, but I'd warned him that it was being watched and that he definitely didn't want to cross my dad.

"I'd been away at Columbia for college but recently called back because I was lifted in ranks and expected to take over the business. That's how I ended up at the university in Winter Park alongside you."

I moved my hand over one of his and patted it as I giggled. "You know you're off on a tangent again, Van."

He kissed my earlobe and lightly bit it. "Sorry, love. As you've seen, my family's story is complicated to some degree. Anyhow, when Dad found out Trent was in the coffee shop sleeping on a cot in one of the rooms above it, he called the campus and the health inspector and almost put Mark out of business by forcing him to kick Trent out or be shut down. That's why we were there that day, to check to make sure Mark complied, and then to set up my transfer to the school.

"Since that day, I couldn't stop talking about you to Trent. I praised your work in class, your brilliant mind, and how beautiful you were to me. I also told him about how I almost forgot to breathe when our eyes met, and the shock that went through my arm when our hands touched. Once Dad passed, Trent got curious and decided to go visit Mark and check out the woman who stole his brother's heart."

I could feel Van smile against the back of my neck as one of his hands slid up and caressed the bottom of my breast, which sent waves of pleasure throughout my entire body.

He seemed to sense my unfamiliarity with his forward gestures, because he paused to make sure he didn't go too far. I did gasp as his fingers lightly grazed my breast, but then relaxed back into him and wondered. "So you didn't send Trent?"

"No. He went on his own accord. I'd given him a description of what you looked like but not your name." I was happy to hear Van admit this. That meant it must be fate drawing us together.

I smiled remembering the events as they transpired. It was the day my life and goals were saved. "I remember that day vividly. Trent came in asking to speak to Mark. I saw the two of them talking rather intensely about something. They held hands for a time, and I thought how romantic it was that the two of them found each other. A few minutes later, Mark had a delivery to accept in the back of the shop, so he went off to take care of that, and I went on break while Jean took over for me. I sat a couple tables away, trying to figure out what I was going to do for room and board since my dad had frozen—and stolen—most of my mom's money. He'd been furious to find out she'd been helping me with expenses.

"I guess I was close enough to Trent that he overheard me, on the phone, begging the school for options so I could finish my final year and receive my degree. I wasn't just short on room and board; the university, somehow, found out I'd been working extra hours for Mark and holding down a couple of other odd jobs to help pay for things, so I was not so kindly reminded that my scholarship was on the line if I worked over a certain number of hours. I had to abide by their rules and restrictions to keep it." Letting the anger I was feeling toward my father and the injustices of the situation out, I punched the bed.

Van held me tighter. "That's it, angel, let it out. You'll feel better." He leaned over, kissing me on the side of my mouth before taking a deep breath. "I'm afraid I have a confession to make: that was my father interfering. A few days before he died, he learned I was still infatuated with you, so he talked with the chancellor of the school to come up with a reason to cut your funding. Once Dad passed, however, I had Luke put some fear into the chancellor, citing we'd cut funding to the university if he dared follow through with his threat to you."

He pulled my head back toward his, kissing me gently on the lips. I deepened the kiss, trying to convey that I knew it wasn't his fault, not directly, and to thank him for coming to my rescue even though I didn't know it at the time. "I don't know who has the worst father, you or me."

He laughed. "I agree."

"Trent came over to my table and asked to sit down. He inquired about my situation before telling me about himself. I couldn't believe the well-dressed man before me had gone from wealth to living on the streets." I didn't need to add anything more to my story, because Van already knew it by heart...Trent had gone from the streets, to Mark's, to a homeless shelter for a few days, and then on to a weekly-rate motel, thanks to his mom and Van slipping him money via a friend.

Trent also had explained to me how he'd walked into a bar one day desperately needing a drink. The bartender, a woman named Cassidy, befriended him and asked if he could wait tables and dance on stage. I remember laughing that he hadn't realized there were women dancing on a stage. Cassidy then informed him that a few nights a week it became ladies' night, where it turned into an all male revue for the women to have some fun. He took the job but four months later, when an agent came in to see the male revue and took a fancy to Trent's look, was offered a chance to model. The rest was history with him getting one modeling job after another, buying a condo, making some investments, and building a nice little nest egg before his trust fund had been restored, thanks to his mother.

Van continued to place kisses all over my face and neck, below my ears, down my chest, and before I knew what was happening, he threw off our covers and was hovering over me again, taking possession of my mouth and making my mind melt.

I vaguely remember opening my legs for him to lie between my thighs, and his hand slipping up under my shirt and fondling one of my breasts and rolling my nipple, which caused me to cry out in a mixture of pain and pleasure.

My mind kept telling me how well we fit together, how we didn't have to twist or turn to line up perfectly with one another. I was lost to the bliss Van was providing my body, when he began to rub his hardness against my shorts. He was so hard and so tempting, but the idea of doing it scared the shit out of me. When he uttered the word "Mystique," it was like a bucket of cold water splashed over me, bringing me back to the moment. I realized I had subconsciously wrapped my legs around his waist, seeking him out, too. But I couldn't go through with it, not until I knew him better, so I broke loose from his lips. "Please stop."

The moment the words were out of my mouth, he jumped off of me and out of bed. One of his hands came up over his mouth in alarm. "Oh my god, what have I done?" He realized he pushed a bit too far, too fast.

I shook my head and raised my hands. "It's okay; you stopped. We didn't take it any further than I wanted. I can't believe you got my body to respond like that."

I motioned for him to come back to bed, but he shook his head. "If I get near you right now, I'm afraid I won't be able to stop, Kaelin." He looked a bit distressed for a moment and glanced over at the clock. I followed his line of sight and realized we'd talked until after 1 p.m. "I need to take a shower to cool off. Besides, we need to get dressed, get some lunch, and do some work in preparation for the meeting we have with the security and computer experts tonight."

I nodded in agreement, but something kept bothering me. "Why did you call me Mystique in the heat of the moment? Is that who you see when you look at me, or do you see me as Kaelin?" I was confused and a little pissed. I didn't want to be with him if he only wanted my other persona. He had to know that wasn't me, not entirely. I was more Kaelin than anyone else.

He ran his hand over his face. His breathing was still ragged, and his cock was still tenting his boxers, leaving nothing to the imagination. The sheer size of him was shocking. I'd never seen anyone naked, up close and personal, except for Trent. Once, after a shower, his towel worked loose in the kitchen when he bent for a drink in the refrigerator. So I really didn't have any comparisons, but from what I gathered, Van was an impressive size, which made me wonder if we did end up in a sexual relation if he'd even fit.

I waited for him to slow his breathing.

"I fell for you first, Kaelin. Your outer appearance attracted me—your smile, your eyes, and those curves. Mystique enticed me with her body and her willingness to try some new things in play, but even then, it was the way you articulated yourself, the way you carried your body, as Kaelin, which caught and held my interest. My apologies if I made you feel uncomfortable. I can't help that I'm drawn to you in ways I've never experienced before."

As he moved toward my side of the bed, he motioned his hand, silently asking permission to sit. I nodded. His hand came up and held on to the side of my face as his lips came forward to kiss the end of my nose. "It's you I want, Kaelin. Forgive me for my error. I'm only human, after all, walking new ground. I don't want to rush you, but I do want to protect you and see if what we feel for each other can lead to more."

"I'd like that, too." I moved forward to kiss him gently on the lips, but Van moved off the bed and held his hands up in surrender.

"I'm going to get that shower before we go too far. It's all I can do to resist you right now."

I watched as he lifted his t-shirt over his head and tossed it in the hamper as he walked toward the shower. *Damn, I knew it...he definitely had a six-pack on the way to becoming an eight-pack.* His chest was lightly dusted with hair, not too much but enough for someone to run their hand through. He had a trail of dark hair that started just below his navel and ran down under his boxers to his manhood. His back showed every muscle carved perfectly into his skin, as if the Greek gods had carved them. And that ass...I bet you could bounce a quarter off of it. *Girl, you have it bad for him.*

I couldn't disagree with my inner thoughts; I did have it bad. I was just happy Van hadn't noticed the moisture seeping from my underwear into my shorts. How did he know how to play my body and get it worked up so quickly? *Your webcast, duh. Or was he just that good in bed?* He nearly had me willing to break my rule of waiting until marriage, or until I met the right one, to lose my v-card. Is he the one? With us being thrown together in close proximity, I guess only time would tell. So far I liked what I saw and felt.

I heard the shower come on and saw his silhouette through the hazy glass door designed to allow you to see someone was there but not see any details. I looked over at the clock and twiddled my thumbs, before realizing we needed to eat lunch, so I decided to head to the kitchen and see what I could find while waiting for my turn for the shower.

Chapter 8

Van

I CAME OUT OF the bathroom in a towel. I didn't mean to do that, but I'd been so worked up over Kaelin that I'd forgotten to take my suit with me so I could dress in there.

I panicked the moment I realized she wasn't in bed, until I heard, "I thought you were trying to cool us down, not amp me up with what you're wearing." I turned toward the kitchen and noticed Kaelin putting something together for lunch.

"Sorry, forgot to take my clothes with me. What are you doing?" I wondered.

"I couldn't sit still. That's just not me. I'm used to doing something, so I figured I'd look in the kitchen and make us some lunch. Hope you don't mind. I found the ingredients to make tuna nicoise salads. I also hope you weren't saving the ahi tuna for something special." Her voice was low, as if she was afraid I might get upset over her helping herself.

I stayed my distance, because the act of a beautiful woman fixing me something to eat had always been just a fantasy for me. No one had ever gone to the trouble. It was a simple act, but it meant the world to me and was turning me on. I had to hold my suit over my privates so she wouldn't see. *So much for getting off a few times in the shower to try and get my cock under control.* "I should've explained that my place is your place and to please help yourself to anything you need. If there's something you'd like that I don't have, we can let Luke know, and he'll get it for us."

She breathed a sigh of relief. "Thank you, Van. I wasn't sure if you'd be mad, or if you'd even like what I fixed."

I nodded. "Understood. You're in a new place, under straining circumstances. Just know I could never be mad at you, and, by the way, I love nicoise salad. I actually bought the tuna with that in mind. You'll find our tastes in food don't differ much. I'm sorry to say that I have the advantage of knowing what you like, thanks to Trent telling me your preferences." I stared straight at her. "I know I sound like a broken record, but you and I have much more in common than you'd like to believe."

I turned and went back into the bathroom, dressing in record time. We'd only been together for a day, under trying conditions, but a moment out of her presence felt like an eternity. I'd been infatuated with Kaelin from a distance, but now I was hooked. *Reel me in, my angel, make me yours.*

When I returned, she'd eaten a few bites of her salad but got up off her barstool to head toward the bathroom. "Where are my work clothes, again?"

Putting my hand on the small of her back, I directed her over to the closet and pulled open the doors to show her one side was mine and the other was hers. I watched her eyes go big. "You didn't bring much of my wardrobe for me to pick from."

"We couldn't. We needed the stalker to believe you didn't run from the apartment. We pulled a couple of items that he might think were at the dry cleaners, but mostly you have a new selection of clothes to choose from." I moved away and opened a couple dresser drawers, revealing where her new undergarments were.

She was in awe over the selection. I'm glad I had the foresight to have Luke remove the price tags. Hopefully, she wouldn't recognize the Agent Provocateur lingerie or any other designers' names and, therefore, the actual cost of her new wardrobe. I may not have spared any expense. "Feel free to wear whatever you'd like."

I watched as she pulled out a light gray dress along with a darker jacket, which made the outfit look more professional, and a pair of black Louboutin shoes. I had to look away as she selected her lingerie. I didn't want to know what she had on underneath, or I'd be fanaticizing about it all day long. There's nothing like trying to hold a serious meeting with security personnel while sporting a major boner. I wanted her—there was no doubt about it—and we were meant to be together, but I wasn't out to buy her affection. No, I wanted to earn her love and her trust.

Sitting at the bar, I looked for a bottle of dressing but didn't find anything. Did she forget to put it out? I noticed she drizzled a little dressing already, which looked to be the same stuff sitting in a small bowl near her plate. I pulled it over cautiously, sticking my finger in to taste it. Damn, she made homemade vinaigrette dressing. I didn't even know I had the ingredients to make something this tasty. I quickly drizzled some on my salad and took a tentative bite. The salads I made failed miserably in comparison to this one. I usually overcooked the tuna, had the potatoes too hard or too soft, and usually turned the green beans to mush. Trent had raved about what a fine cook his roommate was and how he was hitting the gym more often because of it. Now I knew what he was talking about. I guess I'd have to dazzle her with the couple of dishes I knew how to cook, thanks to mom's chef showing me how to prepare a few meals.

I was lost to the flavors playing on my tongue and relishing each bite, when I felt a soft touch on my shoulder. I turned to see Kaelin sharply dressed in her new attire. The dress, causing my manhood to stand up and salute, was more form fitting than any of the items she tended to wear to work. She definitely was a knockout.

I got up out of my seat, which, according to the gentlemen who served our household, was proper etiquette when a woman was near the table for a meal. I leaned forward placing a small kiss on her cheek. "How is it that you look amazing in everything you wear?" She cast her eyes down at the floor as I watched the blush spread from the small amount of cleavage she was showing, all the way up to her face. "There's nothing to be ashamed of, angel. You look wonderful." I motioned toward the stool and then helped her take her seat and gave her another peck on the cheek. "And the salad is truly amazing. I've never had one this good before. Where'd you learn to make dressing like that?"

She was adorable, continuing to redden under my praises. "My maternal grandmother is highly allergic to some of the preservatives in mass-produced products, so we were always making things from scratch."

I'd just finished taking my last bite when Luke texted me. He had a few issues he needed to run over. "I'm sorry, but I must leave you for now. Would you like to rest and relax, maybe watch some television?"

She shook her head. "I need to be doing something; otherwise, my mind goes back to those nightmares." She put her fork down and looked up at me. "Can I work more on the financial comparisons? Maybe I can be of some help when you talk to the accounting expert tonight."

"That's not a problem. I'll have Luke help me bring in as much as you want." I opened the door sealing us in and left it open before calling for Luke's assistance in fulfilling Kaelin's request.

The moment the boxes hit the floor, she bent down to take some of the files she'd stopped at yesterday and carried them over to the bar to look through while she finished her salad. I put my hand on my chest in admiration of this woman. She truly was someone after my own heart. I couldn't sit still either. If I did, my mind would travel back to all the negative aspects of my father's life.

Pulling me to the side, Luke leaned in and whispered, "We picked up Kaelin's webcast camera yesterday, and someone definitely tampered with it. We gave a brief explanation of some details to Peter and his team—the one Titan Security recommended—but weren't sure how much you'd want to divulge at this point."

He looked at me like he wasn't sure how to approach the question playing on his lips. I could see him open and shut his mouth a few times, when I finally had enough, demanding, "Spit it out, man."

"Peter wants access to her computer and suggested we provide her a new one for now. The computer expert can copy whatever she needs off the old system onto the new one. They believe it has been compromised. And they'd like access to her webcast account to trace things there as well." He looked relieved once he'd gotten it all out and I hadn't reacted.

I could have yelled at him, but the reality of it hit me in the shower this morning. They needed to be aware of everything, but I'd keep her privacy by demanding non-disclosure agreements from everyone. I wouldn't have her name ruined as a result of her stalker. Since he blew up several of my laptops, I suspected he infiltrated her system despite the firewalls and safeguards my people built into her computer.

I leaned forward, grabbing ahold of Luke's shoulder before whispering, "Get everything that is needed. I'll discuss it with her at the meeting, if not before then. Her safety and privacy are imperative. Draw up NDAs for everyone working on this case. I will not have her or my family compromised."

"Consider it done, Van." He started toward the door, before turning. "I almost forgot. Mr. Walters is a bit early for his appointment. He was wondering if you could go ahead and see him. He's got a couple employees out sick with the stomach bug and is short-handed today."

"Give me five minutes and send him in. Thanks, Luke."

"No problem, Van."

I tried making it out the door a number of times but fell short, because I felt the pull back to this hidden apartment. I didn't want to leave her, but I knew she was safest here. There were no other ways into the place except through my office. Once the alarm was activated, and we were sealed shut at night, anyone attempting to enter through my workspace would trigger hidden sensors, letting me know of an impending threat before it happened.

I walked over to Kaelin, spun her around in the chair, wrapped my hands around her waist, and pulled her to me, taking her lips prisoner, not wanting to let go. The searing kiss flooded my body with an intense passion I couldn't even consider explaining, and I knew I needed to relish in this endearment, since it'd have to last me over the course of the next several hours.

I finally made it to my meeting, and Mr. Walters was very enlightening, with copies of issues he discovered in our computer system along with copies from the bank showing cash withdrawals from our accounts. We installed fail-safes to avoid such issues after we noticed this happening regularly while my father was in charge. But they were starting to occur again, somehow getting around our attempts to stop them.

Mr. Walters found the same concerns as Kaelin with accounts having incorrect data, causing a backlog of work in the department and needed correcting immediately. Either someone was messing around with our files or they intended for me to look bad and discredit me as the new CEO. I wouldn't officially be appointed until I had my master's degree and the board voted on my work to date, deciding whether I could lead them into the next era of management and bring this company about.

I took the paperwork with his concerns and explained that I hired someone to look into it, but I'd hold him to the NDA the company had on file, so he couldn't tell anyone what was going on. I wanted him to do business as usual and keep correcting what the department could until we got a handle on things. Thankfully, he agreed with my plans.

It was nearly the end of the workday when Mr. Walters left. I was put off a little regarding him showing up early, but was now thankful his appointment wouldn't bleed into the next, and I'd have time to see what Kaelin had discovered.

Surprise was what I felt when I entered the hidden apartment. There were papers everywhere, like a tornado had come through my space. In the midst of it all was my sweet angel running and glancing back and forth at different piles, pulling several pieces together into a new pile, and making notations of things on the laptop we'd given her to use, with passwords for the more intricate details of our financials.

"Did you find anything new, Kaelin?"

She jumped, turning around so quickly that papers went everywhere. She placed her hand on her heaving chest as I raised my hands to show I meant no harm.

"I'm sorry, love. I didn't mean to frighten you. I finished meeting with Mr. Walters about some of the same concerns you've presented and wanted to check on you to see if you've found anything new before we head into the meeting with the security team, computer expert, and accounting guru."

I knelt on the floor to help her gather the papers that finally floated down. As our hands touched, I felt the static of our closeness.

She jerked her hand back. "I'm sorry. I didn't mean to make such a mess." Her eyes finally met mine and she nodded. "I think I might have found a pattern to things."

We finished cleaning up her papers and stood. She quickly put them in order, looked at me and then back at a small stack over on the bar area. She opened her mouth to say something, only to close it again. I'd been around her enough to know she was having difficulty finding her words. "Just ask whatever it is you're planning to ask. Nothing is off limits," I finally stated with curiosity.

"When exactly did your dad decide you'd marry that Heather Thresher lady?"

I was caught off guard, never expecting that to come out of her mouth. I shrugged my shoulders and tried to think back on things. "I was free to date a few young women, per my father's approval, toward the end of high school. While at Columbia, I was able to get away with dating a few he hadn't consented to." I tried to remember when exactly he called me and told me to start communicating with Heather. Our families had been friends for the longest time, but Heather and I never had any romantic interests for one another.

"I think he told me around Thanksgiving a couple years back that I was expected to date her a few times. We hung out at Christmas when I was home on break, and my family had her family over for a few meals, but we didn't have much to do with each other after that, until a couple months before I was pulled back here, close to the end of the summer semester, to register locally. That's when my father stated an engagement ring had been delivered to her and she'd accepted. We were to be married as soon as I graduated the master's program. Why?" Okay, now I was really curious.

"According to the transfers of cash to the Threshers's accounts, your marriage was set up two years prior to your so-called engagement. I'm beginning to think your father, possibly to avoid some form of blackmail or something, was paying people off and arranging marriages for you and your siblings. The same notes—about keeping secrets—that were found on the back of the financials for Freidmont Pharmaceuticals and Hollings Shipping Industries were also found on the Thresher financials." She pulled a piece of paper from the stack she was holding and pointed right at the note. I recognized Mr. Thresher's handwriting instantly. Kaelin then pulled another note agreeing to unite our families dated two years ago and in my father's script. What the hell?

I shook my head in disbelief, before grabbing a pillow off the sofa and punching it several times, wishing it had been my father's face. "I was nothing more than a damn pawn for that bastard. My life, my existence meant nothing more than a business deal to him." I threw the pillow across the room, where it bounced off the side of the wall and landed on the floor.

I felt Kaelin's arms wrap around me from behind.

"He's not worth your frustration, Van."

I turned in her arms, loving how the feel of her body against mine was calming. I lifted her chin with my hand to give her the kiss I'd been craving the past couple hours, when I saw the hurt in her eyes. She'd been in my shoes. She knew exactly how I felt. *No wonder we're so perfect for one another.*

My lips were gentle against hers, not wanting to scare her. When she went up on her tiptoes to deepen our kiss, I took that as a positive sign and began to pour all of my emotions into her. I wanted her to know just how much I needed her, just how much she meant to me.

Caressing her face with my hand, I leaned my forehead against hers. "I'm sorry for my little fit. I don't normally act that way...it's just...I can't believe how manipulative my father was."

She shook her head. "It's understandable. You didn't scare me. Remind me later to enlighten you about how many pillows I ruined the first year I was away from my dad."

I couldn't help but laugh.

We sat down on the sofa, and she showed me all the illegal transactions that had been made to numerous accounts. I thought my family ran a legitimate business, but what Kaelin uncovered was proving differently. I couldn't figure out whether my father was being blackmailed for his indiscretions or was dirty dealing with the family business. Either way, we'd soon find out.

I marked the areas of interest I wanted the new team we'd hired to look into. I was still so impressed with all that Kaelin had discovered in such a short time. I couldn't comprehend how the other firms had missed it, unless they were companies my father had paid off with past audits of our books and were holding to their previous agreements. Who knows? The man wasn't beyond pulling anything to get what he wanted.

A couple of hours passed while Kaelin and I pored through the paperwork to see if I noticed anything out of the ordinary that she might've missed, when a text came in on my phone. It was Luke letting me know that Peter, his team, and the two experts were in the waiting room. I told them to go ahead and meet me in my office at the conference table. I wanted Luke included in this discussion.

Shit. I had all this time to tell Kaelin the team needed full disclosure and about the news of her equipment from my brother's apartment. How we managed to keep the police from realizing she was doing a webcast of an adult variety, I had no idea, but I was definitely giving Luke and his team a raise. There wasn't any time left, so it was now or never.

Kaelin had the papers gathered, in order of importance and date, in a nice little box. She started to move off the sofa to pick it up, when I stopped her. "Angel, I need to tell you a little something about the security team."

"Okay?"

"Luke talked with Peter earlier today and had to give him a heads up on a few details that we tried to keep private from the police."

Her eyes held sadness. "The team needs to know about the webcast, right?"

I nodded. "Luke has already had all the members of Peter's team along with the technical experts sign Non-Disclosure Agreements. I wish there was another way, but they feel some clues might be in your equipment."

I turned from her and waved my hand around at everything. "This maniac has caused us to live in close quarters and be cut off from the rest of the world. He figured out where you live, the alarm code to your place, he beat up my brother—your best friend—and he managed to send viruses to blow up a few of my laptops—"

She raised her hand to stop me. "I came to the realization a few hours ago. He's somehow tracking me, and we need to find out how." Her hand came to rest on my chest, right over my heart. I'm sure she could feel how frustrated I was with how fast it was beating. "It's going to be okay, Van. I'll do what I have to do."

I shook my head, pondering how I'd gotten so lucky to end up with a woman who was not only beautiful but also brilliant. I knew we still had a lot to learn about one another, but the fact that our minds were already working nearly as one...that just sealed it for me right there. I wouldn't let this amazing angel get away from me.

We walked out of our hidden room to find everyone standing around the table waiting for us. Peter was as I remembered him but with a short military-style haircut and definitely had bulked up from serving in the Navy. He and his team along with the experts took up one side of the conference table, while Luke stood on the other side with three chairs pulled out for us to sit.

Luke used his hand to gesture between us all as he made the introductions. "Peter, everyone, this is Donovan Meyers, the new CEO of Meyers Corporation, and Ms. Kaelin Richards, one of his interns and..." he was at a loss for words on how to introduce her.

Leaning over, I whispered in Kaelin's ear, "Is it okay if I call you my girlfriend?" With her eyes wide, she turned her face to mine, revealing a slight tint of rosiness to it. I watched as she bit her bottom lip for a moment, pondering the question, before finally nodding. *Did she not know how enticing she looked when she did that thing with her lip? Did she not know I wanted to whisk her back into my hidden apartment, lock the doors, and suck on that lip, marking it as mine? I prayed this meeting would be quick. I didn't like the idea of her being around so many strapping young men.*

I extended my hand to Peter. "It's good to see you again, my friend. Long time no see." I guided Kaelin forward as I settled my other hand on the lower portion of her back. "This is my girlfriend Kaelin." I watched as she leaned across the table and shook his hand.

"It's a pleasure to meet you, Ms. Richards. Anyone who can snag Van is okay in my book." He motioned at his team. "My teammates are Russ, John, and Michael." They all leaned across the conference table to shake her hand. Then Peter motioned to the two guys—thankfully sporting wedding bands—on the end. "The two freeloaders over there are Nate Lawson, who's the accounting genius, and his buddy Ethan McDonald, who's a whiz at the computers. They mainly work with Prescott International but freelance with Titan Security."

I motioned for all of us to take a seat. I didn't know who should start first, when Kaelin piped up, "I'm sorry to ask this, but I heard you don't really work for the security company that Van wanted to hire; you're an extension of them. Why is that?" The statement had only been made once and brief at that. I didn't know she'd picked up on such a minute detail.

Peter smiled. "We get asked that question a lot, ma'am. While we are no longer full-time with our unit in the Navy, we still have another year to fulfill with the reserve team before we are finally discharged. When we were offered this case, we had to call our handler to make sure nothing was coming up so we could commit full-time to helping you and Van figure out who this stalker is." He waved his hand back and forth between Luke, myself, and him. "Luke, Van, and Trent have known me since childhood; they can vouch for me." Peter then slammed his fist into his other hand. "All I know is that I want a few minutes with this jerk for going after your roommate. The way the man attacked Trent shows he's a coward hiding behind a strong fantasy of possession."

He went on to add, "Once we're fully discharged from service, we've already been offered contracts with Titan Security. We've done several jobs for them already. Feel free to contact Rick, who's the new manager, if you'd feel more comfortable. I'm sure he can put your mind at ease."

She held up her hand. "That won't be necessary. I can see by the way you look me in the eyes and don't bullshit around the question that you're telling me the truth. I just wanted to make sure you're legit." She waved her hand at his peers. "They're all Navy SEALs?"

He nodded. "Yes, ma'am."

"Please, call me Kaelin." She laughed before adding, "Too bad Russ isn't named Paul. All of you would make a good representation of the Four Horsemen of the Apocalypse." That seemed to lighten the mood in the room, as everyone laughed at her reference. I hadn't realized just how right she was until I looked at them in a new light.

"So where shall we begin?" I asked.

Prepared to take notes, Peter and his team opened up notepads, while Ethan opened up a laptop. Peter spoke first. "Let's begin with when this guy started talking with you. We need to know how long you were online before he came around. Was he aggressive at the start? Did he try anything initially? When did his demeanor change? What kind of setup do you have? What days did you broadcast? And can Ethan have access to your equipment so we can check for a backdoor?"

Kaelin looked like a deer caught in headlights. Her eyes were wide with fright, and she wasn't speaking, so I asked, "What do you mean by a backdoor?"

Ethan spoke up. "We know the guy is tech savvy, but we don't know to what degree. Regarding Kaelin's laptop, we can see if he had enough knowledge to create a backdoor or a weakness in the firewall, which would allow him to get into her system to track her, etc. We also need to see both of your cell phones to make sure there aren't any viruses attached to them as well." He looked pointedly at me. "I need to see your old laptops, the ones the stalker destroyed with viruses. I might be able to neutralize them and trace them back to a source."

Ethan held out his hands and shrugged his shoulders as a gentle expression formed on his face. "I know it's asking a lot, and it might feel like an invasion of your privacy, but this will help us profile the person and give us a better understanding of his knowledge and also help us develop a way to catch him."

Kaelin started to shake a little in her chair. I reached over and put a hand on her shoulders. "Are you okay, angel?"

"You have to know everything?"

Peter and Russ seemed to exchange some sort of silent communication along with some hand signals. Then Peter nodded, "Go ahead, sailor."

Russ began speaking. "Ms. Richards, Kaelin?" She looked up to see a gentle smile on his face and his hands in a surrender position. Her shaking began to slow. "No one is here to judge you. We all signed agreements that none of this will be discussed outside this room. As part of the Navy's most elite SEALs team, we all have levels of classified information, and yours are safe with us." He winked and said, "I actually have a secret that may help you feel a little more comfortable around us."

I found myself nodding with her while my eyes encouraged him to continue.

"My brother and I aren't from a wealthy home. I had a partial-scholarship to college but stuck around for my brother to finish high school so we could focus on his education first, because he had a full-scholarship to study pre-med in Gainesville. I worked odd jobs to help save money for us to move out and give our parents their space and a chance to enjoy some traveling and each other's company.

His eyes were somber, and I was beginning to wonder if there was a point to this story. "Two days after my brother's graduation, we gave our parents a gift card so they could go enjoy a nice meal on us. On the way home, a drunk driver struck them; everyone died on the scene. We moved to Gainesville to start anew, but the job potential was non-existent, so I joined the Navy and was later recruited for the SEALs. I had enough money to help my brother get through the first four years of college and pay for most of his needs associated with medical school. He didn't have time for a full- or part-time job while in school, but one of his dental school roommates was a high-priced gigolo on the side. My brother didn't want to compromise his morals, so he ended up dancing on stage in a member's-only club that catered to women certain days of the week. They helped him don a disguise so no one would recognize him, and he made enough to cover the rest of his expenses and then some."

I looked over to see Kaelin nodding. "Where is he now?"

Russ had a smile of pride on his face. "He's set to finish his surgical fellowship in another couple of months, and he's already accepted a local position at one of the hospitals." Russ raised one of his hands in the air gesturing between himself and Kaelin. "See, there's nothing to be ashamed of. I'm not happy that my brother had to resort to that, but he did what he had to in order to survive, without sacrificing the moral code our parents instilled in us. You're doing the same thing to get where you need to be in life. You're not doing anything illegal, and you're not sacrificing yourself for anyone, so there's no need to be ashamed. I actually applaud both you and my brother for being creative so you could pursue your goals in life despite your hurdles."

Kaelin touched her hand to her heart as some tears formed at the corner of her eyes. "Thank you for sharing your story, Russ. It helps to know I'm not alone in what I've had to do."

She started opening up willingly, answering every one of their questions. Apparently, Eagle Eyes started following her within the first month of her webcast going live. I could only see that I was in the main broadcast or private session room with her. It wasn't until he started kicking me out that I could see his name at all.

"He wasn't aggressive at first, just asking more questions than I wanted to answer. The main one was why I didn't allow my voice to be heard," she admitted.

Peter spoke up, asking, "Can you elaborate?"

"I didn't want to be recognized by my peers or anyone who knew my family, especially my father, so I donned a wig, fancy lingerie, a decorative mask, a couple of faux tattoos, and even used backdrops to make it look like I was in different parts of the world. I had a strong southern accent when I first started, a very distinctive one, so I used talk-to-text to communicate with my viewers. I would never answer any questions anyone asked, at least not until I stumbled across Van." Her hand reached out and caressed the side of my face.

All eyes were on me as the smirks ran down the line of the other side of the table. I shrugged my shoulders. "What? I'm a man, so sue me. I offered to help my brother with his roommate's webcast, since I enjoyed watching a bit of porn for relaxation. He needed some advice on how to help her set up her website. I didn't know Kaelin was Untouched Mystique, and she didn't know I was one of her favorite viewers. We just hit it off in reality with our college classes and online with her broadcast. It wasn't until later I discovered the truth, but I was already lost to both of them." The guys seemed to nod, understanding filling their eyes.

Kaelin jumped back in. "Eagle Eyes started getting more persistent with his questions and demanding I answer them. When I didn't, he blocked everyone's requests for me to do certain things, even throwing a few viewers out of the room. I didn't realize he was doing this until they started complaining. That's when Van's persona suggested private sessions, and then bought them all so Eagle Eyes didn't have as much access to me." She turned to me and smiled. "You were watching out for me this whole time and didn't even know it."

I shrugged my shoulders and shook my head. "No, angel, I didn't at the time. All I knew was that I was drawn to you."

I was getting angry remembering how things played out. "It was at that time Eagle Eyes started entering the private sessions on my end, booting me off at first, but then about a month later, he started sending viruses to blow up my laptops." I tried to remember the date this happened and just shook my head. "I'm not exactly sure of the date. But Kaelin—Mystique—didn't know this was going on. She only knew that one minute I was there, and the next I was gone. I always logged back on as quickly as I could, just to make sure she was okay and that he hadn't threatened her. A couple months ago when he blew up my computer, she wasn't online when I got back on, so I called Trent to go check up on her. He found her in the tub trying to soak off the tattoos and crying her eyes out, trembling." I slammed my hand down on the conference table hard enough for it to sting and loud enough that everyone jumped. "I never want to see her tremble or be frightened of this psycho again."

"Neither do we, Van." Peter said, his tone of voice taking command of the situation. "We talked with Trent, and he helped to fill in some of the timeline. He estimated around Christmas was when Eagle Eyes started showing his possessive nature and then proceeded to get worse as the New Year progressed. Trent also said the deliveries started a couple weeks back?"

My shoulders tensed as I saw Kaelin turn to me. She was aware of a few deliveries but not all of them. "There were more?" Her eyes were filled with hurt that I hadn't confided in her. "You and Trent kept them from me?"

"We didn't want to worry you at first. We wanted to see if we could figure out where they were coming from and put a stop to it. Unfortunately, the guy was clever and paid for someone else to go in and set up the delivery for him. That's when we had Marcus and a couple of our other personal security guards for the company and my family come on board to watch the building and keep whoever this is away from you," I admitted sheepishly. "I didn't want you frightened."

She sat back in her chair with a huff and crossed her arms, which made her breasts lift even more, causing some of the eyes in the room to be diverted. I shot a look across the table and saw every one of Peter's team shift their attention elsewhere. "I thought we had honesty here, Van." Her voice was exasperated.

"If it helps, I wanted to come in and tell you everything right away. It was Trent that kept you at arm's length, ensuring me he'd keep you safe. If you want to be mad, be pissed at him. I know I am. I love my brother, but sometimes he doesn't think, which is why he's in a hospital room recovering; he refused the security guards I wanted to put on both of you."

She couldn't look at me, instead, looking at the floor. "I'm sorry. I didn't know."

I reached out to her and tried to loosen her crossed arms, finally getting ahold of one of her hands and giving it a squeeze. "I'll give you full disclosure of the items delivered. I wanted you to know how sick this guy was, but Trent thought it was best if you didn't know Eagle Eyes had found the building you lived in. He wanted to keep your life as normal as possible, given everything."

Kaelin looked up as tears streamed down her face. "He shouldn't have. I'm stronger than he thinks."

Luke passed her some tissues to wipe her eyes, and we got down to business answering everyone's questions. Peter's team needed to know the details of her dating history, any former boyfriends in high school, college, and so forth. They discussed her family life, her dad's issues, being attacked at work by Roger, the deal her father made with Roger's father, Mr. Chadwick, all the way up to the present. They even included anyone at work and at the university who might have tried to talk with her, asked her out, or got upset with her for any reason. They left no stone unturned.

I was surprised to find that a couple of guys on campus, from our classes to be exact, had called her a bitch and tried to have Mark fire her for turning down their advances. One was a bit pushy and had followed her around for a while. His name was Hayden Michaels. I noticed, more than once, girls looked a bit uncomfortable around him. He definitely liked to bully people. The other, who seemed to back off, was Pierce Montgomery, basically a wimp, but he definitely had the computer skills, because he offered to change students' grades for a fee by hacking into the university's mainframe. I made a point to pass this information on to Peter's team.

Ethan asked for the computer equipment Luke had requested from Trent and Kaelin's condo so he could go ahead and get started on things while Peter's team continued their questions. Peter explained that they'd go over the information we gave them and have Ethan look up any potential suspects on his main computer—which had access to some of the most sensitive servers in the world—back at home base.

Ethan asked for our phones, just to run a program off his computer that would identify any potential threats there. According to him, all it takes is one opened text message from the wrong person to activate a virus in the phone that can turn the thing into a tracking device or a microphone, pending the person's intent. *Scary to think some people had nothing better to do with their time.*

Two hours of questioning from Peter's team, an hour of pointing out accounting issues with Nate, and several program checks from Ethan gave us a good start on profiling our psychopath.

Chapter 9

Kaelin

I was surprised when Van and Luke had introduced the head of the security team as one of their childhood friends. During the course of the discussion, it was a bit amusing when I learned the leader of the team used to be a hellion growing up. But wasn't that the way? Here I was the wallflower with a webcast for people to watch me get off. Irony can sometimes be a bitch.

The hours ticked by, and I felt like a prisoner being interrogated by a hostile enemy. I realized they needed what only I could answer, things that Van and I hadn't discussed yet, and I felt naked for the first time in my life, exposed to a roomful of men who could judge me in any light they wanted. I only hoped they'd all listen and wouldn't be critical, because as Russ pointed out, sometimes we have to do things we aren't proud of in order to get to an end result. But being able to do so without compromising our moral integrity, that's the trick, one in which I'd held on to so far.

I gave them an approximate timeline of when Eagle Eyes started talking with me and when he started getting a little more demanding and aggressive online, and then Van provided the details about deliveries I hadn't known about. After my spiel, I mostly listened to them all strategize what would be done. Peter's team put their heads together with Luke and discussed the details from every potential angle.

Wait a minute. Did I just hear correctly? "There was no match to the DNA left at the crime scene." My attention quickly went to Luke's words. "What DNA?"

I wondered. No one had told me anything other than my stalker beat up Trent before he got into the apartment.

I glanced back and forth between Van and Luke. They were communicating some silent message, and I'd had enough. I held up my hands, one in each direction, to indicate for them to stop. "I want whatever this silent communication you have going to halt immediately. I'm a grown woman. I have a right to know what's going on in *my* life."

Van nodded as Luke started filling me in. "The perpetrator wrecked the apartment. He didn't leave any fingerprints that we can run against databases for a match, but he did leave some DNA evidence."

"What kind of DNA?" I was repulsed thinking of the various options and hoped it was blood or spit. Somehow I knew it wouldn't be, because Eagle Eyes had become very perverse with his dialogue. *"One day soon, I'm going to be up inside that delicious cunt, break through your virginity, and mark you with my cum."* Recalling his words made me shiver, so I prayed it wasn't as bad as I feared.

Out of the corner of my eye, I noticed Van's face became enraged as his fist clenched and he tried to contain himself. Luke looked pale and sick to his stomach. He ran a hand through his hair, trying to stall.

"Just spit it out, Luke," I begged.

The words came fast. "There was blood on the mirror, saying 'She's Mine,' and he ejaculated all over one of your more popular outfits on your bed. We've run the DNA evidence with the state's database, but we didn't find a match."

A wide variety of emotions passed through me, revulsion being the most prevalent. I didn't know if I wanted to scream, wanted to punch something, or wanted to throw up at the idea of someone in my room, my personal space, getting off on my clothing while imagining me there. I knew this degenerate wanted me. He told me numerous times how he intended to take my innocence; how he wanted to spray me with his seed and impregnate me, tying me to him; how I belonged to him; and how he owned me. I always thought it was just part of the act, a part of his make believe world. Most of the men who watched me probably got off to me rubbing myself to completion, Van included, but to intrude into my space...no words could describe how I felt. I was truly violated.

"Thank you for your honesty, Luke." I turned toward Van, Nate, and Ethan. "Can we please get back to the accounts, change the subject, something?" I shook my head, trying to dispel the image formed in my mind. "I can't handle this right now."

The talk of accounting had my mind refocused in no time. I might've made Van a little jealous when I kept talking Nate's ears off. He was famous in the forensic accounting field for the issues he found in multiple companies, but mainly for taking down a major monetary hacker at the company he now worked for. He and Ethan created numerous programs in the accounting world to find issues and alert the accounting departments to potential errors. Ethan had gone one further to create firewalls that were nearly impenetrable. He continually reworked his systems to make them iron clad, and then sold them for a small fortune to multiple companies around the world.

Nate wanted permission for Ethan to install their software on the company's mainframe to have it run a silent check of where the mistakes in the accounts were coming from. The system they designed would not only highlight any changes made to finalized data instantly, but it would also keep the old copy and pinpoint which computer the changes were being made from, providing it came from an internal source.

Van shook his head. "What we have now works just fine." You could tell Nate and Ethan were getting frustrated at their suggestions being shot down.

Ethan also added, "Your firewall isn't as secure as it should be, neither is your Wi-Fi. There's code written into your programs giving someone backdoor access to your systems. We need to upload this software, both accounting and protective, to eliminate further risks until we can get this straightened out." He pointed to his screen and turned it around. I wasn't quite sure what I was looking at, since there were a bunch of numbers and characters written on the screen. "The perpetrator's signature is all throughout your system. This is how the virus got transferred into your computer, causing it to blow up. I can see a path from the backdoor right into your Wi-Fi. Thankfully, you were the only one logged in that night; otherwise, there'd be other blown electronics."

Looking over to Van, I noticed him running his hand through his hair. I'd been around him enough at school to know he only did that when he was getting stressed out. He looked up at Ethan. "And our phones?"

I had the same question. I noticed when we handed our phones over that Ethan pulled out a small metal-like box, placed our phones inside, hooked up some wires, and then ran some tests. It was fascinating on some level, but scary as hell, too.

"Your phone is fine, sir." Ethan looked over to me and shook his head. "However, it's a good thing your phone was turned off, Kaelin, or you would have been transmitting a signal to your current location. Your GPS had been turned on externally, and a virus had been uploaded into your phone via a text message, which turned your phone into a listening device. Whoever did this was using it to detect your every movement."

I was dumbfounded by the news. How in the hell could someone have managed to do this to my phone? Then I remembered getting a text from a number I didn't recognize. Mom sometimes bought burner phones to keep in touch with me so my dad wouldn't know where I was. As far as he was concerned, I still lived in Louisiana and was going to school there. The façade we'd created had worked, or at least I thought it did. The moment I opened that text must've been when it happened.

Van spoke up, asking the question I was about to. "Was her computer compromised?"

All eyes in the room focused on us as Ethan spoke. "There was a backdoor written into her computer and a program put into place. Every time she used the computer, he had access to everything she did and any information she placed on the system, including the webcasts."

The room was silent for a long time as all the information sunk in. *He'd been watching me. Not only was he viewing my broadcast through the webcast camera system but with my computer's cheap built-in camera when the other one was turned off.* I felt violated. "It all makes sense now."

Van looked at me flabbergasted. "What makes sense?"

"Do you remember how I had a list of songs I liked to listen to and how the viewers could add to the list, making their own selections for when I was on camera? It was set up to play like a jukebox—whoever put in the selection first, played first."

He laughed with a small smile playing on his lips. "Yes. I used to always pick Ed Sheeran's 'Shape of You.' Why?"

"He must've been watching me through the crappy camera on my computer the whole time. He added and kept picking that song by The Police, 'Every Breath You Take.' The lyrics say right in it that 'I'll be watching you.' Is it possible he could've also taken over my professional broadcasting camera? It was on the other day while the computer was down, and I know for a fact I turned it off after the last session." I shook my head in disgust, not only at this guy's actions but also at not realizing it sooner.

I opened my mouth with a gasp, throwing my hand over it. Everyone turned to me.

"What is it, angel?" Van grabbed ahold of my hand and gave it a squeeze.

I looked over to Ethan for confirmation. "If he had total control of my laptop, then he knows where I'm from, where I go to school, what my class schedule is, and my intern schedule?"

Ethan nodded. "Unfortunately, yes. I have no way of knowing exactly how much information he ascertained from your system. Anything and everything on your computer was accessible to him."

How could this have happened? How did I not see what was right in front of me? I slammed my hands down on the table, frustrated by what I'd just learned. "What about the so-called computer experts Trent used to make sure my signal bounced all over creation? Is it even there anymore? How could this monster have found me?"

Van put his hand on my thigh and gave it a squeeze of reassurance, letting me know he was there. Ethan shrugged for a moment, while everyone else looked shocked that I do, indeed, get pissed from time to time. Granted, I'm a wallflower, and a lot of people mistake me for being easily walked on, but don't push me or I'll push back—hard!

"I'll need to take a look at your broadcasting camera to see if he gained access to it, and I'll also need to take the computer with me to run some diagnostics to see when someone last worked on it, what they did, and at what point in time it was disabled. He's had a direct line to your laptop for a while now. I just need to figure out how long. Is there anything you needed from your system?" Ethan asked politely.

"I can access my email from any computer, but I do need my schoolwork. I can show you which files they're under."

He walked around with the computer so I could point them out. "I'll have a USB dropped off to Luke tomorrow afternoon after I ensure the files are safe to be loaded to your current computer. Right now, I have a scrambler hooked up to block any incoming and outgoing signals from the affected laptop."

There were a few more topics discussed. Van finally conceded the company needed new software and an upgrade to the firewall. Ethan and Nate volunteered to install the systems personally and to train the Accounting and IT departments on how to use them to get the full benefit of the system and increase productivity.

Everyone began to get up to leave, when I realized something no one had addressed. "What about my webcasts? I can't just disappear, wouldn't that raise suspicion?"

Peter's team looked at one another, then at Ethan, and then at us. Finally Van spoke up, saying, "I don't want you putting yourself in harm's way by doing those webcasts. That's just inviting him to provoke you."

"I agree with Van," Peter added. "Do you have a message board to communicate with others when you're not online?"

"Yes, but I rarely do that. I have an online schedule posted of upcoming webcasts. Most times and dates are locked into place, only a few need to be moved around. When that happens, I usually put up an apology post welcoming them to come back later. Why?"

He looked over to Ethan. "Can you go out as her and post that due to a family emergency all webcasts have been cancelled until further notice, while leaving an option for anyone to comment?"

Ethan nodded. "I'm doing it right now." Everyone watched as he took out his personal computer, accessed the internet address for my webcast, and logged on as me. I wondered how he figured out my password, but then again, the backdoor he spoke about might have had the answer there all along. I was over it at this point.

Peter then looked my way. "Let's buy ourselves some time to see if we can create a list of suspects and narrow them down. In the meantime, Nate and Ethan can work their magic on the computer systems while we track down any leads. We'll meet in a week, earlier if needed, to see if we're riling up Eagle Eyes. My thought is that by denying him his pleasure, he will leave messages, ones we might be able to track. I'm hoping we can avoid the need to put you online with a webcast to draw him out."

I didn't like it, but I'd have to live with it for now. God knows I didn't want anyone else hurt from this mess, myself included. "Okay."

The group began to leave, when I remembered a couple things. I held my hands up waving them back. "Wait. He had an accent."

Peter looked back. "The perpetrator?"

I nodded. "It wasn't there all the time. I'm not even sure if it was his real voice. Can you create an accent with a voiceover machine?" Heck if I knew.

Peter shook his head. "Machines can alter the sound of one's voice, but an accent is hard to reproduce." He wrote a couple lines down on his note pad. "What kind of accent was it?"

I shrugged my shoulders. I wasn't a linguist who could place people's roots based on their dialect. "He seemed to talk as normally as you and I are right now, but when he got upset with me, a Southern undertone slipped through. I almost want to say it was slightly familiar, almost sounding Cajun or Creole, but I might be mistaken. For all I know, he could've been hiding a French accent."

Peter's eyes widened. "Was the voice one you've heard before, from another point in your life perhaps?"

I shook my head, not sure how to answer. This was all so confusing. "I'm not sure I can answer that. I want to say yes, maybe, but I really don't know." Then it dawned on me. "You said you checked the state database for a DNA match. What if he's not from here? Is there a way to check the DNA evidence nationwide?"

Peter nodded. He came over and put his large hand on my shoulder and gave it a slight squeeze. "Don't worry about it tonight. We'll do another search on the DNA and open it up to other agencies to see if there's a match nationwide. For now just keep it in the back of your mind, and if you remember anything more have Van or Luke call us."

Luke followed everyone out, escorting them to the elevator, before returning. "Van, Kaelin, is there anything more you require tonight?"

I looked over at Van, encouraging him to answer. He held his hand up to Luke. "No, man, you've done well with getting a sharp team together in such a short time. Take the rest of the night off. We'll lock ourselves in the apartment and call it a night."

Luke nodded. "Sure thing. Marcus is on duty if you need him, along with Russ, who offered to stay behind just to be on the safe side. They're going to rotate one of their guys out at all times as added security to ours.

"I almost forgot. Trent is doing better. He called just before our meeting to see how things were going. His doctors are looking to release him in the next day or two. He's planning to go to your family's estate where a physical therapist and full-time nurse have been hired to help him heal."

We finally said our goodnights to Luke, and Van locked up his office with a security code before guiding me back through the hidden entrance to his apartment. "Are you ready for some food?"

I looked around, thankful we'd picked up all the paperwork I'd thrown about trying to dig for reasons why Van and Trent's father had bought up worthless companies. We'd shown Nate the figures, and everyone seemed to think Mr. Meyers had been coerced. All of us assumed it was his sexual proclivities, but who knew. Maybe there was something else he'd been hiding. Maybe the team could make some sense of it.

Pushing a couple of boxes to the side, I headed toward the kitchen, when Van grabbed my hand and spun me around, locking his arms around my body and pulling me as close as possible before sealing his lips over my mouth. The kiss was searing, possessing every inch of my mouth. *Why did it feel so good when he took control like this? Any other man scared the shit out of me.*

My stomach began to rumble, so Van pulled back, leaning his forehead against mine as he tried to catch his breath. "Why don't you go take a shower, love, and let the water wash away the stress of today while I fix us a pizza."

I made a face.

"What was that for?" He asked, laughing.

"I'm good with pizza, as long as it's not the frozen junk you get at the grocery store. Those things taste like cardboard." They did. I couldn't help it. I wasn't always a snob about my pizza, but after Trent introduced me to one of the pizza places he loved when he indulged in carbohydrate-loaded goodness...let's just say I thought my taste buds had their own food orgasm that night. I couldn't eat any other kind of pizza from that point on.

"Not to worry, angel. I don't like that junk either. If I know my brother, he's got you hooked on Little Anthony's Pizzeria."

I nodded. "Yes."

"I love the place, too. I even struck a deal with the owner. He partially cooks some pizzas for me to take home and freeze, which I can later cook the rest of the way here in my kitchen. I don't go to the pizzeria often, because normally by the time I stop working, they're closed, and they usually don't deliver to the downtown area."

My stomach started rumbling at the thought of eating. "What kind of pizza are we talking about?"

He shrugged his shoulders. "What's your favorite?"

"Don't make a face or laugh at me because most people think it's foolish, but I like..."

Before I could get the words out of my mouth, he started smiling, looking like the Cheshire cat. "Let me guess, ham and pineapple?"

I was in shock. Had Trent told him? "How?"

His fingers came up and caressed the side of my face. "I can tell that mind is working overtime to figure it out, but Trent didn't tell me much about your food preferences. If he had, I would've wanted to meet you sooner.

"When are you going to trust me when I say that we're more alike than you give me credit for? We don't differ that much in backgrounds or anything else for that matter. I know your dad's family had money, a fairly impressive amount at one point."

I skipped right over the piece of information he just let slip and focused on something else. "But what about my past, my father kicking me out, and what I've been doing to get by?"

With a look of infatuation playing across his face, he cradled my head gently with both hands and looked deep into my eyes. "I don't care about your past. I already know everything I need to about you. As for your father, I'd like to give him a taste of his own medicine for treating you so unjustly. And what you're doing now may not be ideal, but it brought our paths together."

He tenderly moved one of his hands to the side of my head and gently intertwined my hair between his fingers, making me want to lean into him. If I were a cat, I'd be purring. He pointed his finger toward my forehead. "All I care about is what's in here," he then moved his hand down over my chest to my heart, "and in here. You aren't your online persona. You, Kaelin, are a rare gem that's had me enraptured by your shining quality, clarity, and shape since the moment I laid eyes on you. I adore everything about you...I love you."

I started to open my mouth, when his finger came up to stop me. "I know I'm saying things too fast, too soon, but I can't help how I feel when I'm around you. I think that one song by Selena Gomez says it perfectly: 'the heart wants what it wants,' and mine wants yours. But don't tell me you feel the same way until you know with absolute certainty that you love me. I know we still have a lot to learn about one another, and I'm willing to wait for you to say it, because I know you will. When your heart is ready...I'll be waiting."

I was speechless. I couldn't say a word. My heart was too overwhelmed by the knowledge that this man, a man who looked like he walked off the cover of GQ, a man who could have any woman he wanted, desired me.

He was right. My heart was confused. I was fearful of the stalker, not feeling I could let my guard down to explore what was right in front of me. Van was offering me a future, one I never knew could exist, but I wanted it. I just needed to open my heart to the possibilities.

Van turned to walk toward the kitchen, when the reality of his first words hit me like a ton of bricks. "How do you know about my father's family? Did you have me investigated?" *How dare he do that!*

Shaking his head, he stopped in his tracks and headed toward the closet. I watched as he entered the walk-in, and then heard some kind of mechanism open. Maybe a safe? He walked back out with a folder and handed it to me to scrutinize. "It was my father, not me, angel. He had you investigated the moment I met you in the coffee shop. He wanted to find some dirt so I wouldn't be interested in you; instead, he almost threw out the plan he had with Heather's family in favor of you and your grandfather's fortune, until he had your father's parents investigated, too. He changed his tune when he realized your grandfather lost most of his wealth during the recession. Dad didn't bother to investigate further to see that your grandfather is now worth a lot more, thanks to some wise investments and the recent turnaround in the market."

Van leaned against the back of the sofa, his arms crossed and a look of distaste on his face. "When Dad found out we had a few classes together, he tried to get my schedule changed, only to discover few professors taught the subjects we were taking in the master's level. The bastard even tried to railroad a few professors into pulling me off our group assignments, but they refused to budge."

I looked at him with cautious eyes. "So you didn't have any part in this?" I held up the folder and found myself looking through the detailed material again.

He lightly lifted my chin, stared me straight in the eyes, and shook his head, so I knew he was telling me the truth. "I only found out about it because Dad had Luke do the inquiry. However, Luke kept one crucial piece of information from all of us: that you lived with Trent. Father would've been furious. He would've tried to destroy both of you."

The folder was more thorough than I could've ever imagined. It had a copy of my birth certificate, my parent's marriage license, information about both sets of grandparents, my father's siblings, and so on, right down to bank accounts, statements, and net worth for each individual.

How they could find information about my grandfather's offspring not wanting to take over the family's restaurant chain throughout the South, I have no clue. He ended up selling it and making a huge profit, even retaining a large chunk of stockholder shares with the new company. Unfortunately, the recession had taken most of that and over half the chain folded. My dad had bitched, moaned, and groaned that he would have gone into the business had I not been conceived and born.

My grandfather had often said it was my dad's immaturity and inability to take responsibility for his actions that caused him to sell the business. He couldn't trust him, and the rest of his kids didn't have any interest in running the company. He and my grandmother were the only ones on that side of the family to show me any love and affection. Everyone else treated me like an unwanted bastard child. Oh how I wish I could talk to my grandparents to tell them I'm okay. Mom said they'd been upset with their son for running me off. But Dad wanted what he wanted, and he wasn't about to change for anyone, not matter what. If I dared to contact them, my father would know I wasn't living in Louisiana.

I couldn't look through any more of the folder tonight. Some of the information in there brought back bad memories of my father constantly yelling at me, while others made me long for the familiarity of those who loved me. I had enough stress and chaos to last a lifetime. The past couple of days alone were enough to send most people over the edge. I needed that shower and a chance to unwind.

Placing the folder down on the edge of the coffee table, I turned toward the bathroom, ready to escape reality for just a few moments and bask in the glory of a hot shower to wash away my cares. "I'm going to take that shower. I just can't deal with anything else right now." I needed to get away from Van, so I grabbed a nightshirt and some fresh panties from the dresser drawer and then closed myself in the bathroom. I didn't want him to see the tears that were streaming down my face. I needed to forget everything for the moment, and the only way I knew how was to make myself come.

Chapter 10

Kaelin

I LOVED THE OPAQUE glass feature of the bathroom door. I could see Van's shadow stripping out of his business suit and wondered if he could see me. My mind instantly pondered how he looked without his shirt and, even better, without his boxers. Feeling my body heat up at the idea of us being naked together, I quickly dismissed the thoughts.

Girl, get your mind out of the gutter. You need to make yourself feel better before you try anything with that hunk of man. My subconscious was right. My life was in chaos, and I couldn't focus on anything but the need to feel myself surrender, to let an orgasm cast out all the negative thoughts and fears in my life, giving me just a few moments of peace.

Stripping quickly, I stepped into the water and let it flow over my body while soothing me with its warmth. The weight of today slammed into me, making my legs give way, forcing me to lean against the tile wall. Every moment of the day, good and bad, played through my mind. *How did it all come to this?*

Feeling detached for the first time in years, I slid down the wall onto the floor of the shower. The only other time I'd been numb was the night I finally had the courage to walk away from my father. His behavior indicated it might be coming, but I never thought he'd try to sell me to someone. Talk about a shock to your system. My father was a lost cause and everyone knew it. Mom and her parents, with what little they had to offer monetarily, helped me set up an escape out of town and out of the state to start a new life. I hated that man. He forced me to leave everything I cared about behind, but I was free now.

Who are you kidding? You think you're free, but here you are on the floor of a man's shower. A man you haven't known very long. You're isolated from society, from life, hiding away from a maniac while you put your trust in others. Can you trust them? Will you be saved? Will Van be your white knight ready to save you from whatever evil follows you? I shook my head, not knowing how to answer my thoughts. They always turned dark when I was down, when I needed to escape from reality. But did I trust everyone? It's not like I had a choice in the matter. Either I go out on my own and a psychopathic sex fiend gets me, or I wait it out, protected by someone who claims to love me as I am.

The water continued to rain down on me from above, cleansing me in more ways than one. One of my hands found its way toward my slit, parting it to find my nubbin hard and waiting for release. Thoughts of Van had my nipples hard and erect and my center aching to be touched. My fingers walked the path they'd walked many nights over the past year, but I didn't have his voice guiding me to completion. I tried time after time to get myself off. I could feel the buildup deep within me. I managed to get right on the edge but faltered.

My attempts were futile, and my center ached for release. I vaguely became aware of someone crying. While trying to quiet my mind and figure out where the noise was coming from, realization hit: it was me. There was pounding around me, but I was too caught up in my own world to know what it was. The bang of something hitting the door caused me to curl up into myself as the warmth of the shower began to escape.

I didn't look up to see why I was shivering. I knew I'd been in here for a while. How long? I didn't know. I could hear Van saying something, but the words didn't quite make it through to my mind. I was dazed, confused, and ready to give up. I needed out of this nightmare and it needed to be now.

The shower door closed and I saw his feet as he stood close to me to adjust the water's temperature. It had started to cool before he adjusted the setting but then warmed my skin again; although, my shivering didn't stop. I heard something hit the floor and saw Van's waterlogged t-shirt in the back corner.

His warm arms encircled me and lifted me onto his lap. I assumed he stripped completely, but he retained his boxers, though the feel of his cock beneath me told me why: he was hard. I guess he didn't want to scare me.

He pulled my head against his shoulder while his other hand drew me tightly against his chest.

The dam broke and I cried like I'd never cried before.

"Get it out of your system, Kaelin. It's unhealthy to harbor everything inside you."

The tears gushed for what seemed like an eternity. They finally started to ebb, and through it all, Van continually held me close, dropping kisses to my forehead, my hair, and my face while his hand ran up and down my arms to comfort me. Never did he once try to touch me inappropriately while I sat naked in his lap. *How did this man keep such restraint? Didn't he suffer from blue balls? Is that what he called it?*

My first words, "I'm sorry," were choked out and barely audible.

He wrapped both arms around me and hugged me so tightly. "It's okay, love. You've been through so much in your lifetime, especially the past few days." His hand lifted my chin, and he gave me a chaste kiss on the lips. "I'm here for you through all this and more. I just hope we can put this nightmare behind us soon, allowing us the chance to get on with our lives, together."

I know he'd explained why he was drawn to me. We shared so many likes and dislikes that it was almost scary. I mean, who has that much in common with another person? Wasn't the old expression that opposites attract? So why did it feel as if we were one person, merely split in half and finally having found the other half of our missing soul and could both breathe again? And why couldn't I just let my guard down and be happy for once?

Staring into Van's crystal-blue eyes felt like diving into the warm waters of the Gulf of Mexico. It felt like home, and it scared me. I watched as his eyes traveled down my body to the hand I still held between my thighs. A small smile played on his lips as realization hit him. "Are you like me, angel? When you're stressed, you need to surrender your anxieties out to the universe with a sexual release."

I nodded but then shed a few tears I didn't think I still had. "It's been days since I've come. I know I'm wound up tighter than a guitar string ready to break, which isn't allowing me to get there."

Van kissed my forehead and pulled me against his shoulder as he rocked us on the floor of the shower. His voice lowered, taking on the seductive tone he always used as DaLuvMaster online, the tone that always drove me to the edge of reason and made me climax harder than I'd ever done in my life. "I think I know why, darling. It's come to the point that I need you in order to get off, and I think you need me, too. We've been there for each other over the internet, guiding one another to the height of sensual pleasure, a pleasure only each of us could give to the other."

He hastily changed the topic, asking, "Have you washed yet?"

I shook my head, wondering where this was going and knowing I looked baffled by his question. He moved me off of his lap and stood, offering his hand to assist me. I tried to cover myself, but he grabbed me under the arms, which exposed my body to him as he lifted me to my feet. His tone was soft, yet stern. "I don't want you to ever cover yourself around me, angel."

I looked down at the shower floor, not wanting to meet his eyes, but he forced me to look at him anyway.

"You're more beautiful than a Greek goddess."

I blushed while looking anywhere except directly at him.

He moved his head around until my eyes finally locked on his. "Besides, I've seen you naked countless times over the last nine months. I've memorized every inch of your glorious curves. My only regret is that I've never felt those curves until now."

I started to speak, but he shook his head and placed a finger over my lips. "I don't want you talking, not just yet. I'd like your permission to help you bathe, and in return, you can do the same for me. We've already used up a lot of water. It would be shameful to waste anymore when we could just shower together."

Van looked quizzically at me. "Is that okay with you?"

I nodded in agreement but feared what it would do to me to feel his hands washing my body.

He walked me back into the stream of water and guided my head back so my hair got completely wet. I closed my eyes and enjoyed the feel of the water cascading down my body. I jumped when I felt his hands start to work my lavender-scented shampoo into my hair. "Your hair is so soft. I love the feel of its texture. I can imagine it wrapped..." His words trailed off, and I could feel his manhood stir underneath his soaked boxers as he moved close to rinse my hair.

"Why don't you remove your boxers?" I wondered.

He stood back from me a bit. "I don't want to scare you. You're naïve, to a point, about sex. Have you seen a cock?"

I blushed a bit. He was right. I hadn't seen one in person before, other than his brother's and only by accident, but I wouldn't admit it. "I've seen them online." His eyebrows quirked with amusement, so I figured I'd better explain. "My roommate in the dorms was addicted to watching free porn. She watched almost anything and everything from masturbation to the physical act of sex. That was her way of relieving stress and what ultimately gave me the idea of doing my webcast. She became so addicted to it that she started paying to watch the films, not being satisfied with the free clips."

Trying to hold back a laugh, he bit his lip.

"What?" I wondered.

Van shook his head. "It's nothing, Kaelin. I always wondered how you got into this. I would've never guessed it was from an example set by another student." Stepping back, he lowered his fingers into his waistband and slowly worked the water-laden briefs off his body.

I was mesmerized the moment his cock sprung free from its confines. My eyes were bulging at the sheer size of him. I'd seen men with huge pieces online, but this put all those guys to shame. I caught myself reaching out to touch it but then realized what I was doing and stepped back.

Grabbing my hand, Van guided me to him. "It won't bite, love, not unless I tell it to." He laughed. *The bastard.* "Go on, touch it. You won't hurt me unless you grip it too hard. Besides, I do expect to get to wash every inch of your body, and I want the same in return, including my cock."

His hand rested over mine as he pulled me to his manhood. It was standing strong and proud, curving up toward his belly. He was huge. I'd heard people call a penis a rod, but his cock didn't feel like hard metal; instead, it felt soft to the touch but hardened underneath the silky texture of skin. I was shocked to see he was clean-shaven, just as I was down there. I'd been told I should remove the hair because that's what men wanted. Actually, it's what Van told me in the beginning of my webcast. *"Men desire their women clean-shaven so they can see their pussy dripping with the juices of desire. It also provides more sensitivity to the man and woman during oral sex."*

I ran my hand down the length of his shaft and marveled at the feel, when his cock twitched in my hand, causing me to jump. After a few more caresses, it began to grow in my hand, and his hips starting to thrust ever so slightly as a moan escaped his lips.

He pulled back abruptly and spun me around. His breath was uneven, his voice throaty, "Enough, love. I can't take the feel of your touch. It's too tempting. If you keep this up, I'll want more than what you can give me." He leaned forward, placing a kiss on my neck just below my ear. "If you tempt me any further, I'll need to take you against this shower wall. I wish for your first time to be special, Kaelin, and would like it to be memorable for you, for both of us. I yearn to be not only the first man to climb inside you, taking your virtue, but the only man to ever know how it feels to have those walls clamped around my dick as I take you to heaven and beyond in sexual bliss."

His hands were now soaped and washing over every inch—and I do mean every freaking inch—of my body. He was turning me into a wanton creature as he held the weight of my breasts in his hands, tweaking the nipples into hardened peaks. They hurt so badly. I needed him to relieve them, but he didn't, only pinching them before moving down my body to my mound. He cupped it in his hands as he washed between my folds and up around my backside. He left no portion of my body untouched. My internal temperature had reached boiling, and my body was vibrating with need. My breaths came hot and heavy as I found my ass rubbing, on its own volition, against his hardness.

"Patience, Kaelin. I know you need to come, but it won't be here in this shower. We'll give each other pleasure out on the bed."

I stiffened at his words, knowing I wasn't ready for actual sex, not yet at least. The idea of his size entering my small, untried center scared the hell out of me. He must've read my thoughts.

"No, love. I'm not going to take you, at least not tonight. As I told you before, I'll only take you when you're ready for me. You'll have to be the one to tell me when you're set to accept my cock," his voice dropped to a heated tone, "and it will be me that takes your virtue. I'm laying claim on that pussy right now."

His words sent a shiver down my spine. "You like it when I talk dirty to you, like I did online. Does it get you hot for me?"

I nodded. He knew me too well. It was his words and his self-assurance with his own sexual needs that got me to come. I didn't require a toy and didn't have to use my hands, but I did need him to get me off. No other person online was able to get me to the edge.

His hand slipped down between the apex of my thighs before he traced between my folds with his finger, feeling my juices already drenching me. He dipped it at the edge of my opening and gathered the moisture before bringing his finger up where I could see it glistening with my desire. "Look at you, love. You're soaked."

I turned around and watched in amazement as he sucked on that same finger.

"Mmm. You're more delicious than I ever imagined. I could easily get addicted to your taste."

Without warning, Van's lips crashed against mine, and my mouth opened in surprise. I thought I'd be repulsed kissing him after he'd sucked on my juices, but the taste shocked me. I was further getting turned on by his actions. If he kept this up, I'd be going off like a firecracker on the Fourth of July. He already had the fuse lit.

The kiss was scorching. So much so that I didn't even realize we changed places in the shower, until he grabbed my hand and poured some shampoo onto it. "Lather me up, angel."

He bent down so I could reach his hair. I lathered him up and guided the water over his head to rinse him clean. He poured the bodywash onto my hands next. I rubbed them together before washing his body. I loved feeling the lines of all his muscles. Damn, the man was ripped beyond belief. His clothing hid so much of his shape that it was ridiculous. He had the face of GQ but the shape of a bodybuilder. His pecs were hard, and his nipples poked out, enticing me to lick and bite one, but I refrained. His chest had only a light sprinkling of hair while a darker line of hair trailed below his abdomen down toward his clean-shaven cock. His hips were that perfect V that every woman swooned over, while his backside was the tightest ass I'd ever seen on a man. Trent was quite the cover model, always in demand because of his physique, but I wondered why Van hadn't considered doing the same. He was Adonis personified to infinity. I felt light-headed just looking at him. His arms and his legs were straining with muscles, solid in their form, but it was his cock that got my attention, drawing me to him.

Van's eyes closed often during the time I washed him, with primal moans escaping from his throat as I slowly finished. "You have no idea what you do to me, Kaelin."

I pushed him under the flow of water to rinse him off, and his lips found mine once again. "Thank you, love," he whispered as the water poured over our bodies, creating a protective cocoon and allowing us to escape from the world for a few moments.

I pulled back to see the head of his cock dripping with a touch of pre-cum. I swiped at it with my finger, and before I realized what I was doing, my finger was in my mouth so I could taste his essence.

His eyes closed as he drew me into a hug. "What am I going to do with you? You entice me to no end. Do you have any clue the number of times I've jerked off in this shower to the thought of you? And now you're here, teasing me. I'd love nothing more than to see your lips swollen with my kisses and wrapped around my dick while you suck every part of me into your soul."

His words had an unusual effect on me. I felt power for the first time in my life. I didn't know how to respond to his declaration. "You taste salty and sweet, which reminds me of salt water taffy I used to get when we went to the beach."

Laughing a bit, Van shook his head as he smiled down on me. "Feel free to have all the free samples you want, love. I have an infinite supply, and it has only your name on it."

My breasts pressed against his chest as I reached behind him to turn off the water. I could feel his heart beating uncontrollably, much like my own. "Towels?"

He opened the shower door, grabbed two towels from the warmer, and dried me off from head to toe before asking the same in return. He then wrapped his towel at his waist and wrapped mine around my center, just barely containing my breasts. He walked me over to a stool and gestured with his hand—an indication for me to sit.

I watched as he pulled out a hair dryer and brush and began to dry my hair like an expert. "Where did you learn how to do this?" I asked a bit harshly. I'm not sure I wanted to know the answer, for a little bit of jealousy crept into my system.

Turning the dryer off, he leaned down and kissed me gently on the cheek. "My sister, Alyssa, broke her arm once. Mom was busy with society functions, Trent was off at college, and Alyssa was too old for a nanny, so I helped her style her hair."

"Oh," was the only thing I could utter, because I felt ashamed of myself for jumping to conclusions.

"By the way," he whispered into my ear, "this little streak of jealousy is such a turn on. Be careful. My beast already wants you and is barely contained by his leash. Don't make me break my promise, love."

I didn't say another word as he turned on the dryer and finished styling my hair to perfection.

He held his hand out to assist me standing. As soon as I was upright, he bent down and flung me over his shoulder, carting me out to the bed and plopping me down right in the center, but not before removing my towel completely.

My voice was shaky. "Whhaattt arrre youuuu doing?"

Van's eyes darkened with desire, his breath increased, and he resembled a godlike predator, and I was his prey. "Something I've only dreamed of doing. I got a taste of you in the shower, but you and I both need to find release to ease our suffering, to wash away the shit the past two days have brought. You need my voice to come, right?"

I nodded. "Yes."

"Well, I need to touch you. I won't ask you to reciprocate, but I need to bring you to the edge and push you over into the biggest orgasm you've experienced to date."

To anyone else, his words would seem pompous and too self-confident in their ability, but with me, I knew he had the power, and so did he. Van had done it before, but to finally feel his hands where mine had once been, to enact the scenario we'd done time and time again... "Please. Make me come, Sir."

Chapter 11

Van

HER WORDS, *"MAKE ME come, Sir,"* went straight to my cock. This was going to be hard at best. The scent of her arousal was already calling to my inner being, demanding the alpha side of me come alive to satisfy my own needs. I was going to have to keep my towel wrapped around my waist; otherwise, I might be tempted to dip into the pleasure of her warmth, which I knew would easily be addictive.

Thinking back on some of our earlier interactions, I'd once asked Kaelin, or rather Mystique, if she was saving her virginity until marriage. Her answer was astounding. *"I've had numerous offers to 'tap that,' 'get my v-card punched,' and even offered money to take away the 'burden' I was bearing. To me, it isn't a hardship to wait for the one who isn't going to 'get it and go.' I don't need to be wined, dined, and romanced to an extreme, but the person I let in is the one who has my heart. It doesn't have to be a forever romance, but I do require some kind of connection with the person."*

As I watched Kaelin adjust to the sudden changes in her life, I couldn't help but be awed by her incredible strength. Her resilience and courage were nothing short of captivating. I had been drawn to her for longer than I could remember, and every moment spent in her presence only solidified my feelings.

Our connection went beyond mere friendship. At university, we shared a special bond that had carried over to our professional lives, and even to our intimate moments online. But I yearned for more. Could we build a life together that would fulfill us both? My mother used to say that living together was the ultimate test of a couple's compatibility, and I couldn't agree more.

Only two days had passed since we were thrown together, but I knew that if—no, when—we finally came together, it would be at Kaelin's behest. I was willing to wait as long as it took for her to feel the same way I did. The thought of being with her filled me with a passion that burned like a flame, and I knew that no matter what challenges lay ahead, I was ready to face them with her by my side.

"What's going on in that mind of yours?" She asked shyly, still trying to cover her nudity.

I checked to make sure my towel was still tightly wrapped around my waist. I wanted her to have access to my cock, to hold it, to touch it. I wanted her to start getting acquainted with it personally, since it would soon become her new sex toy and best friend.

Crawling up on the bed, I pushed one leg between hers to open her to me. I leaned forward and kissed the edge of her nose and smiled. "I've been dreaming of this moment for a long time. To have you here in my bed naked for my viewing pleasure is one of my deepest fantasies come to life."

Her sharp intake of breath filled the air, and my senses heightened as I watched her bite down on her lower lip. My cock pulsed with desire, and I couldn't resist reaching down to pull her lip free.

"No biting your lip, my sweet angel," I murmured. "They belong to me now." And with that, I began to shower her with soft kisses, trailing my lips along her forehead, her eyes, and her cheeks. I savored the way her body responded to my touch, reveling in the soft moans that escaped her lips.

But it was the spot underneath her ear, the spot that drove most women crazy, where I licked and softly nipped at her skin, causing her body to shiver. As she moaned, I whispered in her ear, "Remember how I used to guide your hands as if they were mine, urging you to close your eyes and let your mind go? Well, tonight, it's your turn to let go and surrender yourself completely to me."

Her eyes changed color to that of a darkened forest green. Her voice was deep and throaty. "Yes."

"Remember how you closed your eyes and imagined it was me hovering over your body guiding your hands to the places I wanted you to touch? How I wouldn't let you come until I gave you permission? How all your pleasures belonged to me?"

Her voice was barely audible. "Yes."

I had her on edge, right where I wanted. With my hands, I lifted hers back toward the headboard and placed them around two of the decorative spindles. "Tonight, my father won't stand in our way, and your dad is but a distant memory. We'll forget about the world around us and focus on you and me. There will be no personas to hide behind, and our eyes will be wide open to everything around us. I'll show you that same scene, only this time it will be my hands, my lips, my touch that'll make you come."

I held her hands in place as my eyes looked deep into hers. "I want you to hold on to this headboard. If you move, I'll stop, denying you your pleasure, and we'll start all over again. I'm sure you don't want to do that, with both of us needing to come."

"Yes, Sir."

Kaelin's breathing was elevated, her nipples hardened into peaks, and the aroma of her essence was sending me into meltdown mode. I needed to touch her, to taste her in the ways I'd only imagined.

I ground my knee up into her crotch, feeling the wetness and heat emanating off her pussy and wished it were my dick feeling it instead. I bent down and began to kiss her, nipping at her lower lip, pulling it until she finally opened. Our tongues met in a frantic dance of seduction, tasting every inch of one another's mouths until my mind was filled with every possible way I planned on taking her.

I backed off and leaned into her ear to whisper. "It's my turn to feel you, to touch this delicious body, to see how mad I can drive you before you come all over my tongue and my hand."

She arched her back off the bed and moaned as I licked my way down to her neck, where I purposefully sucked her luminous skin into my mouth, marking her, wanting ownership over her so others would see she was mine. That word:

MINE. For my father it meant what he could possess with money, but for me, I wanted it to mean my connection to Kaelin, my possession of her body, my control over her orgasms. For the first time in my life, the word had meaning to me.

My tongue trailed down to one of her breasts. I licked around the outer edges of her nipple, teasing it, feeling it harden and extend even further. Wondering how she'd respond, I began to massage her other breast, rolling the nipple between my fingers, pinching it lightly. A low moan escaped from the back of her throat as her body arched up against my hand and my mouth. She wanted more.

I began to lightly bite and suck on her luscious globes, teasing her with what we could be together and imagining one day I might have a son or daughter sucking on this very nipple. I never fancied myself a family man, but with Kaelin, I began to see things that I once despised about my father. I wanted to be the man he couldn't. I wanted to show a wife and children the love he'd failed to give. I was determined to break the cycle.

Kaelin's hips began to gyrate against my upper leg. I'd never been with someone so responsive. I'd almost bet that if I played with her breasts long enough, I could get her to come, but I didn't want to waste an orgasm on second base. No, sir, I wanted to skip second and go right to third.

I released her nipple with a pop and then blew on it to cool it down, causing her to shiver. I moved over to her other breast to show it equal attention. I licked my way down to her navel and bit it lightly, causing her to jump.

My leg was covered with her slickness. It was all I could do to refrain from pulling the towel off and entering her. But the need to taste her, to bring her pleasure was more overwhelming and ruled my brain. She didn't trust easily, but I was determined to earn her reliance on me, and it didn't hurt to drive her wild in the process.

When I moved down the bed, she squeezed her legs together to try and control her desire. I popped her lightly on the side of her thigh before pushing my hands between her legs and opening her to me. "I didn't get enough of your flavor in the shower, angel. I want to taste that sweet nectar and sear the flavor into my memory while driving you over the edge."

"Please."

My lips hadn't even touched her clit, and she was already needy. My sweet Kaelin needed help to fly, and I was about to give it to her. "Please, what? Tell me what you need, darling, and I'll be more than happy to help you soar."

"Touch me...make me come, Sir."

"Your wish is my command, Kaelin." Her hardened clit protruded from its cover, seeking out my touch. I lowered my tongue and brushed over her nubbin lightly, which caused her to buck against my face. I tightened my grip on her legs to hold her down. "You'll need to keep still for me, angel, and remember, you're not to come until I give you permission."

I didn't wait for her to respond. The flavor of her was all over my tongue and driving me crazy. I felt like a wolf deprived of his snack for too long, and now I intended to feast until my inner beast was satisfied.

I used my thumbs to open her folds and expose her clit for my pleasure. I licked her up and down teasing her clit a couple times to ensure she'd stay put. Her moans were getting more intense, but she held her position, so I moved her legs over my shoulders, which forced her to open wider. Slipping one hand underneath her gorgeous ass, I lifted her to my mouth to devour.

My tongue ran the full length from her clit to her ass and back again, before settling on the warmth emanating from her center. She hadn't come yet, but her juices were flowing and too intoxicating to ignore. I lapped at her core, licking up every ounce of her pleasure. The more I tasted, the more I wanted to dive into her and make her a part of my soul. I moved my free hand up to rub circles on her clit as I pushed my tongue forward into her center and felt her walls clamp down on it.

I watched as her head thrashed against the pillow, but her body remained unmoving as I continued my pursuits to drive her toward her release. I reached out for a pillow to push up under the ass of this angel I desired so that I could use both hands to drive her mad with desire.

With Kaelin firmly in place, I dipped one finger into her moisture and began spreading it against her puckered back hole. I knew she wasn't unfamiliar with touch to this area, because I had insisted she try small plugs in her backside for her webcast. I pressed one finger against her ass and pushed forward. Her restrictive ring gave way to allow one finger deep inside her forbidden hole. She sighed as I pushed my finger in and out of her ass while I continued to rub circles against her clit and eat out her pussy.

Her body began to vibrate, signaling her release was building. I pushed two fingers into her center, and her body stilled as her virginal walls clamped hard against my fingers, not allowing them to move and seek out her g-spot. "I'm not going to touch your hymen, angel. Your purity will remain intact. I'm only after a little bundle of nerves that'll have you seeing stars." I managed to move one finger just enough to find the tissue I was looking for and pressed into the area, causing a low groan to come from her throat. "Relax, love, I promise only utter enjoyment and relaxation."

Her stiff posture relaxed, and I continued in my pursuits. I pushed my fingers up against her pleasure center and pumped one finger in and out of her ass while I latched onto her clit, sucking it into my mouth. When I felt her body tense, holding right on the edge, I finally said, "Come for me, angel. Let the heavens hear your sweet release," before biting down on her clit, causing her to scream out in pleasure.

Kaelin's eyes rolled back in her head. Her body stiffened and then jerked as her vaginal walls and her ass milked my fingers. Seeing her take her pleasure nearly caused me to spill my load. It was a true sight and honor to behold. I would love to see her lose herself with me over and over for the rest of our lives. This was one thousand times more satisfying than watching her online.

When her body started to calm, I removed my fingers and began to lick the juices from her pussy and inner thighs, which kept her on edge for a little while longer. Kaelin finally begged for mercy.

My heart swelled with emotion as I moved up to lie beside her and gently removed her hands from the headboard. I couldn't bear to see her in pain, even the white-knuckled grip she had shown from our intense passion. As I gazed upon her, my eyes filled with adoration and love. I wanted nothing more than to spend the rest of my life with this woman. I had the ring in night stand drawer, waiting for the perfect moment to ask for her hand in marriage.

I couldn't help but run my hands over her body, feeling the warmth of her skin, the beat of her heart, and the depth of her soul. I knew that she had been through a difficult life, with a father who had never shown her the love and support she deserved. But I was determined to prove to her that not all men were the same. I wanted to be the one to make her feel cherished, loved, and adored.

My brother had told me about her past and how untrusting she was of most men. But I was different. I would do whatever it took to win her heart and show her that I was the one she had been waiting for. I had hoped to take things slow and date her the old-fashioned way, but fate had other plans for us. We were forced together in this intense moment of passion, and I couldn't be happier.

When I had promised my brother and her that I would protect her with my life, I meant every word of it. She was the missing piece of my heart, and I would do whatever it took to make her mine forever.

Kaelin's breathing settled, and she tried scooting back against me, but I stopped her. "Be careful, love. My cock is still at attention and in beast mode."

Her head turned to me. "You didn't get off?"

Leaning forward to kiss the end of her nose, I shook my head. "Don't worry about me. I got plenty of pleasure watching you."

The next words out of her mouth hit me hard.

"I want you to take my virginity, Van."

Under normal conditions I would've jumped at the opportunity. The idea of being with the woman of my dreams had me harden to an uncomfortable state, but I couldn't act on it, not yet anyway. I wasn't a virgin like Kaelin. While I was getting my bachelor's degree, my old man encouraged me to tap anything with legs. Granted, I didn't sleep with tons of women, but I wasn't a saint either. I took precautions with the women I was with, but the moments were fleeting, only serving the purpose of seeking a release. I didn't feel anything for any of them.

My mom and my brother fully believed that we are born of one soul and are split apart, thanks to the inherent evils of life. It is only when we find our other half that we truly feel the joy life has to offer and the true promises of the flesh. It was what I felt with Kaelin: the ability to breathe, be whole, and love with my whole heart. Everything my father had said about love being for suckers...well he was the damn fool. I'd rather spend my life wrapped up in the love of a beautiful, caring, and intelligent woman than feel the emptiness of a casual fuck. They did nothing for me, while she...she set my soul on fire.

"Van?"

I snapped out of my thoughts and looked into Kaelin's concerned face.

"Don't you want me?" Her voice was shaking, uncertain of what we meant to one another.

I reached over to move her hair out of her face and behind one ear. "You have no clue the depth my soul craves you. I would love nothing more than to be your first, your one, your only in this life. But right now I feel it wouldn't be proper. You're terrified of this stalker. He's after your virtue, and you might not be thinking straight."

Her facial expression was one of hurt, of pain. I needed to elaborate. I rose over her so our eyes were in direct alignment. "I want you more than I've ever wanted anyone. I'm not trying to put you off or offend you, but I want you to be certain you're ready for this. Once you've relinquished your virginity, you can't take it back. I don't want you doing this just to try and get this guy to stop pursuing you. I don't want it to be a means to an end. I want it to be real between us. When I take you—and YES, I will take you—I want it to be because there's a love growing deeply between us. I don't want it to be a one-time thing, a momentary weakness." I shook my head. "No, I want to take you because I'm making you mine, not just for the moment, not just for a while, but for an eternity. When you can tell me you want me without any reservations playing on your face," she blushed knowing I unmasked her, "then I'll be more than happy to sink myself deep into you and let our bodies become fused together as one."

She was speechless but seemed to understand what I was saying, as a small smile formed when she nodded in agreement. I couldn't refuse those lips any further, so I crushed mine to hers and let our tongues and mouths speak for us.

I was surprised when her hand came down to loosen my towel and grab my manhood. I pulled back suddenly, trying to escape her reach. "Whoa there, love."

"I..." She couldn't quite form her words, so I nodded, encouraging her to continue. "I want you to have pleasure, too, but I've never touched a man's cock before. Can you show me how to bring you pleasure?"

This woman was a gift from the gods. No other woman I'd been with had offered to show me pleasure, without asking or demanding it. They were greedily seeking their own releases, not caring if I had mine. For that reason, I couldn't make myself feel anything for them. Well, that and the fact they knew my name, knew I belonged to money, and wanted ten minutes of fame at my side.

Kaelin was the exact opposite of everything I'd known. She wanted to be treated as an equal in the workforce, wanted to please others, and help in any way she could. In the bedroom and in my apartment, I found my brother's words ringing true. *"She's a giver. She doesn't care about money or status, only happiness. That's what she longs for and wants to provide in return."*

"Let me pleasure you, Van." Her words were endearing, touching my heart where no other woman had ever dared to tread.

I leaned forward, placing my forehead against hers. "You don't have to reciprocate."

"I want to." Her words were adamant, and her desire to please reflected in her eyes. I couldn't deny her the new experience, and, if I were being honest, I wanted her hands on me.

Rolling over onto my back, I undid my towel, leaving it to rest underneath me on the bed. I was hopeful it would catch the mess I was sure to make. I watched as she got up on her knees, her breasts hanging full and heavy in my sight, as her hand hovered over my cock.

She seemed reluctant to touch me at first. "I don't want to hurt you. Can you show me how you like to be touched, what makes you feel good?"

I nodded, not able to speak the words, as I was already holding back a groan at the site of her glorious nudity. I reached out for her hand and guided it to my manhood, which stood at attention, curving towards her, wanting inside her heat. Pre-cum was already visible, so I took the sticky substance and smeared it all over her palm. "You want to use that to lubricate your hand. Now hold on to the base of my cock and gently squeeze."

Her touch was hesitant but soft. She squeezed my dick tenderly, making me jump at first. *How many times had I fantasized this while I was on the computer with her?* The feel of her was more intense than I could've ever imagined. My hand fell over hers to adjust the grip and guide it up and down my shaft. I showed her how to press her thumb against the underneath of my head and to swirl the pre-cum around the tip and squeeze lightly.

Once she got the hang of that—oh my god did it feel like nirvana—I asked her to cup my balls and give them a little tug while caressing here and there to add to the sensation. She was a natural. Within minutes, I found my hips jutting forward off the bed into her grip while I moaned my approval into the air.

I closed my eyes, allowing myself to enjoy the moment, when I felt a tentative lick against the tip of my head, followed by the warmth of her tongue surging down on me and sucking me in. "Oh, God!" escaped from my mouth on its own accord. My eyes shot open to see her still working the base of my cock while her mouth latched on to my tip and devoured it.

"Mmm. You taste good. I'm seriously craving salt water taffy now, but your dick is satisfying my hunger." Her words were garbled around my cock, but I got the gist of what she was saying. I hadn't expected her to suck me. I wanted it, sure, but wasn't going to push her too far too quickly.

I reached up to run my hand through her hair, holding it and guiding her pace against my cock. "You're a natural at this, angel." I didn't even have to tell her to suck her lips in over her teeth. She was doing everything right. "You haven't done this before?"

She shook her head ever so slightly, but enough for me to understand I was her first.

"You're doing fine..."

At that moment, she pulled me further into her mouth and swallowed, causing me to let out a moan of desire. "God you feel amazing, baby."

A small smile played at the corners of her mouth. She was gaining confidence to try something she'd never done before.

Holding her hair, I guided her further and further onto my dick. Kaelin didn't seem to have a gag reflex. I was already hitting the back of her throat, adjusting her angle ever so slightly so she could take me further yet.

After a short time, my mind began to melt as all the blood rushed south, and the intense, burning need to come had almost reached nuclear proportions. I tried to pull her off me, to let my dick shoot off like Mt. Vesuvius, but she refused to budge. "Angel, release me if you don't want me coming in your mouth."

She didn't move and latched on to me tighter as my dick exploded in a cataclysmic eruption sure to put any volcano to shame. I came harder than I'd ever come before. My field of vision blackened with white flashes of light shooting off behind my eyes, leaving me blind with desire. I could feel myself spurt out rope after rope of cum into her mouth. To my surprise, she was swallowing as quickly as I was going off. Only a small amount fell out the corner of her mouth and onto my thigh.

My vision finally cleared, and I could feel the last couple spurts leak out into her mouth. She dutifully cleaned every inch of my softening manhood before releasing me and lapping up what had spilled against my thigh.

Kaelin started to move back to her spot in bed, when I pushed her onto her back and kissed her with every ounce of love I had in me. I wanted her to know just how much she meant to me. "Thank you for that, angel. You didn't have to."

She kissed me back with enthusiasm. "I wanted to, Van. You've done so much for me. We're both used to getting off... It just seemed the natural thing to do." Her face blushed. "Plus, I wanted to try something new, and I'm glad I did. You're everything I've ever wished for in a man." She licked her outer lips, the little minx, making me want her all over again, before realizing what she just said. It was funny to watch her throw her hand over her mouth in embarrassment. "I'm sorry. I don't know what came over me. I didn't mean to say—"

I put my finger over her mouth to silence her. "Rule number one with me: never apologize for speaking your mind, especially when it comes from the heart. I always want to know what you're thinking, how you're feeling. I want us to have the utmost honesty with one another. Agreed?"

We didn't have any time to discuss anything further, as both of our stomachs groaned in demand of food. I hated the interruption. I wanted only to bask in the glory of our release. Que sera, sera. At least she was here with me, in my bed, and her taste was still prevalent in my mouth—a taste I was definitely getting addicted to. I had to be thankful for the distraction from our lives and could only hope the security team could put a quick end to this mess, giving us some resolution and the ability to freely explore, within the normalcy of dating, where this relationship was going. But then again, nothing about the way we'd met, our paths crossing, or us being thrown together had been commonplace. Who knew?

Chapter 12

Kaelin

T HE FIRST WEEK WAS both a nightmare and a dream. I still had bad dreams about Roger and my father. They were my norm, but I also started dreaming of a masked stranger following me, claiming ownership of me, and corralling me into a corner where he took whatever he wanted from my body while Van was forced to watch. The dream ended with both of us being killed.

I often awoke screaming from the intensity of the dream, only to feel the warm arms and soothing words Van offered to comfort and assure me that we were obscure to the outside world. We'd fall into each other's arms and give into the temptation of needing release. We were both on edge, seeking out more from one another to calm our harried souls.

My heart kept telling me to protect it, to keep Van at arm's length. I didn't want him falling for me if I was to be taken from him, but I found his charm and persistence endearing to the point my own heart wasn't listening to reason and, instead, was falling head over heels for this man. I came close to whispering words of love and asking him to make love to me, but Eagle Eyes would wield his hand and force me back to the reality that I needed to keep Van safe. I was still shaken up from having my BFF nearly beaten to death. I couldn't go through another scare like that. I needed to be strong and protect my heart and body from that psycho.

Right now Eagle Eyes had power he didn't realize. He kept me from happiness. He kept me from wanting to hope for a future filled with the potential of love—something I wasn't that familiar with but suddenly craved.

As far as the campus knew, Van and I each had family emergencies that forced us to view our lectures and submit our work via computer. Thankfully, each of us was committed to succeeding and had completed the majority of our remaining assignments, only needing to submit one or two papers each, and then sit for our final exams, which we would work out closer to that time. We still had a little over a month and a half left before graduation.

As for the security team and the computer/accounting team of Ethan and Nate, they worked feverishly the first week. Somehow, and I don't even want to know what they did to pull it off, they managed to secure a copy of both Hayden Michaels's and Pierce Montgomery's computer hard drives.

Hayden had turned out to be nothing more than a bully. He'd been actively surfing the internet for free porn and was even part of some free dating websites, but he was all talk and no action. Apparently, his bark was much worse than his bite, so to speak, so the team ruled him out as a potential threat.

Pierce wasn't as lucky. His computer had some women complaining about him stalking them, harassing them, and threatening to get a couple restraining orders if he didn't back down. He had, indeed, been to my website and paid to watch me numerous times, but the screen name HawkEye436 was one I remembered. He'd been pleasant in his requests. In fact, he almost sounded afraid to ask me to do something he wanted.

Further inspection showed he had another computer, a small mini-laptop that he carried on his person at all times; although, when he slept, he locked it up. We couldn't figure out if this was the computer he used to hack into the university's computer system to change students' class grades or what. There were plenty of money transfers into his account, and his major had been computer programming.

Ethan discovered Pierce's hacking abilities were top notch and was quite impressed with his skill level. With the security team's help, Ethan secured a guest speaker position in one of Pierce's computer programming classes. The idea was that Ethan would test the students' ability to hack into a dummy computer set up at the front of the room. The top three would win some minor prizes while his other computer would be actively searching and pinging for a specific type of code.

There was another name, one I never would've imagined in a million years, added to the list of potential suspects. Mitch—Gina's husband and one of the head IT guys from work—used a company computer after hours to log on to my website a few times prior to the birth of their child.

The security team set up surveillance on Mitch and acquired a copy of his home computer's hard drive, along with his laptop and a couple of other electronic devices. They wanted to see if he could be the culprit.

I was shocked to learn Mitch had a portion of the culprit's code written into his system. Either he was Eagle Eyes or the bastard somehow knew who I was, where I worked, and slipped in through the cracks to keep an eye on me.

My website, or I should say Untouched Mystique's site, received a few messages of encouragement from men, and some women, to take my time and take care of life, and they'd be back when I returned. There was only one threat, in the form of a song by Eagle Eyes. He'd posted the video of Duran Duran's "Hungry Like the Wolf," listed the lyrics, and highlighted "I'm on the hunt, I'm after you."

The idea that Eagle Eyes was searching for me scared the shit out of me. Trent, who we'd talked to over Skype, assured me that no one would be able to find us. The security team backed him up on that. The only people who knew we were here had been sworn to secrecy. As far as the world knew, just like the character Mystique, we were ambiguous. No one could find us, not even my own mother, who'd been freaking out and calling Trent. He assured her I was just fine.

Over the next couple of weeks the team managed to uncover more dirt about Pierce and ruled out Mitch, who was happily taking care of his new daughter and set to return to work soon. The DNA evidence was run through a national database and came up empty-handed, only proving the perpetrator had no criminal record that we knew of.

Nate and Ethan installed the accounting software and some other diagnostic testing and discovered the changes within the system had come from two separate sources. One was external and came in through the backdoor of Mitch's computer. Apparently, when he accessed my website on a company computer, a link was created for Eagle Eyes to slip through and sidestep the firewall. Once he was in the system, he managed to create a backdoor in the firewall, allowing him access to more than just one or two computers. A few viruses had been sent into the system to corrupt the company's data and set up some transfers. For what reason, we didn't know. *Was this guy trying to keep others from watching me? Was he that possessive? Or did he have an agenda with Van, because he saw the amount of time I spent with him online?*

Nate assured Van they'd put a halt to any further damage, but had set up a decoy system for the culprit to enter into, where they would hopefully attach a virus that would guide the team back to the perpetrator's location. We only needed to wait for him to log back in to try and track him.

The odd thing about all of this was that the hits on the accounting software and the banking transfers had been set up internally at a station designed for vendors assessing our systems to utilize, so it would be hard to pinpoint who it was. Both had similar code written into them. What were the odds he'd be the one causing some of this shit? *Had he slipped in here under the guise of a vendor, like he'd done with the security at our condo?*

Van was livid. Apparently, the man who was trying to steal money from his company was the same man who'd beaten up his brother and who'd been stalking and threatening me. The only questions were "Why?" and "What purpose did it serve?"

The security team seemed to be focusing on one angle, but Ethan wasn't convinced we were headed in the right direction. He said the code written into the back of all the systems indicated someone with similar skill sets, but every hacker likes to put their own little spin on things. "They're very proud of their ability to hack, steal, and even destroy systems, so they want to leave their own fingerprint, therefore, making it impossible for others to take credit for their triumph. From what I'm seeing, this may be two people, but I can't be certain."

Under an assumed name, Ethan decided to go into the online underground hacking community, called the dark web. He admitted he'd have to do some things he wouldn't be proud of, but it wouldn't be illegal to gain the trust of the community in order to get some answers. If anyone could help him find the person or persons involved with the two slightly differing codes, it would be the hacker elite. The only problem, the time needed to get answers. This just meant the whole ordeal, unless we caught a break, would continue on for an indefinite amount of time.

Another week came and went with no further leads. The security team expanded their search to include other employees at Meyers Corporation, classmates at the university, teachers too, and even past girlfriends of Van's. There was a small theory that maybe a former flame realized he'd been in love with me, having overheard one of his many talks with his brother, and as a result, felt I was a threat and wanted to neutralize me by pretending to be a man.

I wasn't buying the last theory, but I was told stranger things had happened. The team was looking into every potential lead, but so far most hadn't panned out.

Ethan had been into the hacker community for a week now. Only a couple people were talking to him. He still hadn't gained their full trust, not enough to ask any questions, so we were still biding our time on that option.

My stalker, Eagle Eyes, was definitely starting to get more desperate. He left online messages every couple of days demanding to know where I was hiding. "I'll find you. I own you. You're mine to claim, mine to have, mine forever." Only this time he left a more sinister song by Nickelback, "Follow You Home." He highlighted the words "Mississippi Queen" in the lyrics. I wasn't from Mississippi. I was born and raised in Louisiana, but my grandfather did have a chain restaurant throughout the southern states, Mississippi included, which provided Peter and his team a new angle to follow. They couldn't rule out a disgruntled employee from his former franchise.

Before long, the team managed to uncover more dirt, but, at that point, I wanted out of Van's apartment and out of the office. I couldn't take being pent up behind closed doors any longer. Eagle Eyes continued to flood my site with messages stating he was close to finding me. The last one he left was Def Leppard's song "Two Steps Behind," highlighting "you can run, but you can never hide," and "turn around and I'll be two steps behind." I guess he was waiting for me to mess up, and with my current state of mind, I doubt it would be hard for me to do.

The security team promised me it was all mind tricks. Luke explained it was a common tactic to play on the person's emotions and physical state of mind. All the messages, songs, and threats were a means to try and draw me out of hiding. In all likelihood, Eagle Eyes had no clue where I was and was still actively searching.

Nate pored over the financials regarding Van's father, as well as the misappropriations of the company's funds to buy failing businesses who were beyond help. To date, we all agreed he must've been hiding his sexual preferences from becoming common knowledge. But something bothered me about the situation. Ethan mentioned that the recent transfers into offshore accounts were not to the companies Van's dad purchased, but to some other entity, unless they were the same companies hiding under false identities.

The team still needed to figure out the person behind the accounts, but encountered roadblock after roadblock with the countries' banking authorities, not to mention the timely process to secure the documentation to allow them to access the accounts.

I posed questions to Van's team. "Wouldn't the money be sent directly to the former company heads to ensure their silence and not to various fake accounts?

And why would the pattern continue after his death? Is there something else going on that we just aren't seeing?"

We pored through the information about the companies that were purchased and tried to find out why. But what if... "I don't know if this is me just thinking aloud, but could a vendor with access to the guest computer have the skills to uncover what Mr. Meyers was doing and potentially blackmail him? Are there any deposits in these accounts coming from the other companies in question? Do we have blinders on and are just looking to the road ahead and behind us. Do we need to look to the crossroads and dirt streets along the way? I feel like we're missing something."

Van was all smiles with my way of thinking and leaned over to kiss me on the cheek. "Babe, I love the way your mind works." He looked over to Luke and requested copies of all the vendors who had access to the guest computer or who stepped foot in the office within the past few years when the questionable purchases happened.

I didn't know if I was pulling ideas out of thin air just to have something to contribute, but the attempts to block transfers from the bank to new offshore accounts kept failing and the withdrawals continued. Whoever this person was, whether it was Eagle Eyes or some freaking computer mastermind, they were giving Nate and Ethan a run for their money. Everyone seemed to like my idea and thought it possible.

More days passed, and I became pent up emotionally and sexually. Every moment Van and I weren't talking with Peter's security team, the computer guru, or the accounting genius, we were naked in each other's arms, giving into the temptations of orgasmic bliss. We found a common fondness for getting each other off at the same time in the sixty-nine position. It quickly became one of my favorite treats. I don't think there was an area left in his apartment where we hadn't succumbed to desire.

After Van, with his talented tongue and skilled fingers, enticed me to come for the fourth time that day, I was nearly asleep in his arms, each of us as naked as the day we were born.

He whispered, "I love you with all my heart and soul, Kaelin. I want you in my life forever."

My heart and my mind took over, reciting back, "I love you, too, Van. I need you with me always," before I fell into the first peaceful night's sleep I'd had in weeks.

I woke up the next morning to a burning desire building in intensity within the center of my body and spreading outward at a fast pace. Van was eating me out and talking, between licks, about a surprise for me. I asked for him to spill the beans, but he wouldn't. I held on, begging for release as he kept me right on the precipice, before finally letting me shatter. He'd taught me to scream out and release any negative thoughts I'd had from the night before, as well as any pent up frustrations from our situation, and free them from my body. As a result, I wasn't having as many nightmares. He sure knew how to play my body and my heart. I'd fallen for him hook, line, and sinker.

Van was the one who shattered the walls I had built around my heart and allowed me to experience raw, unfiltered emotions. Every second spent away from him felt like an eternity of agony, as if the very air I breathed was infused with torment. His presence was my solace, the balm that soothed my soul and made me feel alive. Though I was a woman of fierce independence and self-reliance, with him by my side, I no longer had to carry the weight of the world on my own. He was my rock, my protector, and my confidante, and I trusted him with every fiber of my being.

You're not alone. You have Van and Trent, along with their mother and sister, whom adore you. Your mother and grandparents are there for you, too. For the first time in your life, you are surrounded by unconditional love.

When Van finished licking me clean, he moved up my body, kissing every inch as he came closer to my face. He hovered over me, leaving his lips only inches from mine. I couldn't resist him any further. "I love you with all my heart, Van. I truly do."

"Oh, Kaelin." His eyes were filled with delight as his chest breathed a sigh of relief. "I've loved you for what seems like an eternity, and each day, my affection for you grows exponentially."

I couldn't help but smile. "Exponentially, huh? I love it when you talk dirty to me." He knew my love of math, accounting, and statistics.

He moved his legs between my thighs, forcing them apart and grinding his impressively sized manhood against my hip. A devious smile played on his lips. His eyes were heated and looked like two cavernous pools of water that I wanted to swim in. "You want dirty, angel?" His lips began nibbling and sucking on my neck, marking me to let others know I was taken.

I nodded. "Yes, please. I want your filthy mouth and your dick inside me."

He rocked against my hip again. "You don't know how long I've waited to hear you say that to me." He let out an exhaustive sigh. "I wish your timing was better. I'd love nothing more than to sink deep inside you and spend days wrapped up in your heat." Van moved to the side of the bed, hung his feet over, and rubbed his face hard.

"Don't you want me, babe?" I felt hurt. The sting of rejection was a bitch, and I wanted to swat it away. The love I had for my father had been continually discarded, and he turned my sister against me as well. I didn't need to experience more dismissal in my life.

He turned, putting both hands around my face. "I do want you, so badly it hurts. You don't know how much I'd like to blow off plans today, but I've arranged for us to go visit my family. Trent's been asking for you, and I know my mom and sister want to spend more time with us, especially now that we're officially a couple. My mother is over the moon. She loves you so much."

Yes, we were together. He started calling me his girlfriend from the start. I finally caught on to the term of endearment and agreed he was my first real boyfriend. Our commitment to one another extended beyond that. My soul felt connected to his, merged in a way that when one of us was excited or hurt, the other sensed it. I almost felt married to him, but I couldn't hope for something like that, not this soon.

I was still feeling a sense of rejection, but my mind began processing what he'd said, and then realization slammed into me. My eyes were wide. "We get to go out?"

He nodded. "Yes, angel. We get a few hours outside our prison, our pleasure dome, or whatever you want to call it. To me, wherever you are is home." He stood up, offering me his hand to stand. I noticed his erection had started to ebb, until his eyes perused my body.

I kissed him on the cheek and caressed his cock with my hand. "Down, boy. We need to get ready, but who knows, maybe we can do something about this later?"

Wondering if we'd have time for other things, I looked at him in a questioning way and loved when he reached out and pulled me close, pressing his body flush against mine. "Count on it!"

The security team showed up with a couple sets of doppelgangers ready to lead whomever on a wild goose chase. They asked us to pack a couple of overnight bags just in case we needed it, like in the event we had to travel to another safe location.

My heart pounded in my chest as we were instructed to don hoodies and were led away from our doppelgangers. The three identical town cars with matching tags pulled out of the building at staggered intervals, the tension in the air palpable. Luke and Peter were our guides, with Russ and Michael trailing us in a car, ever-vigilant for any suspicious activity.

As we made our way towards Van's family estate on the outskirts of town, I couldn't shake the feeling of dread that hung over me like a dark cloud. The security around the property was tight, and I couldn't help but wonder what danger awaited us behind the walls.

My nerves were shot by the time we pulled up to the front door of the house. It had been weeks since I had seen Trent, and I was desperate for answers. Van had been in constant contact with him lately, discussing everything from business to personal matters. I was itching to get my hands on him, to interrogate him and find out what was really going on.

But as Luke and Peter flanked us and ushered us inside, my stomach twisted in knots. Their eyes darted around the property, scanning for any signs of danger. It was clear that they were on high alert, and the sense of unease that had been building inside me only intensified.

I took a deep breath as we stepped through the threshold, bracing myself for whatever lay ahead. But nothing could have prepared me for what I saw on the other side.

Chapter 13

Kaelin

M Y BREATH WAS LITERALLY taken away at the sight of Trent standing next to my former boss at the coffee shop, Mark. They were both dressed in tuxedoes; Mark in a solid white one and Trent in the typical black and white one. Each of them was quite handsome, but the two of them together were drop dead gorgeous.

I shook my head and blinked, wondering if I was seeing things, but they were still there. Mark's arms were around Trent's waist, providing him some support to stand. I ran up to Trent as a smile spread wide across my face. His face was a reflection of my own when he leaned down to kiss my forehead. "I've missed you, sweetie bear."

Allowing me to get a good hug from my bestie, Mark stepped aside. I looked over to him and mouthed, "Thank you," for which he politely nodded. You could see the love Mark had for Trent reflecting in his eyes. "Are you feeling better? You look better. I'm not hurting you, am I?" My mouth was operating a mile a minute. Trent, and now Van, understood I did this when I got nervous.

Trent pulled back to look at me. "I'm doing much better. There are still some pains to work out, and I still have this stupid cast"—he lifted his arm to show it was present—"but I'm better than I ever could've imagined." I watched as he pursed his lips. "I'm getting married today, sweetness."

Holy shit! "You're getting married? Today? When did...What...How?" I was tongue-tied.

Mark motioned for all of us to take a seat in the next room. It was only then that I realized Trent and Van's mother along with their sister, Alyssa, were also present. I waved to them and smiled as I followed Trent to a comfortable sofa. He sat down and patted the seat next to him while Mark took up the seat on his other side. I watched as Mark laid his hand over Trent's cast and stroked his exposed fingers. A contented sigh escaped Trent's lips. My friend was happy, and I was happy for him. My eyes began to tear up.

Mark was the one to speak up. "Trent scared the living daylights out of me. We fell for one another in high school but weren't allowed to be together, so we secretly hooked up a couple times during college and afterwards. Trent was the one who helped bring my dream of owning a coffee shop to fruition. I submitted the idea to the company for review, showed the potential for growth, and revealed that the university's closest coffee shop was over five miles away. If Trent hadn't invested his own money, all of our lives would not have crossed paths.

"As you know, his dad wouldn't accept our preferred lifestyle and nearly closed my shop, forcing us apart. However, we've been dating on and off since he died, and we were debating taking it to the next level, but I was the one holding out, fearing some other form of retaliation from Mr. Meyers, even from beyond the grave. The day Trent got attacked was the day I realized I'd rather take the risk of losing everything than live another moment without the man I love." Mark put his hand to his chest and was breathing a bit hard. I'd never seen him so emotional before. He usually had an iron-clad determination about him.

It was funny when Ms. Ellingsworth, formerly Ms. Meyers, spoke up. "Years around that bastard of a husband can make you paranoid beyond belief. I hope he's rotting in hell for the torment he caused everyone. I know he'd hate today with a passion, which is why it gives me such pleasure to welcome you into our family, Mark, my son." I watched as Mark got up to hug his future mother-in-law.

Rounds of "Damn straight!" went up all around the room causing everyone to laugh, myself included.

Trent took the opportunity to lean close to my ear and ask, "Are you doing okay? I know the attack shook you up quite a bit. Has my brother been treating you well? You look happier than I've seen you in a long time."

I looked into his eyes and answered with my heart. "I'm nervous about the stalker being on the loose still. He's been hounding my website and posting songs to send a message that he's trying to hunt me down. So, yes, I'm doing as good as can be expected.

"As for your brother, Van has been a most gracious host, treating me more like a queen than someone in hiding." I leaned in closer to him so no one else could hear. "I think I'm falling in love with your brother. I hope you aren't upset."

Trent leaned in even closer, giving me a kiss close to my ear and whispering, "He's loved you from afar for nearly two years now. Just looking at him, I can see his love for you has grown. You're the only person he's ever let in and the only one to capture his heart. You're both good for one another, baby girl. You have my blessing for whatever direction your lives take you."

Van stood up for a moment before coming over to give me a quick kiss on the cheek. "I'm going to quickly run upstairs to use the bathroom and get ready for the wedding. Mom's informed me that a dress she and Trent picked out is waiting for you, but go ahead and enjoy talking to my bro. I'll be back in a few minutes." He kissed me again, giving a wink to Trent as he left the room. *What the hell was that about?*

Trent kept me occupied with idle chatter, letting me know that he and Mark planned to start slow with their lives together but intended on having a family either through adoption or surrogacy.

When I asked about his modeling career, concern flooded his facial features. "They understand that accidents happen, and they're giving me time to heal, but I've lost several modeling jobs and others are starting to pull out, too. I don't know if I'll have anything to go back to." He shrugged his shoulders the best he could. "It's not like I had many years left at the gig anyway, but I did enjoy it. Although, now with my marriage to Mark, I know I don't want to be away from home too long at a time, and you, my dear, have firsthand experience with how busy I stay flying off to different parts of the country and the world."

I nodded in agreement. At first, I was happy to have his place to myself when he was off to work. But as our bond deepened and our friendship blossomed, I found myself consumed with loneliness every time he was away. Our daily phone conversations were a poor substitute for having him there with me, especially when I was plagued by nightmares. He was my security blanket, until Van had come crashing into my life like a force of nature and everything had changed. Trent would always hold a special place in my heart. He was the brother I never had but always wanted.

Trent's face was almost flawless. No one would be the wiser that he'd been beaten up and swollen only a few weeks ago. The only mar to his perfect chiseled face was a small scar inside one eyebrow. To me, it added to his allure, but I wasn't a modeling agent. "What will you do if you can't go back?"

"I've already decided to only take a few gigs here and there if they'll have me. Otherwise, I'm devoting my time to Mark and the family business."

My whole body twisted toward his on the couch as excitement and hope filled me. "Are you saying what I think you're saying?"

Trent nodded.

I heard footsteps coming down the stairs.

"That's right, angel."

Van had finally entered the room, looking dapper as hell in his tuxedo, which matched Trent's.

Trent laid his good hand on mine. "Van and I have been talking a lot the past week. I want to stay closer to home, but I don't want to come back and run the business by myself." He looked over to Van, who was sitting on the coffee table in front of us. "Van doesn't like handling the deals, and I'm not one on finances and marketing, so we've opted to be co-CEOs and use one another's strengths to bring the company into the next decade. But we'll need a CFO to help us understand the finances and ensure we're not buying crap like our father did."

I was happy to hear they'd decided to work together and utilize each other's best traits to secure the business and propel it forward. Hopefully, Van and I could get the financial wrapped up neatly so there'd be no further bumps in the road. "Who do you have in mind for the CFO?"

They each smiled wickedly hot grins. I looked around the room and was wondering if they were looking at Mark, their mom, or their sister, but everyone was staring at me. My eyes went wide when realization dawned on me. Feeling like I'd hyperventilate, I put my hand to my chest. "You're not suggesting..." I couldn't even finish the sentence.

It was odd seeing them side by side, nodding in unison. Van spoke up to explain. "Kaelin, my love, your eye for detail is exactly what we need. Everyone else is running around trying to dig down through a haystack to find that damned needle, while you whip out your magnetic knowledge and find it instantly. I've talked with mother, the board of directors, and with Trent. We're all in agreement that you'd be most suited for the position. Granted, you'll just be out of college and may need a couple people to guide you during your learning curve, but you've already outperformed seasoned accountants. They couldn't find in months what only took you days."

I shook my head. "I can't. I'm not good enough for that kind of position."

Van reached out and placed his hands against both sides of my face to still my objections. "Nate, the forensic accounting specialist we hired, said if we didn't hire you, he would. You are just that good. 'A natural talent,' as he called it, and we all agree."

"But with that kind of job right out of the gates, everyone will think I slept my way to the top. I mean what will people think going from intern to CFO?"

Van and Trent looked at one another, silently saying something. I noticed Trent nod as Van began to sink to one knee. *Oh my freaking Lord!*

Van grabbed on to my left hand and held it between both of his. "I know this is sudden, but I can't think of a better time to tell you exactly how I feel."

He swallowed hard as a fine sheen broke out against his forehead; he was nervous. *He wouldn't. It's too soon.* "Kaelin, I've been in love with you from the moment our eyes met at Mark's coffee shop. That day, Cupid must've needed his caffeine fix and decided to shoot an arrow straight into my heart, because from that day forward, you were the only woman I could think of and the only woman that ever made me forget to breathe.

"My father tried to keep us apart, but fate kept bringing us back together. First with classes, and then being tasked to work with each other on assignments, and I'm guessing you figured out that I had Luke come to class to try and convince you to apply for the internship we were offering. I wanted to keep you close to me, affording us the opportunity to get to know each other better."

His hands were shaking, and he took another nervous swallow as he continued. "When Father passed, I wanted the opportunity to date you, to see if what I felt with you every time we were around one another was real or just a figment of my imagination." He looked intently into my eyes. "You can't deny the strong magnetic pull that exists between us. I know we both feel it. But life got in the way with the demands of running a business, trying to finish up school, and then your stalker happened."

I blushed with embarrassment, feeling ashamed that he was talking so freely around his family. He caressed the top of my hand. "Don't worry, love. We had to tell Mom the details of why we were hiding and what had happened. She's okay with things."

Ms. Ellingsworth reaffirmed. "I wish I had your spunk and persistence to stand up against my parents and not have allowed the marriage to that asshole to take place. Thankfully, I got three amazing kids out of the deal, a wonderful soon-to-be son-in-law, and, hopefully, a new daughter-in-law. You have courage and strength, dear, which I look highly upon. You needn't worry about any objections from me."

Van kissed my hand and continued on, "The past few weeks I've come to discover a deeper love for you. Trent would often tell me how much we had in common, and I usually dismissed it, but you and I have had plenty of time to talk and get to know one another on a level that most couples never get, even after years of marriage. I don't know what will happen next, but I can't imagine going through whatever life throws at us without you by my side. You make me a better person, someone who believes in the hope of love, family, and, with some luck, a happily ever after. Please say you'll marry me, be my wife, be my partner in this crazy mixed up world and come work alongside us as part of this family. Marry me, angel, because I don't know how to live without you."

The tears began pouring down my face. I was speechless as I watched him pull a ring from his pocket and present it to me. It was a heart-shaped diamond surrounded by rubies—my birthstone—in a platinum setting.

He held the ring up to me, encouraging me with his eyes to answer. I still couldn't find the words. *This is crazy. It's too quick. But you love him with all your heart. You've fallen hard for him, and face it, you couldn't go on if he weren't in your life.* My mind was right on all counts, so I let my heart answer for me as my head nodded up and down.

Van slipped the ring, which fit perfectly, onto my finger before kissing me hard on the lips. Applause filled the room as he took my breath away.

When we finally came up for air, his mother and Alyssa were standing, holding their hands out to me. "Let's get you ready, dear." His mother grabbed hold of me and started pulling me toward the door.

I planted my feet onto the tile. "Wait a minute. Today? We're getting married now?"

Trent smiled. "I told you my brother was impulsive. Did he tell you he's had the ring since the day he figured out you and Mystique were one in the same? He's known that long that he wanted to ask you to marry him. I don't think he can wait another day, sweetness, so please put him out of his misery. Let's have the double wedding we always talked about having. Two BFFs supporting each other on their special day." Trent always had a way of putting my mind at ease. No wonder we got along so well.

All of their words hit a soft spot in my heart. I couldn't deny that I was scared about the stalker, always wondering if he'd truly come for me and afraid of what he'd do if he found me. But I could live in this moment, a cherished contentment that no one could strip from me. This was a point in time where I could be surrounded by happiness. I would be married to the man of my dreams, my own Prince Charming, who'd come to rescue me from the evils of the world, who'd protect me from harm, and who'd cherish me in this life and into the next. I just hoped we would have an eternity to find out. Fate obviously wanted us together, so why not?

I nodded to his mother. "Please lead the way, Mom."

Her face lit up with a radiant smile while Alyssa's arms wrapped around me. "You're going to be my sister. I've always wanted to have one, and now I will." She was so giddy; whereas, internally, I was wishing that I had this kind of relationship with my sister and that my mom and some of our family could be here. But life isn't always perfect. I learned to be grateful for whatever I was given, and right now, it was more than I could've ever hoped for.

"It's my wedding day!" I yelled out.

Van responded immediately with, "Damn right it is! I love you, angel. I'll see you soon."

Chapter 14

Van

I PACED THE HALLS the first hour that Kaelin was upstairs with Mom and my sister. "What's taking them so long? Are you sure you got the right dress size and a design she'll like?" I looked to my brother for answers.

He held up his hand. "They shouldn't be much longer. I just got a text from Luke that the minister, our lawyer who brought the marriage certificates, and a notary have arrived and are being escorted out back by the pool, along with a few special guests. We had the gazebo decked out earlier today."

I put my hands in the air. "But you didn't answer me about the dress." I was anxious.

My brother just smiled and laughed. "I get it, bro. You feel like you're underwater. You can't breathe when she's not around, like your life ceases to exist. I feel the same way about Mark."

"And?"

He nodded. "The dress is amazing. It should fit her figure perfectly. After all, I've been helping Kaelin pick out her clothes and lingerie for the past year. I know her figure and her size almost as well as you do." He winked at me and added, "I'm sure you'll love the little number from La Perla I picked out to go underneath. Let's just say it's my wedding present to you both."

The mere thought of her in sensual lingerie had my blood heading south-bound on the expressway, leaving me slightly light-headed. She'd asked me to talk dirty to her, to take her earlier, and I'd finally have my chance tonight to ravish her body. I hope she remembered to pack her bubble bath, because we definitely would get filthy, I guarantee it.

Trent cleared his throat and raised one of his eyebrows to me in a knowing look. "Be gentle with her, brother." My thoughts were consumed with all the ways I could take Kaelin, and there were many. My brother had no clue how kinky my sweet, innocent Kaelin could get, but I did. I listened to her desires and let her body guide me where we could both seek bliss in one another's arms. I'd make love to my wife, that was a given. However, with the stress we were both under, we'd also fuck like rabbits. We'd already been going at it pretty intensely, albeit with oral sex, hand jobs, and finger fucking.

Breaking my steamy train of thought, Alyssa came down the stairs dressed in a soft pink flowing gown. I'd never seen my sister looking more lovely and relaxed than now that she was divorced and free of her arranged marriage. Rushing into the kitchen, she whizzed past us, but quickly returned with a box full of boutonnieres—a faint pink rose for each of us—along with a larger box containing two bouquets of pink and white roses.

She helped us pin our boutonnieres on. "I'm so happy to be here for you guys today. I never thought I'd see the day when one of us got married for love, and both of you managed to find it."

I reached out for her, giving her a gentle hug. "You'll find your happily ever after when the time's right, sis. Dad doesn't control us anymore. We can live our lives any way we see fit."

"Thanks, Van. Kaelin's ready, and she's a vision. I'm really happy the two of you found each other. Who knows, maybe I've already found my prince." She gave us a wink and then walked back upstairs. Wondering what that was about, I threw my brother a questioning look, but he just shrugged his shoulders and shook his head.

Trent was the one to suggest the dual marriage. He knew I was ready to bind myself to Kaelin but wasn't sure if she'd be open to the idea, at least not this quickly and without her family members here. I had to admit that the idea of making her my wife and consummating the marriage had quite the appeal. Plus, it would, hopefully, discourage Eagle Eyes. I'd love nothing more than to show him he couldn't own her, because she would belong to me. Although even without the psychopath hounding us, I could still see myself here today ready to take the plunge.

Kaelin was a free-spirited woman, one I wanted to challenge me at work and in life. The only place I'd ask for control would be in the bedroom and only with her permission. I wouldn't take what wasn't freely given to me.

I shook my head to dispel any bad thoughts. Today we wouldn't talk about stalkers, financial issues with the company, or our families' pasts. That would all be sidelined for now, allowing the focus to be on the love surrounding us in this moment with the hope of a brighter future.

Only a short time had passed since Kaelin was in my arms, but every minute that ticked away on the clock felt like an eternity to my soul. My heart didn't beat with the same joy, and as my brother so adequately put it, I felt stifled.

The click of heels on the marble staircase gave notice that they were approaching. Mom had changed into a silvery cocktail dress, elegant as always. Alyssa was carrying her bouquet and looking much happier today than on her wedding day a few years back.

When Kaelin appeared on the steps, I swear the clock stopped, the world stood still, and it was just she and I in the room. How did I manage to convince this gracious beauty to become my wife? I was one lucky bastard, that's for certain. I'd do everything in my power to give her the happiness she deserved, her happily ever after. I just prayed our nightmare with the stalker would soon end, and we could put all this mess behind us.

Kaelin took the steps carefully, floating on what looked to be glass slippers, but I knew that to be impossible. She was definitely my Cinderella dressed in a floor-length pure-white strapless dress with a long sleeve lace jacket overlay cinched at the waist. I guess you could call it a jacket. Trent knew fashion much better than me. He'd definitely picked the ideal dress for Kaelin to have her fairy-tale moment. The lace covering floated the full length of the dress, accentuating her tiny waist and providing additional coverage to her generous cleavage. She was a vision.

Mark helped Trent to stand. He was doing much better than I expected. I could tell his ribs still hurt, with the small breaths he took, and the cane was a sure sign his leg was still sore, but he looked happy, and I was happy for him. He didn't give in to Dad's demands, held true to his beliefs, and found happiness with Mark in the process. It was nice to see them holding on to one another as they headed out of the room.

Walking over to Kaelin, I extended my arm. She quickly wrapped hers around mine as she held on to her bouquet. I liked that Mom and my sister didn't put a veil in Kaelin's hair, keeping it all natural and free flowing, adding only a few ringlets here and there. "You take away my breath, angel. I've never seen you look lovelier. Had I known you'd be this much of a knockout, I would've asked for your hand in marriage sooner."

She smiled, but concern was etched on her face.

"What's bothering you, love?"

She shook her head in dismissal, but I withdrew my arm, stood in front of her, and held on to her chin until she stared me in the face. "I want to know."

Kaelin took in a big breath and released it. I could see her shoulders were sagging a bit. "I just wish my mother and grandparents were here. I'd always envisioned one of my grandfathers giving me away." A small tear escaped the corner of her eye, so I reached up to wipe it away.

"I know, angel. I wish they could be here, too, but things are too risky right now. The fact that we're getting married today is a miracle in and of itself." I took in a deep breath, wishing I could give her all her dreams come true. "I only want your happiness, so let's have another ceremony, a traditional one, when all this is over, along with a huge reception where everyone can party together. How does that sound?"

A small smile spread across her face as she nodded. "I'd love that, babe."

I'd never get tired of hearing her call me babe, honey, or any other term of endearment she could come up with. I loved this woman to no end. Now it was time to make her mine.

I guided her arm back through mine and walked toward the back of the house, near the pool area where a gazebo had been flanked with flowers, lights, tulle, and candles. It truly was a sight to see, more romance than I ever thought myself capable of, but I'd do anything to make my angel happy.

My brother and Mark were already to one side of the minister, while my mom and sister stood back a ways. We walked in their direction and nodded. Right on cue, Kaelin's mom and her grandparents stepped out of the shadows. I looked over to my love and saw her glowing with happiness.

I released her to go to her family. The emotions were high, as her mother and a couple of her grandparents shed tears. I went over to shake everyone's hands, though wasn't expecting the women to hug me like crazy.

Her mother was the first to explain things to Kaelin. "A guy named Luke contacted us to let us know who you were dating and about your impending nuptials. We had to leave at different times and go varying directions to throw your father off our track. He has a detective following me around lately, but right now he's trying to track down my decoy in Alabama." She laughed out loud.

"No one knows we're here. Your father is grasping at straws to try and keep some of the money he's stolen from me, but with the help of"—her mother looked over to mine and nodded—"your future mother-in-law, we found enough dirt on him to have him thrown in jail for quite some time."

Kaelin asked. "What dirt?"

"You mean Van hasn't told you?" Before anyone could respond, her mother went into a brief explanation. "Apparently, your father got into gambling and pissed off the wrong people, owing them a lot of money. He went through his trust fund, stole money from work, stole money from me, and tried to pay things off by settling with a loan shark who's now after his ass. He was hoping to find dirt on me, enough to force me into paying off his debts, but with the information found on him, the judge is allowing the divorce and advising him to settle his affairs, because he's headed straight to jail. His company is pressing charges for theft, and the judge advised me to do the same."

Her mother put her hand to her chest. "Look at me going on and on. I'm so sorry, honey. This is your day. Let's forget about all the assholes in the world and focus on the future instead."

I reached out and gave my future mother-in-law a squeeze. "That sounds like a wonderful idea, Ms. Richards."

She was quick to point out, "None of that Ms. Richards crap. You can call me Pamela or Mom, whatever your preference."

Luke came up to us and patted me on the shoulder. "I hate to interrupt the happy reunion, but we shouldn't be standing around out here for too long. Can we go ahead and proceed?"

Kaelin's family had been informed of my family's status and wealth. They were led to believe paparazzi could show up on property at any moment, so we needed to keep things on the down-low. The fact that my angel had a stalker wasn't my information to reveal. If she chose to come clean, I'd support her; otherwise, I'd continue to protect her.

To our surprise, none of them questioned anything. But then again, they were used to outlandish statements, thanks to the pandemonium Kaelin's father created.

Her family took their place alongside my mom and sister. Luke and Peter were right there with us, continually looking up to scan the area for threats.

The minister began. "We are gathered here today to join these two couples in the bonds of holy matrimony. If anyone here sees just cause why these two should not be married, please speak now or forever hold your peace."

After a moment of silence, he continued. "Trent and Mark have decided to write their own vows. Whenever you're ready." He motioned for them to proceed, so they faced each other and joined hands.

With tears in his eyes, Mark was the first to speak up. "I can't believe we're here. All my life, I've been told I'm not supposed to love you, but I never stopped. I know we've had our obstacles, and at one point, I thought they were insurmountable, but fate continued to bring us back together, showing that love *does* conquer all.

"My worst nightmare came true when I got a call letting me know you had been attacked. I knew at that moment that I couldn't risk going another day without you in my life. So I commit to you my love and devotion, asking only that you love me in return, through good times and bad, with all the crazy stuff in between."

I stood behind Kaelin and wrapped my arms around her waist while watching my brother and waiting for his response. I'd never seen Trent at a loss for words, but the emotion of Mark's words hit him strong.

After a few moments, Trent bounced back with a determined look on his face. "I had a speech written of everything I wanted to say to you, but you've already touched on it all, leaving me to speak from the heart. I didn't think this day would ever come for us. I've loved you for as long as I can remember, and I'll love you for a lifetime to come. I want the dream of happiness and a family, and I want that with you. So on this day, I commit to you my love and devotion, too. We've already been through the bad times, and we may have more to come, but with you by my side, I know that anything is possible."

The minister turned to us, asking Kaelin and I to face one another, but she first handed her bouquet off to my sister. "Van has prepared his own vows. Kaelin may choose to do the same, or we can offer a traditional vow." He motioned my way, "Whenever you're ready, Van."

I was transfixed by Kaelin's exquisite eyes and the happiness I saw reflected in her smile. "The happiness on your face right now reminds me of the day I walked into Mark's coffee shop. He was teaching you how to use the espresso machine, and you looked up, and at that moment, I somehow knew we were meant to be together.

"Some say love at first sight doesn't exist, that it's a sham, but Cupid needed a pick-me-up that day, and while he was there, he shot his arrow straight into my heart. The moment your eyes met mine, I felt my heart skip a beat, and I forgot how to breathe."

Hold it together, man. You've got this. "I couldn't explain why, but from that moment on, you were the only woman I could think of. Regardless of my father's plans, I promised myself that I'd only marry you. Obviously fate thought we were meant to be, pairing us in similar classes; though, I will admit to pulling strings to get you to intern with our company.

"Every moment we spent together at the coffee shop, in class, and at work, my love for you continued to grow, and then to find out you were my brother's roommate, it was kismet. The past few weeks have shown that we're two halves of a whole, fitting perfectly to traverse this life together—a life filled with hopes, dreams, and above all, love."

Kaelin was starting to shed a few tears, and I was barely holding back my own. I never knew how deeply true love could touch, not until now. "I give you all that I am. You have my heart, my body, and my soul. I want only your happiness in return. I know the road ahead might not be easily traveled, but I know that together, we can conquer anything life may throw at us. Through good times and bad, through this life and into the next, my heart is forever yours."

I reached up to wipe a few stray tears running down her cheeks. My sister handed me a tissue to help. Kaelin held her hand up. "I'm sorry. I just need a moment." She shook her head and smiled at me. "I didn't know we were writing vows today, let alone getting married. So how am I to follow words that were so perfectly spoken?"

The minister offered her traditional vows, but she declined. Her hand reached up to caress the side of my face. She took a deep breath and began to speak. "All my life, I've dreamed of a white knight or a Prince Charming to come to my rescue, taking me from a plane of mere existence to a realm of happily ever after. I don't know if such a thing exists, but I am standing in front of my prince.

"Until you, I didn't know what love was, didn't know how to express it, yet you've been so patient, so kind in helping me understand there are no conditions for the passion and devotion between two kindred spirits. I don't know what the future holds, and I don't care about our pasts, but here and now I commit to you my heart and eternal gratitude for the love you've shown exists in this world and into the next. You are my everything, and my heart belongs only to you."

Kaelin swiped my face with a tissue. Shit, I was crying. But with the weight her words held, who wouldn't? There wasn't a dry eye around us, including our security guys, and those dudes were hard shells to crack.

I reached out to give her a kiss, when the minister held his hand out between us. "We're not to that part yet, Van. Just a few more minutes, sir."

Nodding my head, I made my apologies. "Sorry." A few laughs followed. What can I say, I was anxious.

The minister asked for everyone to hold up their rings and repeat after him. "Just as this circle is without end, my love for you is eternal. Just as it is unbreakable, my commitment to you will never fail. As I put this on your finger, I commit my heart and soul to you, my trusted partner for life."

The ring felt amazing on my finger, solidifying that I was now bound to her as she was to me.

"I now pronounce you..."

I guess the minister hadn't prepared for this one, so I offered up, "Partners for all eternity?"

He nodded and repeated the words, adding, "You may now kiss your spouse."

Finally! I wrapped one hand around the back of Kaelin's neck and placed the other on her lower back, before pulling her as close as I possibly could. This wouldn't be a chaste kiss like I'd seen at other weddings. No, sir. I hadn't been able to touch or kiss my angel for the past two hours. I needed to feel her surrender her lips and her mouth to me. I guess I wasn't the only one needing this kiss, as Kaelin's hands came up to latch around my neck, pulling me closer and intensifying our endearment.

We only came up for air after the minister cleared his throat. Before our congratulations, the family lawyer, Mr. Hampton, and his notary stepped in. "I hate to interrupt the happy occasion, but I need to get these papers signed so we can be on our way."

Mr. Hampton showed us all where we needed to sign to make our marriages official. He agreed to delay filing both certificates for a month, maybe two, because of Kaelin's stalker; however, we didn't elaborate that to anyone. We let everyone think it was a means to keep the public in the dark, therefore, giving us time to ourselves, which did hold some truth.

Trent and I had Mr. Hampton draw up new wills to include our spouses as our beneficiaries. Both Kaelin and Mark tried to object. They didn't want our money, only our love for them, but neither one of us would rest until we knew our loved ones were taken care of.

I also had paperwork drawn up, with mom's help, proclaiming both my brother and me as co-CEOs of Meyers Corporation and offered a position to Kaelin as our new CFO. We operated without one for too long because Father managed both positions so no one would be the wiser to his false documentation of businesses.

Wanting us back in a secure area, Peter and Luke shuffled us towards the house. We discovered the main dining room decked out to the nines with various salads, fruits, pastries, a couple of small wedding cakes, and a surf and turf meal sure to put any fine restaurant to shame. I didn't know which I was more ravenous for, Kaelin or the food. Her stomach growling made the decision for us. I guess we still needed to be gracious hosts and spend time with our families.

It was nice to see Kaelin's family getting along splendidly with mine. My only wish was that Mark's family would've put their holier-than-thou attitudes aside and been happy for his union to my brother and celebrated this day with us.

I leaned over to give my sweet angel a kiss, when I noticed a couple of tears running down her face. I reached out to wipe them away. "What's wrong, love?"

She shook her head, but I persisted. "Something's bothering you, and as your husband, I think I have a right to know."

As she tilted her head toward the floor, I barely heard, "I wish the rest of my family loved me enough to be here." She seemed almost embarrassed by the admission. "I know I'll never earn my father's love. He's a lost cause. I just wish I could have the closeness you have with your siblings."

My heart was breaking for her. I hadn't thought to try and invite her sister. From what I gathered from Trent and what she told me over the past few weeks, they weren't at all close. "I'm sorry, love. Was I wrong not to extend an invitation to her?"

Kaelin shook her head, and her eyes finally lifted to meet mine. Fear was evident on her face. "No. We've never gotten along. According to Mom, Bethany was ecstatic when Dad threw me out, wishing he'd done it earlier. She's an attention hog and couldn't be happy with just getting Dad's attention. If Mom showed me too much affection, Bethany caused things to happen, which ended with me getting in trouble or hurt. If she were here today, she'd try to hurt me in some way, dragging all the attention onto herself. She'd be jealous as hell of any happiness I found."

Her words sent a shiver of fear through me. I need her to provide more details about their sibling rivalry, and maybe I should have one of Peter's guys do a check on Bethany to see if she's still in Louisiana. But not right now. I wouldn't let today be ruined.

I reached over, planting a soft kiss on my bride's lips. The tender caress of our mouths added more fuel to my barely-controlled fire inside. My mind was reverting to a caveman, imagining me throwing Kaelin over my shoulder, heading to our room, and ravaging her all night. The desire to consummate the marriage was overwhelming.

Stifling my urges, I moved my hands up and down her arms, suggesting, "Let's put aside our fears for now. We won't think about what led us to this point, and we won't try to figure out what we'll do tomorrow. We'll live here, in the moment, and enjoy every laugh, cheer, and feeling of love that exists in this room today."

Trent leaned toward us. "Sorry to listen in, but I think a dance or two for us couples might be in order. Not that I can dance much, but I would like Mark to know how I feel about him today. I can think of two perfect songs that work for all of us." He winked toward Kaelin and got her to blush. "What do you think, sweetie bear?"

She nodded enthusiastically. This was why I loved my brother so, and why I wanted him to come back to work for the company and deal with the potential business clients. He had a way of putting people at ease. He's a natural at it.

Trent leaned over to Mark and pointed to a stereo system just beyond the dining room. They shared some sweet words and a kiss before Mark pulled his phone out and plugged it into the equipment. I stood up as he approached Trent to ask him for a dance. I asked the same of Kaelin. "Would you honor me with a dance, my beautiful bride?"

The room went silent as we moved over to join my brother and Mark on a small area of flooring perfect for a first dance. The song "As Long As You Love Me" by the Backstreet Boys started playing. I was surprised by just how perfect the song was for our current situation. I whispered these sentiments in Kaelin's ear as we danced, wanting her to know that I didn't care where she came from or what she did in the past. It shouldn't matter who we were, only that we love one another.

The music finished and a tinkling of knives against glass signaled us to kiss right before the next song started. When the song "All of Me" by John Legend started playing, my heart soared. Trent knew this song spoke volumes about the intensity I felt for my sweet angel. We swayed to the music as I intensified our kiss. I wanted to pour all my emotion and feeling into her. I could feel my cock harden and tried to remind myself we had company and that I needed to be patient. We'd soon have our special time tonight to make new memories and seal our adoration to one another.

I glanced over to see my brother as affected by the power of emotion. Mark held tightly to Trent as they basically rocked back and forth to the music. *God I love my family! Please let this nightmare we're in be over soon.*

As I glanced around some more, I noticed Luke was standing awfully close to my sister, Alyssa. While we were cutting the cake, I caught the gentle caress of their hands in my peripheral vision. Could they be infatuated with one another? I wouldn't mind if they were. Luke already felt like a part of our family, an extended brother of sorts.

"Everything okay, babe?" Kaelin had a piece of cake lifted in front of my mouth as an offering. I tilted my head toward Luke and Alyssa, so she glanced over before returning her gaze to me. "They're cute. They were flirting throughout the ceremony and now the reception." Wanting my sister to find her own happiness, I nodded in agreement.

During the reception, Kaelin's mom and both sets of grandparents announced they were looking to move to Florida to be close to her. As Pamela explained, "We don't have anything tying us to Louisiana anymore. My marriage will soon be over, and your grandparents are looking to downsize. We just all want to get away from your father and make a fresh start in life."

Kaelin was overjoyed by the idea of her family moving closer. However, I had other feelings I wanted to pursue. The party carried on for well over four hours now, and my desire to be alone with her was increasing with every moment the second hand ticked on the clock.

I finally had enough and pulled her over my shoulder. A surprise gasp came from her lips, causing everyone to turn, including our security detail. I just shrugged my shoulders and smiled, offering a brief apology. "It's getting late and we should get some rest."

I'm sure everyone knew the huge lie I'd just thrown out there, especially Trent, since he was smirking the most. He held his hand out to Mark for assistance. "I think I could use some time to lie down and rest, too. This day has been a bit exhausting."

A few laughs went around the room. I mean, its not like we could say, *"Hey, I want time alone with my spouse to sex them up and seal this union."* Though, I'm pretty sure everyone knew where we were headed and that sleep wasn't on the agenda.

Luke passed me on the stairs and opened a door at the far west wing of the house, away from the family's bedrooms.

I thanked the man and requested not to be disturbed until the following morning when we awoke unless it was vital.

He just slapped me on the back as I carried Kaelin across the threshold. "No problem, Van. We got your back, so enjoy your night." He nodded to each of us before locking and closing the door.

I carried Kaelin over to the king-sized bed—trimmed with rose petals scattered about—and set her gently on the edge. With her hands in mine, I got down on a knee in front of her. "I wish we had the ability to head off into the sunset on a romantic adventure for the honeymoon of our dreams. I remember you told me of your childhood trips to the beach, ones where you seemed to have some happiness. I want to make our own memories, find our own special beach. When all the chaos has been resolved—"

She didn't let me finish before sealing her lips to mine in a kiss that reached deep into my heart, into my soul, saying *"No worries, I'm yours."*

Chapter 15

Kaelin

I HATED INTERRUPTING VAN from expressing his feelings for me along with his desires to provide a perfect honeymoon. Everything out of his mouth the past few hours had been straight from a storybook. It was perfection...and sounded too good to be true. I was waiting for the shoe to drop, so to speak, and wondered when the world around me would shatter. This wasn't my life. I never got the happy ending, never had everything go right for me. So why now? What was this leading up to?

With hesitation, I had to ask, "Our marriage today, did it happen because you truly wanted it, or did you marry me to block Eagle Eyes's attempts to claim me?"

The hurt on his face hit me hard, making me regret the question the moment it had left my mouth. He shook his head. "You don't believe this could happen, do you?"

Shaking my head, I answered honestly, "No, I don't. I know what I feel for you in my heart, but I'm still trying to understand why today happened. Nothing ever goes right for me. Every time I've managed to take two steps forward in life, I end up taking three or four steps back. Look at the facts. You said yourself that you'd set it up where we'd work together on the company's financials and try to figure out the mess your father made. You wanted to spend time with me to romance me and get me to fall in love with you; instead, your brother ended up in the hospital, and we were thrown together, forced to learn about one another quicker than we planned."

Van stood up, pacing the room a few times before landing a punch against the wall and then waving the hand around the room. I followed his motions and, for the first time, saw everything around me.

There were bouquets of my favorite flowers—roses in various shades of pink and red—mixed with stargazer lilies. There were red, pink, and white rose petals covering almost every inch of the room. An ice bucket with chilled champagne, and two flutes with our names and today's date engraved upon them were sitting on the bedside table. There was a tray of fruits, whipped cream, and chocolate for us to nibble on, and there was a bag from the toy store where I'd previously purchased a few sexual toys for my webcast.

I looked at Van with new eyes. He'd tried to make tonight perfect. This wasn't a man just acting on impulse; this was a man who definitely was in love. "When did you know…" I didn't need to finish the question, because he knew what I was asking. I wanted to know when he finally realized it was love.

He ran his hand through his hair, and his face softened as he looked directly at me. "I wasn't lying in my vows when I said Cupid's arrow hit me the day I walked into your coffee shop. Of course Dad was immediately opposed to the idea, but I decided that day we'd be together.

"I wanted to do things traditionally, but nothing about us has been conventional, angel. Life happened, and we both got caught up in it, but I know one thing for sure: each day we've spent together, my love for you has continued to grow. I can't deny what's in my heart. Ideally, yes, I would've liked to romance you, but the end result would still be the same: I'd want us married. In fact, the day I walked into the house and realized you and Mystique were one and the same, I rushed out to the family's jeweler and had him create your engagement ring along with our wedding bands. I knew I wanted a forever with you; I just had to convince you first."

He leaned closer to me, placing one hand over my heart. "Why is it so hard for you to believe in the possibility of happily ever after? Can't you feel your heart speed up every time I'm near? When our hearts are aligned, do you feel your beat sync with mine? Do my kisses not leave you as breathless as they do me?"

I nodded. "They do. I wouldn't have married you otherwise." I stumbled on my next words. "I just have a hard time accepting things are going my way. I'm constantly wondering if this is truly real or if I'm just dreaming. I'm ready for the rug to be pulled out from under me. I'm afraid I might lose you."

His hand came around my face to cradle it. "I'm right here. This is real, and"—he shrugged his shoulders and swallowed hard—"I won't deny the idea of sealing your life with mine to deter your stalker had crossed my mind, but it's an added bonus to what we already share. I would've wanted this day to happen even if Eagle Eyes didn't exist."

The weight on my shoulders had been lifted. I was certain that Van had married me for the same reason I decided to go through with it: love. I reached out my arms to him. "Love me, then. Make me forget about the world around us. Let's seal ourselves away in our own private bubble for at least one night."

Van reached up under my arms to lift me to a standing position before his hands started peeling away the pieces of my wedding ensemble. "With pleasure, love." He paused only for a moment. "If you aren't prepared to lose your virginity tonight, we can wait. I don't want to rush you into anything you're not ready for."

I shook my head while I ran my hand over the crotch of his pants. I felt the hardness of his cock straining against the fabric, waiting to be released. "No, I've waited long enough. I told you earlier today that I want you, and I do. Show me what I've been missing sexually. Be as intense as you want. Leave me gasping for breath and craving more of you, of us."

Van's lips crashed to mine as our hands worked feverishly to rid ourselves of our clothes. I soon found myself in the middle of the bed with his body lying next to mine as his hands ran over my breasts and blazed a trail down to my pussy. His fingers spread my lips apart and dipped into my center. "You're wet for me already, love."

His lips latched on to one of my nipples, circling around it with his tongue before biting it gently, causing it to form into a hardened point that craved even more attention from his mouth. He alternated between each one, while his thumb circled my clit and two of his fingers entered me, seeking out the bundle of nerves he knew would set me off in an instant. "But I..." Those were the only words out of my mouth before his lips sealed to mine. The orgasm hit suddenly, making my body shudder as my vaginal walls latched on to his fingers, milking them as if they were his cock.

"I need you to come a couple times for me, angel. It'll loosen you up so it won't hurt as much when I punch through your virginity. I want your first time, our first time, to be a memory you'll never forget."

The first orgasm hadn't even ebbed, yet he worked my pussy as his lips latched on to my clit, sucking it into his mouth and biting down. "How did you...oh my god, I don't think I can handle it."

His mouth released my clit with a pop. "You can and you will come again for me, love. Surrender yourself to me, let all your pleasure be mine to own." My eyes locked with his heated gaze. He wanted me, and he wanted me now.

It only took one look, one word: come. I felt my body release with a more powerful orgasm than the first. He removed his hand and kissed his way up my body. His legs parted my thighs as his hips aligned with mine.

Van peppered my face and neck with tender kisses as he rocked his manhood against my folds, lubricating himself with my juices. His teeth began to graze the area underneath my ear and worked down my neck, before biting into the soft flesh, causing me to rock my hips against him.

I felt the tip of him begin to enter me, but he held back. "Are you sure, love?"

My hands pushed against his chest when I realized he wasn't wearing a condom. "I want you like I've never wanted anyone before, to feel you deep inside me, but I'm not on any kind of birth control. Did you want to use a condom?"

He was poised above me, a smile playing across his face. "I don't care, angel. I've been waiting for too long to make you mine. I want us to come together without anything between us. If we get blessed with a little bundle of joy, so be it. Right now, all I can think about is driving myself deep within you, spraying your walls with my seed, and marking you as mine."

His words were an aphrodisiac to my soul. I felt my hips move against him, which pressed him in further, causing us each to moan. Van moved slowly, carefully, allowing my body to adjust to his size. To say Van was well-endowed would be the understatement of the century.

He paused for a moment. I could see the strain on his face, the effort he was using to hold back. "You're so tight, love, but you feel fucking amazing, squeezing the hell out of my cock. Just imagine when you come."

I watched as the emotions passed over his face, and he regained his control. To say I felt full was putting it mildly, and he wasn't but halfway in. The pace he was moving was driving me to the edge of sanity. I finally reached my arms around his neck, pulled him toward me, and said, "Do it!"

Our lips locked, and I felt him rear back and bust through. I felt myself rip on the inside and was thankful for his mouth absorbing my cries. It hurt for a moment, but then I felt the desire to move my hips against him.

His tongue found mine and began to push into my mouth and explore as his hips began to move in and out of my center. The pain was only momentary, taking me more by surprise than anything. It was soon replaced with a pleasurable feeling.

Van took things slow, but I soon wanted more. The sensations were too addictive to just stay at a gentle pace. "Faster, babe, take me to the edge and back. Show me what I've been missing."

Smiling and shaking his head, he said, "With pleasure, Kaelin. Remember, no coming until I tell you."

He increased his rhythm, rocking into me faster and harder. My legs flew up to encircle his waist. Driving him deeper yet, I pushed my feet against his ass. I wanted him to climb up so far inside me there'd be no space left between us.

One of his hands lifted my ass, allowing him to rock deeply into me. *Oh my freaking Lord! This felt too good.* His pace increased and my insides were heating up hotter than a volcano ready to blow.

My breaths were coming faster. I could barely get the words out. "Please. I. Need..." I didn't mean to enunciate them so haphazardly, but he was literally taking my breath away.

Sweat beaded off his forehead, and his arm strained to hold his body up as he drove into me harder, nearly pushing me into the headboard. A devilish smile spread about his face.

The hand holding my ass dug in as his thrusts pounded into me. His mouth hovered a hair's breadth away from mine while he uttered the words, "Come for me, love. Let's come together. Let me plant my seed deep inside you."

His words sent me over the edge. I opened my mouth to scream, but he sealed his lips tightly to mine, absorbing my cries as fireworks went off behind my eyes. My vaginal walls squeezed tightly against his dick. He pushed into me twice more before I felt him pulsate, plastering my insides with his cum.

My body felt light as a feather. All my nerves were tingly, giving me the illusion I was floating. It wasn't until Van collapsed on top of me, pressing me into the bed that I returned to reality.

Rolling to his back, he pulled me on top of him without breaking our connection. I tried to move off of him, but he wrapped his arms around me and held me tight. "Don't move, love. Just let me hold you for a while." His breathing was just as erratic as mine. "I want to make sure none of my seed leaks out of you."

I lifted my head and looked him in the eyes, seeing contentment for the first time in weeks. "You really want to put a baby in me?"

His hand ran over my back while the other smacked my ass lightly. "Is it bad that I want to see my wife swollen and ripe with my child?"

"I guess not. I do want to have kids, just wasn't planning on them so quickly, but if you think we can handle it." I didn't know what else to say, so I rested my head over his heart to listen to it beat.

His arms came up and wrapped around my back, holding me as close as possible, as if he were afraid I'd leave. "I know we're moving fast on everything, and I'm probably foolish to want something so badly before we have this mess figured out, but I truly want to tie your life to mine in every way I can possibly think of. I want you as my forever. I want you as the mother to my children, and I want you to work alongside me as my equal.

"I want to create a better legacy than what my father did. We were the fruit of his loins, but we were merely heirs to the empire, when all we wanted was to be the apple of his eye. No pun intended."

Running his hand through my hair, Van grew contemplative for a moment. "I want to be the kind of dad that's there for his children. One who doesn't spend his entire time at the office, ignoring his family. I'm actually thinking about adding a daycare center at work for the employees to bring their young babies and children. I've already talked to Mom about it, and she's on board. I believe it might keep some of our staff from quitting when they have children, and it will go far to show that we're no longer the same company my father created." A laugh escaped his mouth. "The bastard had everyone so afraid to get married or have kids. Damn him and his archaic principles."

I felt Van's cock finally start to soften. This time when I started to move, he let me roll off him. I looked down at his cock, and we both saw the evidence of my virginity there, with the slight tinge of blood mixed with our fluids.

"Let me fill the tub and drop in some fragrance, and we'll take a bath together." I started to object, since all I really needed was to clean up, but he raised his hand in the air. "You'll welcome this bath when you start moving around. I wanted to make love to you and take it nice and gentle, but I couldn't resist. Your pussy felt so amazing. I got lost in the moment and took you harder than I'd planned." His eyes looked apologetically into mine. "I'm sorry, love. I promise to show you what it's like to make love."

A smile played on my lips. I wasn't sure how to express what I was feeling, so I just ran with it. "I'll never forget this moment for as long as I live. You showed me compassion and tenderness in taking me for the first time, but remember, it was I who asked you to go faster, deeper, harder." I reached up caressing the side of his face with my palm. "We can take it slow whenever you like, or we can repeat what we just did. Remember, I'm yours for the taking, and I kind of liked it a little rough. While I'm not a stranger to getting off, I am interested in exploring the wealth of possibilities that exist between us."

Leaning forward and pressing a gentle kiss to my swollen lips, he whispered, "How in the hell did I get so lucky to end up with such an amazing woman?

You are truly a treasure." He lifted my hand to his heart and placed his own on top. "One I intend to protect with my life, keeping you close, always."

His words sent a shiver through my body. "Are you cold, darling? Let me get that bath running."

I just nodded in response to Van's question. I didn't want him to know thoughts of my crazed fan had just run through my mind. I didn't want him to protect me with his life. I only wanted him to love me. I just prayed we got out of this in one piece, together.

Admiring the muscles on his back as they rippled with each step he took, I watched him walk away. And that ass, I could stare at it for days. I had one mighty-fine specimen of a husband. I laughed to myself. The word "husband" still seemed so foreign to me.

Sounds of the water and scents of vanilla mixed with lavender drifted through the air, enticing me to check on my man. Do I hear music playing? Imagine my surprise when I walked into the bathroom and saw not only lit candles flickering in every nook and cranny but also my husband hard and ready for round two.

Memories of the continual love-making sessions through the night played on my mind. Van had me ride him in the tub; then, we managed to get as far as the bathroom counter before he put me atop it, parted my legs, and dove into my center. There was also doggie style in the middle of the bed. I was surprised with his stamina. Just when I thought he was spent, he'd take one look at me and get hard all over again. He was insatiable, and I suspected I was, too. His cock felt so amazing sliding in and out of me all night and into the morning. I was sore, but well sated. Van's just so addictive and dominating, which made me crave him even more.

The light of morning started seeping in through the break in the curtains. I felt my mind begin to drift toward slumber as our bodies finally settled from our last round, which consisted of Van making love to me in a spooning position.

He drifted off first, with his hand still on my breast and his dick still up inside me. I couldn't complain. The need to feel one another this close was overwhelming. I know it doesn't make any sense, but when we're together, I feel whole.

My eyes closed, and the world started to drift away, when someone started pounding on the door. I startled and Van shot upright, separating our bodies from one another. His words echoed my sentiments. "What the fuck?"

He pulled the covers up over me while bending down to grab his discarded boxers. I watched as he huffed over to the door and cracked it open. "This had better be damned important to interrupt us during our wedding night."

I strained to hear what was being said, only getting bits and pieces. "He knows...threat to kill...we need to move...not safe."

Van raised his hand and hit the side of the doorframe, causing me to jump. Shaking his head, he responded back to, it looked like, Russ. *I'm guessing Peter and Russ changed out during the night to stand guard.* "Just give us an hour to wash up, and we'll be ready to go. Make sure the rest of my family's safe. We have a couple locations they can go to. Tell Peter and Rick that I want this fucker caught now, no excuses. This had gone on long enough. Pull in extra men, computer experts, or whomever you need. I want everyone at my office by 4 p.m. today for a status update. We'll also discuss how this all happened and what we're going to do to get a resolution to this once and for all." A few more words were said at barely a whisper.

When he turned around, the fear on his face said a lot.

"He's found us?" I bolted upright, pulling the covers up tightly against me. My breaths were coming fast, and my heart felt like it was ready to beat out of my chest. *Why can't he just leave me alone?*

Van nodded. "The bastard somehow hacked into the security system here at the house. He knows we got married. He's bitching up a storm on your webcast's message boards." Van pointed toward the door. "Russ said the bastard posted a statement saying, 'How dare you marry someone other than me. You're mine, not his!' He also posted a song by One Republic, 'Something I Need.'"

His eyes were frightened, and he swallowed hard as he ran his hand through his hair. His feet shifted from side to side. I could tell there was something he didn't want to state. I tried going over the song in my mind and replaying the words to figure out what had Van looking so haunted. He took in a deep breath to calm himself before finally admitting, "He's highlighted the words 'When I go flying off the edge, you go flying off as well. And if you only die once, I want to die with you.'"

I couldn't breathe. This maniac wanted me dead. I've heard of people obsessed with individuals they loved to the point of committing a murder-suicide. You know the old adage, "If I can't have you, no one will." I never thought I'd be one of them. Hell, I'd only done the webcasts as a means to an end. I needed money for school. I didn't want to be beholden to someone for paying my expenses, so Untouched Mystique was created.

Van's body wrapped around mine, and his hands kept running up and down my arms. "Breathe, angel. Take a deep breath in, hold it, and now let it out." I hadn't realized I'd been holding my breath, but the news just scared the hell out of me.

My first thoughts weren't of me or of Van, but of the life we might've created last night. I knew the chances were slim to none that we'd...what's the baseball expression?...hit it out of the park the first try at bat. But with as much sperm as Van put into me last night and where I was in my cycle, the chances were looking fairly good.

I mean, I don't want to lose my life either, and I want my husband, his brother, and the rest of his family protected, too. I had to ask, "What about our families?"

He held me tighter, as if he feared letting go would cause me to slip out of his hands. "Trent and Mark are going to a secure house that no one knows about. My mom wants to ride things out here with Alyssa. And your family took off early this morning, because your mom needed to get back to her work at the bank, and your grandparents needed to get their affairs in order for their move down here to be with us."

At least something nice came from all of this: my mom would finally be rid of my loser father. His parents and my mother's parents would all move here so we could make up for the years we missed as a family. Too bad my sister was still so loyal to my father.

I was lost in thought as Van pulled back the covers, scooped me up in his arms, and carried me to the bathroom. Kissing my forehead, he squeezed me tightly to his chest. "I've got you, angel. I'm not going to let this bastard destroy what we've found together. We'll come up with a plan later today to try and flush him out."

He set me down on my feet beside the shower, and then reached in and turned it on, adjusting the temperature. As we waited for the water to heat, he rested one of his hands on my hip while the other caressed the back of my neck, causing me to let go of some of the tension. His lips started kissing a small trail against the side of my neck. "I'd planned on us spending the next couple of days locked up here in this room, where I could cherish your body and show you all the different ways I could take you."

His chin came down on my shoulder and a small sigh escaped his lips as his hardened dick pressed against my lower belly. "I hate to say we need to get dressed, love, but the guys have arranged for decoys to be here soon to draw attention away while we slip out. We need to get back to my apartment at the office. The team felt it's the safest location we have right now. Remember, it's essentially designed as a safe room. Although, I never expected to use it as such."

I was about to ask him if we could get some more sleep, since yesterday had been filled with overpowering emotions and, of course, lots and lots of mind-blowing, orgasmic sex. I started to open my mouth, when a yawn took hold.

"Don't worry about sleep, Kaelin. We can get a short nap on the way back into town and then catch a few hours prior to the meeting."

He used his hand against my lower back to guide me into the shower and under the spray; then, he washed every inch of my body. His movements stoked the liquid fire deep within my core. I now knew what it was like to have a raging inferno build to an overwhelming force in the heat of passion, and I wanted it again.

He must've seen the need in my eyes, which was especially apparent when it was my turn to wash him. I latched on to his manhood and simulated the motions of sex, until he finally pushed my back against the wall, lifted my right leg around his hip, and plowed into me, causing me to gasp and cry out, "Yes."

Van shook his head before assaulting my senses with a kiss. His movements were more frantic than last night, as if he were trying to prove a point that I was his. His momentum was fast, furious, pushing me toward the edge at lightning speed. It only took the word "come" for me to detonate around him.

He pumped into me three more times before releasing his load. "You're mine, love. That man will not have what is mine!"

I couldn't argue with Van's point. I didn't want to have anything to do with my stalker. The only thing I did want was my life back so I could take my finals, graduate on time, and spend the rest of eternity with my husband. I just prayed I had a forever and that no harm would come to those I've come to love and care deeply for.

Chapter 16

Van

I WAS IMPRESSED WITH how quickly the Titan Security team, and Luke, managed to get things handled. It only took Kaelin and me an hour to ready ourselves to head back to the office; however, neither one of us really wanted to leave the room, leave what we'd become together.

Peter, Russ, and Luke had four identical cars and three sets of individuals resembling us ready to go as well. Our ride back was uneventful, but one of the other cars experienced a blown tire. Two women stopped to help them and offered to call a tow truck. The team dismissed it as coincidence, but I've never believed in that. I was firm in my beliefs that all things happen for a reason, just like Kaelin coming into my world the very first time I stepped foot onto the university's campus.

Kaelin was quick to fall asleep on our drive back, not even waking once we'd arrived back at our apartment. In order to function, she needed a little more sleep than I did. Not to mention how I'd taken her hard several times during the night. I took off her heels and tucked her into bed.

My body was vibrating with energy, wanting to reach out and grab the sick fuck that was after my wife and now threatening to take her life. I'd just found happiness with her. I'd be damned if I let him take it away.

I didn't want to wake her, so I texted Luke with a couple of thoughts I wanted him to address prior to our meeting with Titan today. My first priority was guaranteeing Kaelin's safety, which included the ability to track her should this psycho somehow manage to get ahold of her. *Not happening on my watch, buster.*

I was working at my computer, handling a few emails, when she started getting agitated in her sleep. I'd been privy to her nightmares the last few weeks and could tell she was in the midst of a doozy. Her body was getting caught up in the sheets, adding to her restless state. I quickly discarded my shoes and climbed in behind her. She settled the moment our bodies touched.

It still amazed me how perfectly our bodies fit together, as if the world knew we were meant to be together right from the beginning. I admit that I could be as hard as nails when it came to business, but I was also a romantic at heart. When you grew up with parents that hated one another, and your father detested the mere idea of love, it made you long for what they didn't have.

My sweet angel started to stir against me. "Shh it's okay, love. I've got you."

"Where are we?" Her eyes tried to open and adjust to the low light in the room.

"We're back at the office apartment. Sorry for the tight quarters, but it's one of the most secure areas I have at hand. We can move elsewhere if you'd like, but this way I still have access to the business."

She shook her head. "No. We need to work. Working will help take my mind off of things. Also, we need to study for our finals." Her eyebrows knitted together in deep thought, before she turned toward me. "How are we going to do the final exams? We can't miss them."

My arms were still wrapped around her body, which was cocooned by mine. "We'll discuss that at the meeting shortly. I had the same thoughts a few days ago and had Luke contact the professors on our behalf to see if we could get some leniency, given the circumstances."

Her eyes filled with horror.

"Don't worry, love. We're not telling them the full story. We only cited a family emergency, initially, but followed up with the need to leave town due to business. They fully believe that you're assisting us with a major business crisis."

The next hour, we just held one another in bed, thinking of only positive things to look forward to. We were happy that school would finally be over, allowing us to pursue our careers full-time. The idea of children was a definite, with each of us wanting at least two to liven up our lives. I asked her for ideas of where she'd like to have a honeymoon once all this was behind us and Trent was back working for the company.

My woman never ceased to amaze me. "I don't need a honeymoon. Just being with you, in your arms, is the ideal vacation for me."

I pushed, until she finally admitted, "I've never seen anything beyond the Gulf Coast of Louisiana and Mississippi. I love the beach but would like to see the world through your eyes." Now this was something I could work with.

I would've rather stayed in bed wrapped up in the love that was Kaelin, but now we were seated around the conference table in my office or, rather, our office. Luke, Rick—the head of Titan Security—Peter and his team, Nate, and Ethan were all in attendance. I welcomed them all on such short notice and asked, "What do we have?"

Ethan was the first to speak up. "My apologies for letting the perpetrator slip into your security system, but that was our plan."

Hearing those words made my hands ball into fists. Kaelin grabbed my hand, forcing it open and laced her fingers through mine. Her presence grounded me enough to ask, "What plan? Why weren't we informed?"

Ethan held his hands up in surrender as he proceeded to explain. "The team realized they had someone tailing them on the way to the property. They lost them with one of the decoys, but you were so close to the location that we were certain they knew where you were headed."

"I'm not following. I get that the person of interest was close enough to my mom's place to know we were headed there, but how did they tie me to Kaelin?" This was all too confusing.

Ethan continued on. "The person who tapped into Kaelin's computer is the same one who managed to create a backdoor on the vendor terminal here at work. However, it looks like we have an additional hand in the pot, stirring up trouble. The code that was similar in nature was the one controlling the bank transfers into an offshore account. We're still trying to figure out the why, but I've found through the underground the coding belongs to a woman in the South, but they're not certain. We are trying to pinpoint where she's located, since some of the hits have come from Orlando, while others have bounced through Mississippi, Louisiana, or Alabama. There are definitely two parties playing this game. One is the culprit who's terrorizing Kaelin; the other is in cahoots with him. Either way, they're out to destroy you both.

"Whoever got into the system here works as a vendor for the company. With you being the new CEO, they were probably able to gather your information from within the system to determine who you were. We're guessing since they were able to penetrate the firewall and blow up your computer through the Wi-Fi connection you had to Untouched Mystique's webcast, they probably put two and two together and discerned you were DaLuvMaster online."

Peter looked over to Rick, getting a nod of approval, before he spoke up. "We also believe they've done their homework. They knew who Kaelin was just by her emails and work assignments for class. Plus the fact that you both work together here at the company and have classes together. Well, it's not hard to add the two together.

"Van, I'd like to apologize for the length of time it has taken us to get where we are today. We'd hoped to have this thing wrapped up by now." Peter looked a little embarrassed about that. "We got a call from our Navy SEALs handler, and we're being called up for a mission in the next few weeks, so we want this resolved just as much as you do. That last post has us all on edge, so we brainstormed all afternoon, coming up with a few ideas we'd like to pass by you."

The team looked over toward Kaelin, and I instantly realized what they wanted to do. I stood, slamming my fist down onto the table, causing everyone to jump. "HELL NO! She's not going to go back online. I'm not going to risk her safety."

Luke held his hands up to me. "Van, bro, you're jumping to conclusions. Let's just hear what they have to say first before making snap decisions."

Kaelin reached out for my arm and pulled me back down into my chair. She leaned into me. Her body heat and presence settled me almost instantly.

"Fine," I grumbled. "Go ahead."

Peter nodded. "Ethan has already piggy-backed a bug onto the computer that hacked into your family's security cameras. As we mentioned earlier, we purposefully let our guard down hoping they'd do just that. When they go to use their computer, the bug will activate and start emitting a signal we can track. The only way they can get it off the computer is if Ethan removes it directly. It's designed to move from one area to another and embed itself deep into the system, making it damn near impossible to remove."

Ethan spoke up. "It's a new tool another colleague and I came up with to try and track criminal behavior. We're testing it out for the first time with your case."

I nodded, a smile on my face. "Good. I hope we get the bastard. Now what about the person tapping into the accounting system? Have you identified which vendor is at fault for letting them through the backdoor of the firewall? And about the security system at my mother's and here, obviously they aren't as safe as we'd first thought."

Rick took the lead on this while Ethan returned to typing away on his keyboard. "As of this moment, Titan Security is installing the latest state-of-the-art equipment at your mother's home, and she's given us permission to update the equipment here at the office. Any attempt to tap into the signals will be met with a virus that will destroy their computer—another new safeguard Ethan's come up with."

I looked to Nate. "What's the status on our accounts? Are they still in shambles?"

He shook his head. "No, sir. The culprit believes you're still operating on the old accounting software. Everything is in place so it looks like the older system still exists, and we've got it set up to look like new data is being entered. There have been no issues with the new system, while the older one has taken several hits from the individual getting in from the backdoor." Nate gestured between himself and Ethan. "We have it set up so the new software is hidden and any changes made to the old system are corrected automatically within a couple days. The person believes they're making a mess of your system and slowing your Accounting and IT departments down, but in actuality, the new software has allowed them to catch up, and they're right on schedule."

Over the next hour, we learned the team had narrowed the potential suspects on the vendor list from over one hundred down to ten. It sucked that we ran a company that had absorbed some other businesses, because it meant more vendors to deal with. The newest list would provide them a start, and we'd be provided a copy to peruse to see if anything stuck out at us.

"Our team will send people out to see if the vendor is where they're supposed to be. Ethan will backtrack any travel agendas and see if the times and dates of specific noted activity matches up. It's not an easy process, but it will get us closer to finding a resolution," Peter provided.

Luke piped up. "Most of your professors are willing to bring the exams to you here at work, so we've reserved time in one of the smaller conference rooms down the hall. Only one of your mutual instructors was reluctant to agree to our needs. We even offered to donate to his research if he'd be a little more accommodating. He wouldn't budge, so we'll need to figure out how to get you both there safely."

Kaelin and I tensed at the idea of having to go back on campus and risk our safety. I gave my wife a gentle squeeze on her thigh before leaning over to tell her, "We'll get through this together, love." In which she responds, with a pat to my hand, "I know. I trust you to protect us."

The idea of going back to campus got me wondering. "Were you able to determine whether Pierce Montgomery was a threat? I believe we last left things with Ethan going to speak to his class."

Ethan nodded. "The computer he carries on him at all times is continually running code trying to break into various systems. That's where he keeps his most prized programs and where he has all of his scrupulous business transactions. He doesn't want to get caught fudging some of the students' grades, so he keeps it close."

"How were you able to determine this? I'm curious." Kaelin was sitting up straight, staring at Ethan with a questionable look.

I had to admit, I wondered the same thing. The man had a mind that seemed to process faster than anyone else. No wonder he was top of his game.

Ethan laughed. "I remembered what I'd done with one of my professor's computers in school. We were all required to hook up to a main system, and then tasked to write code to keep everyone out of their personal computer. The teacher believed his system to be infallible. Well, I proved him wrong, nearly getting myself kicked out of class." Looking toward us and smiling, Ethan shrugged his shoulders. "I just did the same thing, but in reverse. I tapped into Pierce's system without him even realizing it. I have to say, his thinking impressed me. I've even talked with Titan Security to see about bringing him on as an additional hacker. He's definitely got the skill set, but he's harmless. He's been to Mystique's webcast a few times, but not lately, and his coding doesn't match what we're looking for."

A few hours later and we were all in agreement. Kaelin and I would continue as usual while the team looked into the vendors and waited for the hackers to strike again. Kaelin would only go out on the website as Mystique in a week if nothing came to light before then. She would announce that her show was being cancelled since she's now married to one of her viewers and no longer untouched. If the stalker didn't surface before that announcement, he certainly would with that bit of information. The guy was definitely possessive as hell, but who could blame him really? I mean, look at my wife. She's drop-dead gorgeous with curves in all the right places. Just glancing at her had me hard again and envisioning her spread out on the small conference table or atop my desk. *Are you sure you want to share your office with your brother? Think of the potential to take your wife on every surface in here.*

My subconscious was leading onto dangerous ground. I swore I'd hold back from pounding into my sweet angel to give her at least a day to recoup, but all the blood in my head was rushing south to my dick. I wish these guys would wrap it up and get out of here so I could get some relief.

Coming back to the present, I shook my head and followed the last part of Peter's conversation. "...and that sums it all up. We'll stay on top of the perpetrators, waiting for them to screw up. You're going to stay away from campus until the day of the test, and we'll have an extra detail on hand posing as students, just as a safety."

"Good. And the devices I asked Luke to request?" I hated bringing this up without talking with Kaelin first. I watched as my wife looked over to me with a puzzled expression on her face.

She mouthed the words, "What are you talking about?"

Peter pulled a small box from his briefcase. Opening it, he looked at Kaelin and explained, "Your husband is concerned about your continued safety. We're going to provide round-the-clock guard duty to keep you both safe, but this whack job has upped the ante with the threat to kill you. We fear he might want to take Van's life as well, since he took you from the stalker's alleged possession. So, per your husband's instructions, we added a little something special to these watches."

Peter lifted two matching platinum-looking watches out of the box. I'd told them to spare no expense. I wanted to get Kaelin some nice jewelry, since she hardly had any to wear, and figured a watch would be a nice place to start.

She looked back at me with a questionable look. "You got me a watch? How's that going to protect either of us? Is it going to predict the time I need to run or the time I die?" Her voice was laden with sarcasm.

I could tell the weight of the last couple of days was heavy on her shoulders. She only seemed to get snarky with me when she was short on sleep and scared out of her mind. I pushed my chair back, pulled her onto my lap, put my arms around her, and then drew her close to my chest. "The Rolex watches are meant for divers, but they've had some features added to them for our safety. It terrifies me to no end that I might lose you to this maniac. I asked Luke to contact Titan to see if they offered any kind of tracking system that was wearable. It needed to pass as jewelry, be waterproof, and withstand various elements. I gave them carte blanche to purchase the most durable watches on the market."

Peter got up and walked around the table to where we were sitting. He held out his hand to Kaelin. When she put her shaky hand in his, he proceeded to place the watch on her wrist and pointed to the side buttons. "The watch is to stay on at all times. If for any reason you get in an emergency situation, this middle button can be depressed, and it'll activate an emergency signal that goes directly to all of our phones and to Titan headquarters. There's also a tracking chip implanted in the back of the watch that'll lead us to you. The watch is a Rolex Oyster, capable of being wet, so no taking it off to wash your hands, take a shower, or even a bath. It stays on at all times. Understood?"

My sweet angel swallowed hard at all the information provided, but she nodded in agreement with what Peter had stated. He handed over my watch. "The same applies to you, too, Van. We don't fully know the extent this guy will go in order to get what he wants. He might be leading us to believe he intends to kill her, but he might be trying to get you out of the way so he can get to Mystique."

This was true. While the threat had been made against her life, mine was now in the line of fire, too. This sick fuck was on a mission to get to "his" Mystique one way or another, and I guess he didn't care whom he had to kill to get there, myself included.

"Thanks, man." I took the watch from his hands and put it on immediately.

The meeting was over, everyone had left, and we'd just sealed ourselves into the office for the remainder of the night. We were both hungry, not having had much to eat all day, and the smell of the Chinese cuisine was calling to me.

Luke had one of his guys go pick us up a hot meal from one of our favorite restaurants, citing we'd already been through so much that we didn't need to worry about dinner, too. I needed to give that man a raise.

Kaelin started to walk toward the apartment, when I slipped my arms around her waist and pulled her hard against my chest. My mouth latched on to her neck, where I nipped at the skin below her ear before moving up to the earlobe and biting it. "I'm just as hungry as you are, love, but I want a taste of dessert first, if you're up to it. Are you too sore? Because I couldn't get the idea of taking you across my desk out of my mind." I reached for her hand and pulled it against my crotch so she could feel just how hard I was.

"Oh." A smile played across her face as her hand continued to rub against the length of my cock. She bumped her ass into me, causing me to groan. "I guess someone needs a little attention."

She turned her body to face me before leaning in and planting a slow sensual kiss on my lips. Her tongue came out to lick my chin and in her sultry voice whispered, "I could go for some dessert first if you're gentle."

Her hands came down to undo my belt and pants. "I need to touch you, babe. I guess you've created a monster, because the entire time we were in the meeting, I wanted to be in your bed instead."

I didn't know where this was coming from, but I couldn't complain. "I like that you're expressing your needs more freely to me. Would you like to explore a bit?"

She cocked her head to the side, biting her lower lip in the process. *Damn. Did she not know that was the hot button straight to a man's dick?* "What'd you have in mind?" I raised my finger into the air to indicate I'd be right back.

I went into the apartment and found where I left the bag from last night. I purchased some toys for us to play and experiment with, but we'd never needed them.

Taking the bag back into the other room, I carried it over to the desk. "I thought we could give some of these a try if you'd like. Seems a shame to buy them and let them go to waste."

She shook her head, tsking, "That is shameful," as she looked into the contents of the bag. A smile played on her face as she recognized a few items. "You replaced some of the items I left at the condo for the show."

I nodded. "I figured you might want fresh items, since your space was violated. I added a few I'd like to try on you when you're ready. Nothing too intense, love."

I reached around her and quickly felt for the item I was interested in tonight, and then pulled it out to see her response. When I unearthed a blindfold, she seemed to smile. "You're playing to the fantasy we'd talked about online."

"Yes, but only if you're up to it, love."

She took hold of my hand, placing it on her inner thigh. "I guess you'll just have to find out." *The little tease. I loved this side of her.*

My hand drifted slowly up underneath her skirt to the outer band of her thong. I didn't even have to touch the fabric to know she was soaked through and dripping down her thighs. I closed my eyes as I felt myself harden even further, seeking emergence from the confines of my boxers. All anyone had to do was look down to see the tent pole that was pressing against the fabric and pointing straight at its desired target.

Tightening my hand against the delicate lace material of her thong, I pulled hard, ripping the thing into shreds and exposing her dripping pussy lips to my fingers. One graze of my thumb against her folds, and she nearly jumped off the floor.

I caught her off guard when I reached down and lifted her up into my arms, before depositing her on the edge of my desk. I placed the mask over her eyes. "I just want you to feel the love I have for you, Kaelin. I want your mind to let go, focusing only on the love that exists between us, the love we've created. I'll drive you to the edge multiple times, but you're not to come until I tell you, understood?"

Her breathing was already erratic, and the pulse in her neck was beating wildly. A seductive "Yes, Sir" came from her lips. *The little smart ass.* But I had to admit, I did like the sound of "Sir." I don't know that we'll keep that up, but tonight I'd play any game she wanted, as long as we had this moment to create memories. The memories we would be making on a honeymoon if it weren't for that asshole, but that's neither here nor there. Any time spent with my sweet wife would exist as a memory permanently etched in my mind, my heart, and on my soul.

"Lie back for me, love." I guided her back onto the desk. "Reach your hands above your head and hold on to the edge of the desk for me."

The reality of her body stretched out across it hit me much stronger than it did in my imagination. Seeing her breasts barely contained in the fabric of her dress, her ass hanging off the edge, her pussy dripping with the need to have me inside her...I almost came just seeing her like this.

I wanted to bury my face in her sweet center and lick up the moisture surrounding her folds, but her senses were too heightened. We were starving for both the sustenance to our souls and to our bodies.

I reached down to lower my boxers, letting them fall to my ankles. I caressed her inner thighs before lifting both legs up and over my shoulders, causing her center to line up perfectly with my manhood. The heat emanating off of her was intense. My dick was drawn to her, rubbing itself up and down her slit. I didn't need to reach down and see if she was ready to take me inside her. With the amount of moisture now coating me, there was no doubt she wanted me.

I put the tip of my cock against her pussy and started to inch in slowly. I could see the small wince on her face and paused, afraid I was hurting her.

"Please, don't stop." Her words called out to me as her feet wrapped around the backside of my head to draw me closer to her.

Rocking gently back and forth, I managed to work my way inside her. Damn, she felt like a vice squeezing hard around my dick. "I could stay buried inside you forever, love. You feel so tight, so freaking amazing."

We managed to find a rhythm that suited both of our needs, with her hips grinding into me as I pushed inside her. I could feel her walls start to close in around me as a low moan escaped her throat. I reached out grabbing on to the fabric covering her hardened nipples, and then squeezed them, causing her to arch her back away from the desk. "I need to. Please...I have to."

I knew what she needed, but I needed her to build a little more before she released. I wanted us both out of our heads, for even a few moments, just to exist together in our bubble without worry, without fear, without a threat hovering over our heads.

"You can take a little more, my sweet angel." I kept one hand on her breasts, working them over as my cock slid in and out of her center. I rocked at a faster pace, which was driving us both to completion. I slid my other hand down to where we were united and coated my thumb with her moisture before pressing against the rosebud on her ass.

"Yes!" She cried out.

I pushed against her tight hole as she pushed back against my thumb, which allowed me to breach her ass. My thumb went up to the second knuckle before pumping back and forth, feeling my dick sliding inside her through the thin layer of tissue separating her two holes.

"Feels so good...so full...so deep. Please...I've got to..." Her head thrashed on the desk, and her fingers turned white from gripping the edges so hard. Her mouth was open, ready to scream out her release.

I let her legs fall around my waist as I bent over her and whispered, "Come, love. Let your anxiety out with your release. Feel yourself letting go of your troubles as you coat my cock with your juices."

Her mouth opened a bit further, and I covered it with mine, absorbing her scream as we both reached release at the same time. This was the most intense we'd been to date. I could feel myself spurt off rope after rope of cum into her vaginal walls...and hoping I just planted my seed deep within her.

Removing her mask and biting back my fear, I slowly drew her body up against mine. Her eyes were dazed, and a contented smile was splayed across her face. Her head rested against my shoulder as we both caught our breath. *Get out of your fucking head, man. This is time to enjoy your lady. Let the security team deal with things. They've got your back.* My mind was right. If I lived in fear of what could potentially happen, I wouldn't enjoy what was right in front of me—my wife.

Taking a step back, I held on to her shoulders to give her support. I scrunched down to look into her eyes. "Are you okay?"

She nodded happily. "That was wonderful. Can we try that again on other surfaces of your office?"

I couldn't help but laugh. "You truly are a rare gem, Kaelin. And yes, we'll christen every surface of the office and the apartment. I can think of quite a few things I'd love to do with you and to you."

"Me, too." She licked her lip before biting it. *Damn, she was going to be the death of me, in a good way. Going by way of sexual overload didn't sound that bad.*

I helped her down off the desk and grabbed her shredded thong to throw into the trash in our apartment. *Note to self: start looking for potential housing when this is all said and done.*

It was time for us to retire to our humble abode to enjoy a nice meal, take a bath, and get lost in one another. I may sound like a silly old romance novel, but I don't care. If any man saw how my wife looked in the throes of passion, they'd be just as fucking sappy.

I still had trouble wrapping my mind around the fact that we were in love and now married. Most of my dreams had come true. Although, her words about waiting for the shoe to drop started grabbing my attention, which made me fearful of giving into contentment and kept me on edge. I'd worry but not tonight.

Chapter 17

Kaelin

O VER THE COURSE OF the last week, Van and I fulfilled most of the fantasies we'd shared with one another online. One of mine was to suck on him from underneath his desk while he was either on the phone or talking with someone at the office. I loved how the desk went all the way to the floor, so no one could see what was happening underneath.

I got my opportunity when he had a meeting with Luke in regard to my stalker. I don't think Luke suspected anything, since I couldn't get my husband to break his control. However, I could tell I was getting to him from the slow drizzle of pre-cum coating my tongue, but it wasn't until we were finally alone that he grabbed hold of my hair and bounced his hips off his chair to move in and out of my mouth, before releasing his essence down my throat. His taste was quickly becoming my favorite flavor.

It didn't surprise me when he turned things around a few days later, with me in the chair. He ate out my center as I was talking on the phone with Trent. He'd been so worried about both of us that he now called every few days just to make sure we were fine.

Speaking of phone calls, I wasn't expecting the news I received from my mom. Apparently my sister, Bethany, and my father had a huge falling out—about what, we don't know—but she ended up packing a bag in the middle of the night and leaving. She wasn't answering her phone, and no one knew where to find her. I promised I'd keep an ear out for her in case she contacted me, but I didn't put much hope into it. We hadn't talked in almost three years, so why start now?

The week had turned out to be quite productive, both in the bedroom and in the office. We managed to finish the financial analysis of the business, and it turned out that Van and Trent's father had, indeed, falsified financial reports in order to acquire new businesses. The security team discovered Mr. Meyers had been blackmailed. In order to cover his predilections toward BDSM fueled orgies, he arranged for particular companies to be acquired, paying way above market value and sealing the deals with marriages to his kids in exchange for silence.

The only business deal that wasn't completed, thanks to Van's father passing unexpectedly, was the Thresher Restaurant Chain. It gave me shivers to think of Van being forced to marry someone else. To date, they were operating in the red, having closed several locations and selling the less profitable to national chains. Their facilities were spread out across several of the southern states. *I wonder, was this the company that had purchased my paternal grandfather's legacy or was it just coincidence? Note to self: google the Thresher brand and see which restaurant chains they purchased in the past.*

Van inquired about Heather Thresher's current status and was surprised to learn that her manager boyfriend had left her when their pay got cut to save on expenses. Her condo had been repossessed, and she was now living back with her parents, taking over the travel portion of her father's business dealings. She was miserable and apparently blaming Van's father for the mess her family was in.

"I'm glad I avoided that hot mess; although, I do wish her well and hope her family can recover. If they would've come to me, maybe we could've helped them turn things around before it got too bad. With the state they're in now, short of a miracle, nothing can really save them." Van explained she'd gone from being angelic and sincere to greedy in the course of a year, which put a strain on their friendship.

"Forget about Heather and the past, I know I have. You're my present Kaelin, in more ways than one," his eyebrows lifted to emphasis the point, "and you're the only one I want a future with, and in order to do that, we have to get your broadcast behind us, so we can shut down your website for good."

Van was right; it was time for me to do my final broadcast as Untouched Mystique. I needed to announce the site would be shutting down. I hated putting myself on display just to convey a message, but we all believed the stalker needed to visually see me for it to sink in.

Peter's team secured the video equipment and backdrops from the condo I'd shared with Trent. They brought it all into the apartment and helped set it up. Ethan set up one of his laptops to act as a portal to my website to seek out any system with the particular code he was looking for. All he needed was a connection that lasted a short time. Van and Peter worked to provide a script for me to read explaining why I was taking the site down and to make a last ditch attempt to get this whack-a-doodle to leave me alone.

We did the broadcast live without incident. Van had been off to the side watching me with heated eyes as I dressed in character. The rest of the crew was blindfolded, per his request, while Ethan sat with his back to me and monitored the transmission. The moment we shut things down, Van had a blanket wrapped around me and was ushering me to the bathroom, where he proceeded to strip me of my clothing and take me against the counter until we both were sated, before dressing me in my normal attire. My man was fiercely protective of me, something I thought would scare me, but I actually liked the control he exerted...a total turn on.

The stalker remained eerily quiet, causing my emotions to run high. We thought for sure he'd be pissed and respond to the last webcast transmission, but there was nothing.

Van and I kept busy with work, studying, and lots of playtime with one another. He brought out all of my inhibitions and pushed them aside making me feel stronger and more expressive as a woman. Even he grew to possess a more commanding presence both in the office and the bedroom, which personally, my favorite was the latter.

Two days before our exams were to start, Luke ran into the office without knocking, nearly catching us in a compromising position. Keeping one arm around my waist, Van helped me off his desk, and then pulled me tightly to his side. "What is it, man? You look like you've seen a ghost."

Luke walked over to the back of one of the chairs, holding on to it for support. His voice was shaky, and he looked like he had the potential to hurl at any moment. "Eagle Eyes is actively searching for you, Kaelin. He struck last night."

Needing to hold on to something, I quickly wrapped my arms around Van. My nerves were frayed and my legs weak. I just shook my head. "No. I'm here. I'm safe. How could he attack?"

Luke, who was avoiding my gaze, looked solely at Van, "There have been copycat websites pop up by other woman wanting to exploit Mystique's popularity."

I didn't like the sound of where this was going. Thankfully, it was my husband who asked the question playing on our minds. "And? What about them?"

He explained. "Titan Security had someone monitoring the police scanners for activity that might be related to cases they're handling, when a call came about a young woman attacked. A note written in lipstick was left on her body, stating, "Fake. NOT Mystique." Obviously, Titan checked it out."

Luke's eyes looked haunted as he gave us the grim details. "This piece of shit had beaten her to the point of being unconscious, and then tied her to her bed. He left a second note—this one intended for the real Mystique—beside the woman's body." Stating the police took the note into evidence, Luke took out his phone and pulled up a photo of the note. It read:

> You can run but I will find you, Mystique. You are destined to be mine. I OWN you. I'll HAVE you before we're together forever in eternity.

My body began to shake, and the tears began pouring from my eyes. I felt heartache for the woman who'd been beaten in my place. I was terrified that he truly intended to do me harm.

Luke continued. "The good news is that the police are finally taking the attack on Trent and the condo seriously, now that they have evidence this nutcase is still after Kaelin." Luke swallowed hard, "The bad news is they just found another woman, donning the same disguise as Mystique, almost beaten to death, too. However, a camera happened to be rolling during that attack."

Running a hand down his face, he shook his head. "It wasn't a guy who attacked her. It was a woman. She wielded a baseball bat and kept beating the woman over and over. The voice was disguised, as was her attire. We assume it was a female, anyway, as the person was wearing high heels and had womanly curves. There was a second person there as well, a man. He was disguised, but the voice was a definite match to Eagle Eyes. He pulled the female attacker off the woman. You can hear him state, *'It's not her. I don't want a fake. I want MY Mystique.'*"

Van held me so tightly I could barely breathe, but I also didn't complain, since I'd probably be on the floor without his support. "Did the woman say anything that could be incriminating, a clue to her identity?"

Luke shook his head. "Her only words were *'You ruined everything. You took everything I had.'*"

"Angel?" Van moved his hand underneath my chin, tipping my face toward him. "Is there anyone you can think of who'd be jealous of you, blame you for their problems, anything?"

I thought back on things. Because of my father's demands, I mostly kept to myself, so I wasn't popular in high school. However, I tutored numerous classmates, mostly daughters of my father's business associates that were predetermined to go to college to find a man whose family was rich enough to help their fathers' businesses grow.

In college, I mainly talked with one female, my coworker at Mark's coffee shop. We usually talked about our professors or what we'd be doing on school breaks, nothing much really.

I couldn't see my sister being a suspect, since she never really talked to me. She was "daddy's little girl," the perfect child, the one he actually wanted and doted on, while I was as good as dead to him.

Shaking my head, I responded, "The only women I ever dealt with were the ones I tutored in high school, the girl I worked with at Mark's coffee shop on campus, my sister, and the women in the accounting department. I never had any issues with any of them. I mainly did what I had to do and kept to myself."

The words had just left my mouth, when I broke down crying. "Why is this happening to me? Why are these innocent women being beaten all because of me? I want this all to stop."

Van lifted me in his arms, before taking a seat behind his desk and placing me on his lap. "We're working on it, love. We'll find these people. At least now, we've confirmed there is another person involved and the individual is female. It gives us something to go on. Right, Luke?"

Luke stepped forward patting me on the back. A low growl emitted from Van's throat at Luke's innocent contact. It was a bit funny to me, actually. I didn't know if Van was being overly possessive since we were newlyweds or what the deal was, but Luke quickly took a step back and uttered a barely audible, "Sorry, sir." He then added, "The team is already creating a suspect list from Kaelin's past and present. Titan Security has pulled in a few of their contacts to assist in this case and are working closely with the local police department to speed things up."

After a few more minutes of discussion, Luke finally left us alone. Van was quick to lockdown the office door, sealing us in. He tried to be romantic in an effort to take my mind off of things, but I couldn't stop crying. I ended up in our apartment bed with Van's arms wrapped around me as I sobbed uncontrollably into the sheets. I couldn't help it. I wept for how shitty my life had been, for the events that led up to me being thrown into Van's arms, and for the two women who were put in the hospital, thanks to the maniacs. The bawling wouldn't stop. How could someone hate me so much? The tears continued on for the rest of that day and only silenced in the middle of the night.

Chapter 18

Kaelin

I SPENT THE NEXT several days withdrawn. I looked through the vendor list and googled them to see how long they were in business. Most of the vendors checked out, but a few had been known by other names at one time or had been sold within the last couple of years to other brands.

When I wasn't working, I was studying for my exams. The first ones were taken after hours in a small conference room down the hall. The instructors personally brought the tests to us and sat in the room as we took them. Luke, Peter, and his team were present throughout the corridor to ensure our safety.

We managed to get through all the exams except for one, and since the professor wouldn't offer us an exemption on where we took our exam, it was the class I feared most.

Van had several conversations with Luke and Peter in his office, while I remained in the apartment, not wanting to step foot outside its doors. The place seemed more like a bank vault than an apartment. It was only when we were locked in at night did I feel I could breathe, believing no one could get to me here. I firmly believed I was a sitting duck if I exited this place.

The day arrived for the trip to campus to take the last of our exams. To date, we passed all of our tests with flying colors and would be graduating with our master's degrees, pending this exam from the toughest teacher in Finance.

That morning I held the sheets up tightly around myself. When Van tried to lift me out of bed, I held on to the headboard's bars, not wanting to leave the comfort and protection the apartment afforded.

He finally managed to coax me into the shower with the promise of the naughty things we could do in there. It had been days since we allowed ourselves the pleasure of coming together.

Once he had me soaped up and rinsed off, he bent me over, placed my hands against the shower wall, pushed my legs apart, and took me from behind. When he entered me, I felt I could finally breathe again. It was only when we worked together as a team did I feel capable of handling anything thrown my way. Any thoughts I had went out the window as he pumped into me faster and faster. His body bent over mine, with one hand going to my breasts, kneading them, while the other went to my clit, where he rubbed circles against my hardened nub.

"You've been wrapped up inside your head for too long, angel. You and I both know we're better together than apart." His rhythm started to increase, and I could feel the warmth begin to build, turning my darkened core into something lighter, brighter.

"I've missed you, babe." I responded as I reached back and grabbed hold of his ass with one of my hands.

His words came with short breaths. "You. Feel. So. Damn. Good. I need you, love. I can't exist without you."

"I feel the same, Van. I love you."

"I love you, too, my sweet angel." His lips latched on to the junction of my throat and neck while his hand twisted and pinched my breast. "Come on me, Kaelin. Come now."

The strength behind his final thrusts propelled me over the edge and into oblivion. The light going off in my mind, behind my eyes, was blindingly bright, like a supernova exploding in the darkness of space.

I felt myself falling even deeper in love with my husband, if that were possible. He knew exactly what I needed, what the perfect thing to get me out of my head and back in tune with reality was. Van provided me strength, making me capable of standing on my own two feet, while most of my encounters with men left me feeling defeated in life.

My eyes started to readjust to my surroundings. I was surprised to see each of us on the floor of the shower, leaning against one another. I reached over to cradle his face with my hand and give him a gentle kiss on the lips. "Thank you. You knew exactly what I needed."

His hand covered mine while a smile played on his lips. "I needed it, too, Kaelin. This shit has me all worked up inside. I want to be everything to you, protect you with all that I am." He sighed deeply as his eyes revealed the tender emotion he was feeling on the inside. "I'm scared of losing you. I needed to be inside you, to know we're still in this together and to feel connected to you in a way no other will ever experience."

I nodded in agreement. "I'm scared, too. I don't want to go to the campus today. What if—"

"There'll be no what-ifs today. We'll have a couple of bodyguards close by, some plain-clothed security detail, and police hiding in the distance in the event anyone gets close to either one of us. Luke's insisted on us wearing bulletproof vests underneath our clothes as another safety."

I looked more closely at Van's face, realizing just how terrified he was. "Isn't all that a bit extreme?"

He shook his head. There was something he wasn't telling me, and, to my surprise, I was okay with that. I didn't want to hear any more negativity. I'd rather be obliviously happy in my little bubble with Van. "When it comes to your safety, I'll spare no expense." He slapped at my ass. "We need to get out of here and get dressed if we want to have a little breakfast and the chance to get in some last-minute studying."

For the first time in forever, I dressed in casual clothing. It was the only thing that would hide the lightweight vest I was sporting underneath a fitted t-shirt and jeans. It wasn't uncomfortable, but every breath made me realize it was there for a reason. My life was in danger. I wasn't a very religious person, but I prayed for this to be over soon and for us to emerge victorious, keeping everyone that I loved safe.

The car ride to campus was just as crazy as our other outings had been, with several duplicates heading in various directions. Van continued to study in the backseat, while I needed a break, feeling my mind start to turn to mush with all the financial facts running through it.

I whipped out the documentation Luke had handed me as we got into the backseat of the car. I'd asked him for a copy of the detailed background check for the ten vendor companies Meyers Corporation worked with, the one's the security team were currently combing through. Seven came back clean and, therefore, ruled out as suspicious. However, the three remaining companies set off alarm bells. Their names were antiquated, not matching up to the names found in payroll. Peter's team had drawn the same conclusion as I did: something wasn't right about them. But why?

I managed to look through two of the three companies before we reached the campus. We'd hit go-time, and I could tell I was on the verge of a panic attack. Luke had let us off at the back entry of the building our class was housed in. Peter and his team were there waiting for us, along with some college-aged kids talking and yapping away, pausing only to nod our direction as we passed. Wow, the team had gone to extremes to keep us safe. When they'd said they had some plain-clothed people, they weren't kidding. Everywhere I looked, I saw someone watching out for our safety.

The walk to the classroom felt similar to what one might feel when they're walking to the electric chair. Each step took me one moment closer to my life possibly ending. The only thing keeping me grounded was Van's hand interlaced with mine.

Our professor was a real asshole, not letting anyone but Van and me inside. We took our respective seats, while our crew waited patiently outside the door.

The test was easier than I thought it'd be. I finished in record time. Then again, the last three days I'd had my head buried in the finance notes, because I knew the teacher was notorious for testing off his lectures rather than the book. The gamble paid off.

I handed in my test and tried to return to my seat, but Dr. Mendell showed me to the door. "We can't have you sitting around fidgeting in your seat, dear. You'll have to wait outside."

Van looked up, his eyes full of alarm, as I'm sure mine were, too. He nodded toward Peter, and I took his cue to go out into the hallway and wait for him there.

The minutes ticked by as Van continued to take his test. I don't know how many times I'd counted the ceiling tiles. I hated that I couldn't speak up and talk with anyone, since the noise level would interrupt the others taking their exams.

Remembering I'd stuffed the final background check into my rear pocket, I reached around and pulled it out. It would provide some reading material and get my mind off of things.

The company had been known as Trident Computer Technologies. They'd come on board with Meyers Corporation about twenty years ago, supplying the company with both hardware and software to bring it into a new computer era.

As I read on, I noticed that Trident had slipped in their business sales and became dependent upon Van's family's company to keep them afloat.

Nate noted there were a few questionable transactions found in the accounting files. *"We believe the head of Trident may have discovered Mr. Meyers's secrets. Several transactions had been sent to the computer company for 'services rendered,' but no equipment exchanged hands."*

For someone who was too ashamed to love his son, Trent, and accept him for whom he was, Mr. Meyers sure was careless in his own pleasurable pursuits. It made me question if the man even knew how to run a business. It seemed like the last ten years of his life, he was paying people off and letting the board make all the decisions while he collected the money.

Right before Mr. Meyers's death, Trident had been ready to declare bankruptcy, but was suddenly bought by a computer company based in Louisiana. *That's my home state. What the?* Feeling my heart rate increase, I read on, shaking my head, trying to make the words disappear from the page. It was CDR technologies, Mr. Chadwick and Roger's company.

It made sense. Roger had explained how Dad had used me as a bargaining chip. Roger intended to purchase me as his wife. I was to be subservient to all his needs and to be nothing more than eye candy for him. Yeah, that worked out well; I left him choking on his nuts, which I rammed up into his throat the night I refused to accept that life as my fate and walked out. Could it be that to Roger I was the one that got away? Is that why Eagle Eyes kept saying, *"I own you. You're mine to claim."*?

I jumped up from my cross-legged position on the floor while my hand flew to my mouth. I was going to be sick to my stomach. The mere idea that this man was potentially the one after me, coming to collect on the promise my father had made...I needed to find a bathroom and quick.

Luke and Peter looked at me with alarm as they directed me toward the nearest bathroom. I ran inside, leaving one them scrambling to find a female operative to come check on me, while the other one stood guard at the door.

I made it to the stall with just enough time to close the door behind me before the contents of my breakfast came pouring out. My father wanted me to be a sex slave to Roger. It all made sense now. I continued throwing up as the thought sickened me to no end. It wasn't until I hit dry heaves that I finally lifted up, wiped my mouth, and flushed the toilet.

A sheen broke out on my forehead from the amount of force I used to expel the contents of my stomach. Trying to catch my breath, I leaned back against the stall door and panted out to Luke, "CDR is the culprit at work, maybe even the stalker."

"Peter's calling some of his contacts in the area now. We'll also get ahold of the local authorities and send them out to CDR's offices in New Orleans. I'll text to let the team know they aren't to investigate, but to get a search warrant and apprehend the guys for questioning."

With my breathing back to normal and the strength coming back into my body, I opened the door and made my way to the sink. I needed to wash up and rinse the foul taste from my mouth.

The water felt cool and comforting as I splashed it on my face and swished it around my mouth. I closed my eyes and reached out to grab hold of some paper towels, but I, instead, touched another person's flesh.

Thinking this was someone the team sent in to check on me, I grabbed the towel and wiped my eyes. A hand covered my mouth as my eyes opened to reveal my sister, Bethany. She had a gun pointed straight at my gut. *That bitch. She's behind this, too?*

Bethany leaned forward to whisper in my ear, "I need you to remain calm. This isn't what it looks like. I need to get us out of here to explain. Just go along with everything, and I'll try to ensure your safety."

I didn't know what she was up to, but I also wasn't sure how well the bullet-proof vests worked at such a close range. I didn't want to take any chances.

Whispering back, I asked, "What are talking about?"

Her words were barely audible. "I'm sorry, okay? I didn't realize Dad was such a bastard. He was abusive and controlling toward you, he caused heartache for Mom, and he tried to hurt me. I was so jealous of your closeness with Mom that I took all the spoiling and attention, not wanting to see what was in front of me, not until you were gone and Mom pulled away from there." Her face was pained, and the gun was shaking in her hands, though I noticed her finger wasn't on the trigger. "When he couldn't make the deal to sell you to Roger Chadwick, he renegotiated to hand me over to him instead."

My eyes grew as big as saucers, and she released the hand she'd had covering my mouth. I had a hard time finding my voice, but finally managed to utter a horrifying, "No." She nodded, a grim look on her face.

There was a knock on the door before it opened slightly. "Everything okay in there, Kaelin?"

We were hidden from view, so I had no way to give Luke a visual clue letting him know something was wrong. Bethany quickly mouthed the words *"Tell him you're fine"* as she shoved the gun against me, letting me know I needed to play by her rules.

"I'm fine, Luke, just a little queasy."

"Okay. Van looks to be finishing up his test. He should be done soon." He paused for a moment. "I'll be out here if you need me."

"All right." Hopefully, Luke will pick up on my verbal clue. "I shouldn't be much longer. I know I need to get back to my test and finish it." I used the momentary distraction to put my hands behind my back, out of my sister's view, and press down on the emergency button in my watch.

Bethany waved the gun in front of me. "Hands where I can see them." She reached around to see if I had anything in my back pockets. I didn't. We weren't allowed to bring phones to class during tests, so we left them back at the office apartment.

I began to wonder. "Why did you come to find me? And why the need for the gun?"

I didn't get an answer from her, as a door opened at the back of the bathroom. I hadn't realized there was a second entrance to the facilities.

"I can answer that question, Kaelin."

Oh my freaking Lord. Roger! If I hadn't already thrown up, my cookies would be tossing now.

"What are you doing here, Roger, or should I say Eagle Eyes?"

He had a small piece of metal pipe in his hand. I watched as he walked over to the door and pushed the metal inside the handle, not allowing it to open out into the hallway and blocking anyone from entering.

He turned to me while reaching out to caress the side of my face. "I've been waiting a long time for this day to come. You don't realize how well you would've had it with me."

I spit in his face. "You disgust me."

My head jerked violently with the slap of his hand. I'd forgotten how much the slaps could hurt. It'd been a long time since I'd felt one, the last being at my father's hand.

He got right in my face, but his voice was controlled and soft. "You think I'm disgusting? What about your father trying to sell you to my dad?"

"What?" Surely, I was hearing things wrong, but my sister was nodding the affirmative.

Roger continued. "My father runs an underground sex club for swingers and hardcore BDSM fantasies. Your dad had been gambling up a storm, losing everything he had, including some money he didn't. My father was willing to pay off your father's debt if he sold you to him to use as one of his sex slaves."

His hand reached out and traced a path from my face down my breasts before grabbing my crotch. "I've seen how my father breaks young women. I couldn't put you through all that. Your innocence called to me, and I offered to buy you for myself, wanting to thwart my father's goals. I wanted you to be my personal sex toy and, if you played your cards right, my wife. I needed someone who had a good head on their shoulders, who'd be able to talk to other businessmen at dinners. I needed an equal, but NO, you wouldn't spread your legs for me and take what I had to give you. I wanted to lavish you with everything my world could offer." He reached down caressing his dick. "You ran that night, and I was out a quarter of a million dollars."

Holy shit! "That can't be true. You're lying to me."

I could hear the door trying to be opened, but it wouldn't budge. Someone called out my name, but Roger forced the gun from Bethany's hands and pointed it straight at my head. I didn't dare yell out, or my life would be over in an instant. *It might be over already. Your worst nightmares are coming true.*

My sister leaned forward. "When Dad didn't have you to take his aggression out on, he started in on me with the verbal and physical abuse. Roger and his dad came around demanding their money back, but Dad had already spent it paying off a couple of loan sharks that were threatening to kill him.

"I was heading downstairs when I heard Dad, Roger, and his father discussing me as though I were nothing more than property to be bought and sold, only no money changing hands. Roger wasn't interested in having me as his wife, but his dad wanted to put me into his team of sex slaves. Dad refused until I turned eighteen and graduated high school.

"They agreed to the deal, but I was to become educated on the ways in which their club operated and what was expected of me. Roger was to train me for my new position, as nothing more than a slave to men, which would begin the day after I graduated."

I watched as tears streamed down her face. How she managed to keep her voice at a whisper was beyond me. My sister had grown as a person, and her self-control was a tad unsettling because I was used to her being wild and free with her personality. "I was forced to spend hours naked in front of Roger. He'd apologize to me, not liking what his father was forcing him to do. My body was being prepared to handle any of the client's demands. I'm not a virgin in the traditional sense—I'd lost that to my boyfriend in high school—but to be degraded on that level, all because our father owed money." She forced herself to take a deep breath; her control had started to slip. "Roger explained that if his dad had prepared me, he would've beaten me until I complied. So I did everything Roger asked, hoping to bide my time and wait for the opportunity to change things."

Feeling for the crap she endured, I reached out to touch her, but she jumped back. "I wanted to hate you for being thrown into that scenario, but I couldn't. I realized it wasn't your fault. It wasn't your mistakes I was paying for; it was our fathers. You had the right idea by running, so I followed your lead."

She looked up at me. "You know I hated you for a while, because you had your freedom. However, one of the porn webcasts Roger kept showing me over and over again, trying to teach me how to act, how to respond to men's demands, was that of Mystique, which is when I realized the price you'd paid."

Roger started to laugh softly, moving up behind me where I could feel his hardness press against my ass. "Imagine my surprise when Bethany told me I'd been watching her sister all along. Apparently, you have matching birthmarks, and in one episode you failed to cover it completely with one of your fake tattoo's during the taping."

"That's when you started harassing me?" I turned around to question him.

"Yes. Bethany made me a deal: if she helped me find and catch you, then I'd let her go free. Only, she ran away from all of us a week ago. I guess she didn't realize she had a tracking device put in her bracelet, leading me right here, right where I needed to be to make everything I've ever wanted, become a reality."

I wasn't following. "What do you mean?"

I heard heels clicking against the tile floor as a third party, a woman I'd never seen before, entered the room. In a low, malicious voice, the woman spoke. "Don't answer her, Roger." She turned her attention toward me. "All will be revealed in due time, my dear. I'm so glad to finally make your acquaintance in person, Kaelin. Or should I call you bitch?" With that, she reared back her hand, striking me across the face. Roger's slap hurt, but this one...damn! I know understood why no one ever wanted to get bitch-slapped. My face started throbbing.

When I regained my senses, I asked, "Who are you?" *Okay, I'm totally freaking out here, but I know it's best to keep everyone talking and prolong the efforts to save me. I could already feel Van's presence in the hallway and heard quiet chatter and the stomping of feet. I just needed to delay a little longer so they could get to me.*

The woman was beautiful, with long, blonde hair, eyes of the deepest blue, a long, lithe body, and a complexion that made her look like a porcelain doll. She was sex on heels personified. But I could see through that to the evil that was just barely being harbored underneath the surface.

She leaned into me, her face only a hair's breadth from mine. "You stole what was rightly mine. I let Van out of the deal to marry me, because I was in love with someone else, only to have him walk away months later. I tried to seduce Van into my bed on more than one occasion, but he said he'd moved on, found the 'love of his life,' which I assume is you."

"Heather?" I said the word aloud in question. Not sure if I had the right person or not. I knew Van had dated others, had even sowed his oats for a bit, telling me how everything felt empty in his life until he found me.

A smug smile spread across her face. "Well, what do you know? She does have a brain. Now, can you figure out why I blame you and your relatives for my family's fall from grace?"

I thought hard about the information I'd garnered in regard to the Thresher Restaurant Chain. They acquired several business locations throughout the southern United States, ready to revamp them into their own brand. Realization dawned on me, "It can't be."

She nodded. "If our family hadn't bought your grandfather's businesses and just stuck to our original plan, we would've been fine. My father was ambitious, and your grandfather's price was too entertaining to pass up. Getting his chain for a song and dance, we thought we hit the lottery. We hadn't planned on the recession hitting, and then hurricane Katrina to follow suit, pretty much destroying the business."

"And I'm to blame for that?" What was this bitch on, because she didn't make any sense? "I can't be held responsible for the economy or the weather. Those are beyond anyone's control and can't be predicted."

She crossed her arms, throwing her chest out. With a nasty scowl on her face, she continued, "You're right. Maybe I can't blame you entirely for that, but you've been a thorn in my side for some time now. Your family's former business nearly destroyed us. They were mainly located on the Gulf Coast, so the properties took a major hit with the weather, and then the icing on the cake was finding out you were the one Van wanted, not me."

Okay, I still wasn't following where all this hatred was coming from. "I don't get it."

She grabbed hold of my face, squeezing hard. "Our union was supposed to save our family's business. I was willing to walk away from all that for love, but when that failed...Van wouldn't look at me as long as he had you. But luck would offer me up a second chance with Roger's help."

Roger chimed in. "Bethany had already figured out you were Mystique and through some digging at your mother's place, she was able to figure out you were in Orlando. Imagine my surprise when I was checking in with the security desk at Meyers Corporation and saw you walk by and get on the elevator.

"I bitched at Dad for expanding our business by acquiring Trident Technologies, but he saw growth potential, and it did get me out of town, so I couldn't complain too much. I guess fate was in my corner when I got assigned to check in on the companies we do business with here in Orlando, one of which is yours."

Looking back at my sister, I shook my head in disbelief. "How could you?"

She shrugged her shoulders. I looked closer at her and noticed on the exterior she seemed to hate me just as much as them, but her eyes showed compassion toward me. *Who was she playing? Was it me or them? She asked for me to trust her and play along. But could I afford to?*

The door to the bathroom began to rattle some more. Something hard was hitting against it trying to get it open. Roger quickly grabbed me, pressing the gun into my lower back as Heather offered, "This way. We'll cut through the men's room and out the back entrance with the janitor's keys."

Roger was at my ear, threatening, "Make a scream and you're as good as dead, your sister, too."

I nodded in understanding, knowing I was royally screwed at that moment. I began praying for a miracle.

Heather seemed to know the campus like the back of her hand, leading us through one building and into another until we took some steps up to the tallest building on campus, the bell tower. My mind instantly went to the last song that was posted about me flying off the edge. I swallowed hard as I realized I was about to die.

We didn't see anyone following us, and we had perfect views of three sides of the building, making it difficult for anyone to get to us, but not impossible. I offered up a silent prayer. *Please save me and keep Van safe.*

Heather leaned against a corner wall, hidden from all views, while Roger held me against him, the gun still in my back as he continued the story. "I was at your company to check on the status of the computers and see what we could offer in the way of upgrades. I loved how they gave vendors limited access to the system through a separate desktop. Only, I had enough coding experience to bypass the boundaries and access the full server, where I found your current address, knew that you were an intern through the university, and saw the offer they were going to make an offer to hire you on permanently.

"I finished my work and waited around outside to follow you home that day to a nice condo downtown. I tried following you inside, but was blocked by the concierge. He only stopped me for maybe a month, until I gathered the information I needed to enter the building."

"At what point did you start harassing me online?" I wondered. I knew the dates. I just wanted to know where it fit in on his timeline.

He took a deep breath in, inhaling my scent in the process. "You always did smell so sweet, darling." He wrapped one hand around my throat. "When Bethany identified you as Mystique, I wanted to push your buttons. I hated that you'd gotten away from me. You were supposed to be mine. I paid top dollar to take your virginity and train you to be subservient to me, but no, you had to show your little cunt to thousands upon thousands of viewers. You're nothing more than a damn tease." His voice raged in my ear as his breathing picked up and his grip on my throat increased, causing me to gasp for breath.

Heather's voice yelled out. "Loosen your grip on her, Roger. I don't want her to die, not yet anyway. I'd rather play with her a little while longer."

His fingers rubbed against my throat. "It made me so angry how you'd let others watch you come, but you wouldn't let me inside your cunt. It was mine to have. I paid your father the right to own it, and I didn't like my woman shaking her ass for anyone. Why do you think I kicked your lover boy out of the room? I didn't like him seeing what's mine."

I laughed a bit. "It didn't stop him, Roger."

His hand tightened on my neck again, but it wasn't unbearable. "I know. That's why I created the viruses to blow up his system. Imagine my surprise when I discovered the signal was coming off the Wi-Fi servers in your building. I traced it all the way back to the CEO's office and found out who was hiding behind DaLuvMaster name. I was shocked as hell to see it was the same person I'd seen you walking with on campus, and the same one you talked with at work. Who knew it was Mr. Big Shot himself."

I looked around and noticed activity just past the periphery of the building. They knew where I was; they just needed to figure out a way to get to me. So I kept everyone talking. "How did you and Heather team up?"

Licking her lips and giving Roger a seductive smile, Heather filled in the missing pieces. "I was at the bar at my family's downtown restaurant, where I was working on the company's books, trying to figure out how much longer we could operate in the red before we'd be forced to file for bankruptcy. I noticed

Roger sitting down the way from me. He had his laptop open and was watching episodes of you online. As I approached, he flipped the screen to pictures he'd taken of you throughout the city. He had pictures of you and Trent, you and Van, and all the different places you frequented.

"I asked why he had pictures of my ex-fiancé on his laptop, so he enlightened me." Her hands fisted and she swallowed hard. "We got to talking and I nearly fainted when I discovered you were the granddaughter of the man my father had bought his recent restaurant chain from, the one that had us currently sinking."

Her eyes looked straight at mine. I could almost swear they were glowing with a red hue, full of hate. "I proposed he help me get back at both you and Van for what you'd caused. I needed money, and he helped me to get into your accounting software at work. While we were there, we continued to play around with your spreadsheets, trying to cause problems for you and your whole department. We figured you'd never get hired if they thought you were screwing things up. Plus, we decided we were owed a little payback for the money both of us had lost."

She raised her hand in the air between her and Roger. "We made a pretty good team. We managed to skim over half a million off of various entities throughout the organization. Roger even managed to create a portal into the system with the use of the vendor computer. He gave me a backdoor as well, allowing me to screw with the budget to try to dethrone Van as CEO. No one was the wiser, until this butthead decided to go rogue and beat up Van's brother."

I jumped. It was Roger who did that? "Why?"

His hand kept squeezing and releasing my throat, causing me to gasp. "I didn't like that you were living with a man. If you haven't figured it out yet, I'm quite possessive of my property. I was there to grab you, but you never showed, he did. I didn't know it was your boyfriend's brother or that it would drive you into hiding from me, but we're here now."

I breathed a sigh of relief knowing that Trent would be safe. The attack had been nothing more than a fluke. He was in the wrong place at the wrong time.

Roger's words were soft, "You're mine now, Kaelin." As his tongue came out to lick the side of my face, I cringed. His touch made my skin crawl, and the need to hurl was becoming stronger.

I shook my head. "I'm not yours. I belong to Van. We're married, or did you forget."

He released my neck, turning me around to face him. "What? When?"

"You can't be serious. You were the one ranting about me marrying someone else and about how you'd find me." I lifted my hands in the air. "Hell, you even helped beat up two women."

He shook his head and then looked over at Heather. "What is she talking about? I know you said you'd found her, and I met you at the one lady's place, the one you were pounding with a bat."

Heather just shrugged her shoulders. "I have no idea what she's talking about. I only beat up the one woman, because she looked like Kaelin."

He nodded. "You mean you almost killed the woman. Had I not stopped you and gotten you out of there, you would've been arrested for attempted murder. I thought we had a deal here, Heather. I helped you get the money you wanted, and in return, you helped me find Kaelin so I could take her back home with me to make a life together. In return, that left Van open to you. What gives?"

I pulled up my left hand and displayed it for him. "I married Van two weeks ago in a private ceremony, the one in which you managed to connect to the security cameras and watch, the one where you tried to send people to intercept the car we were traveling in to take me for yourself."

He shook his head back and forth. "That's not true. I'd left my laptop open on top of the hotel desk while I went to go get Heather and me some food. We were famished from a night of...well, never mind, you get the idea."

I'd never seen Roger's face so full of hatred and his voice so full of rage. "You used me. I showed you how to do a basic hack, and you did it...with my computer. No wonder that bug hit my system. I wondered what I did to screw things up and haven't been able to use the laptop since then."

His face turned to mine. "What else did I supposedly do?"

I swallowed hard. "The next day there was a post from Eagle Eyes yelling at me for getting married. You threatened to still find me and posted a song about wanting to push me off the edge, and if we were going to die young that you wanted to die with me."

His eyes focused on something over my shoulder. "You double crossed me, Heather. The deal was I got Kaelin, and all this time you had plans to kill her."

My sister yelled out "No!" as I heard the blast from a gun go off. Her body slammed into mine before falling to the ground. Something had hit my shoulder, but I shook it off, until feeling the next gunshot hit me in the back. Roger shoved me to the ground as he raised his own gun and fired, causing my head to bounce against the concrete.

I heard several sets of footsteps climbing up the stairs toward the tower. "Drop your weapon, now! Put your hands above your head where I can see them." It was Peter's voice, strong and commanding.

Roger quickly shouted, "She's the one who started this whole mess, trying to set me up with everything." I'm assuming he was talking about Heather. I heard someone state, "She's dead, a bullet to the heart."

"Where's my wife? I need to see her. Let me get up there." Van's voice was a blessing to hear. I knew he was safe and okay. I tried to open my eyes to look up into his face as he held me in his lap, but my eyelids were heavy. I felt something dragging me down, and I couldn't understand why.

I mouthed the words, "My sister. Is she okay?"

His lips pressed against my forehead. "She's taken a gunshot wound to the chest, but she's got a pulse. Do we need to put handcuffs on her?"

"I don't think so. She came to warn me about Heather and Roger. I don't know the full story, but let's hear her out before we throw her to the authorities." I reached out for his hand, feeling it wrap around mine. "Bethany took a bullet meant for me. She saved me, Van."

I heard the sirens wailing to a stop in front of the building and equipment being moved around. All I wanted to do was to go to sleep. I felt Van move me slightly and then curse under his breath. "Shit! She's bleeding from the back of her head and shoulder.

I felt someone rip the shoulder of my t-shirt.

"There's an entry point just above the bullet proof vest but no exit wound. The slug's still lodged in there. We need to get her to a hospital." It was Peter's voice as he immediately barked orders to the EMTs to get a dressing on the wound.

My body felt as light as a feather as darkness surrounded me, clutching me in its grasps. I could hear the faint words of Van screaming, "Don't you leave me, Kaelin. I can't survive this world without you."

There was light surrounding me and a sense of numbness mixed with peace. So this is what it felt like to die.

Chapter 19

Van

THE RIDE TO THE hospital was frightening, as Kaelin's heart stopped
once. I left the security team to deal with the authorities. My wife needed
me, and I wasn't about to leave her side. I quickly called Trent, who promised
to call Mom and Alyssa along with Kaelin's family to let them know what had
happened.

When we arrived, Bethany was whisked away to surgery. She was stable
enough for the doctors to go in and ascertain the damage left by the bullet
passing through her chest. They feared her lung had been nicked and needed to
go in to repair it.

My opinion of Bethany was changing. We'd been able to listen in on the
conversation Kaelin had with all the respective parties. We hadn't told her that
once the emergency signal was activated, we would be able to listen and record
everything that was said. I knew the team would provide the authorities with
a copy of the tape so they could prosecute Roger and his father however they
saw fit. He'd probably get some leniency for testifying against his dad in court.
I mean, come on, sex trafficking, that's just twisted.

At least his father's underground club would be dismantled and several ar-
rests would probably happen over the next several days. Their computer firm
would suffer, unless the other two partners could separate from him quickly.
A lot of co-owners of companies tended to have morality clauses that allowed

them to negate the agreement so they could save their reputation in the public eye.

I watched in horror as Kaelin's heart rate faltered. They called for a couple units of blood to try and stabilize her but needed to get her into surgery. "Could your wife be pregnant?" The nurse came up and asked.

I just shook my head. "I don't know. We haven't been using any protection." I heard the doctor order a blood test immediately. I didn't know what this had to do with being able to take the bullet out of her shoulder. From what I was gathering, she was bleeding out because it had hit a main blood vessel. They applied pressure to the area, but the dressings were continually being soaked through and rotated.

I shook my head. *This can't be happening.*

Time seemed to move in slow motion; though, I knew they were working fast to save the love of my life. My mind kept wandering to all the different things I wanted to show her, all the places I planned to take her, how I already found some listings online where we could look at houses and find one that suited our needs for our potential family. I spent years of my life lusting after this woman, finally won over her heart and, with one action of malicious intent, it might be over.

Someone grabbed hold of my shoulder. I looked up to see the nurse in front of me with a clipboard. "We need you to sign this paperwork allowing us to operate on your wife, Mr. Meyers. The doctor has her stabilized enough to take into the operating room. He'll remove the bullet and patch everything up. We'll do our best to use anesthetic and medication that won't affect the baby."

I scribbled my name on the areas she pointed to. *Wait! What?* I did a double take.

"I take it you didn't know?"

I shook my head. I knew she was four days late for her period, so we planned on stopping by a pharmacy to pick up a pregnancy test on the way back to the office. We hoped we would be celebrating later, but we didn't want to get ahead of ourselves only to be crushed if it came back negative.

"Kaelin's pregnant?" I turned to see Trent walking in, still with a cane and a limp, but he was there with Mark following quickly behind him.

"Yes. I just found out. I hope they can save the both of them." They wheeled Kaelin out of the trauma room and into the elevator. They wouldn't let us ride up with her, so I kissed her cheek quickly and then held her hand and whispered, "Don't you dare leave me, angel. I need you and that child of ours that you're carrying in my life. Fight for us, love."

One of the nurses directed us to the waiting area close to where the operating rooms were located. "We'll have the doctor come out and speak to you when he's done."

My mother and Alyssa arrived, along with every member of the security team. Roger had been arrested, the taped evidence given over to the proper authorities, and, apparently, a video copy of what happened in the bell tower.

The campus had installed hidden cameras after vandals had struck the tower numerous times in the past. They didn't publicize the fact they were there, but the university quickly offered up the evidence to help out.

We got word, via phone, that Kaelin and Bethany's mom and grandparents were on their way. My mom had rented a private jet for them to be brought in as quickly as possible.

Two hours passed and we were all fidgeting in the waiting area. I paced the hallway several times and, needing to hit something, punched the cushioning of the waiting room sofa. I felt pent up just waiting to hear something, anything. Not only was my wife's life was on the line but also my unborn child's, too.

At the three-hour mark the doors opened and a different doctor came out. All of us were on pins and needles waiting for him to speak. "I'm looking for the family of Bethany Richards."

I stepped forward. "I'm her brother-in-law. Her mom and grandparents are due to arrive soon. What's her status?"

"She's stable and already conscious, asking about her sister. The bullet grazed her heart and nicked her lung, causing it to collapse. We've fixed everything internally, and she's doing fine. Would you like to come back and see her?"

I nodded and was led back into the recovery area, where I saw Bethany's eyes wide, looking for Kaelin. Her breathing was off, and I noticed the tube coming out of her chest. I knew this wasn't the right time, but I needed to know. "Why did you team up with them? Why did you approach your sister in the bathroom?"

The doctor held up his hand. "I don't want you taxing my patient. She's just come out of surgery, and she's short of breath as a result."

"It's okay. He...needs...to know." Her words took time, but she managed to get them out.

I listened intently as she explained everything. She knew she was playing with fire, running to Orlando to find Kaelin, but found her class schedule their mom kept and, therefore, knew when she'd be in class. Bethany hung around campus for a while trying to get to Kaelin, and finally did, thanks to our professor who'd refused to budge on his testing schedule. God forbid the threats on our lives mess up his time.

It turned out Bethany only wanted to warn her sister and get her out of harm's way. Sure she hated her a bit, but it was classic sibling rivalry. "I might not see eye to eye with Kaelin, but she's my sister. She's always showed me love and affection, even when I didn't return it."

I asked about the gun with her fingerprints all over it.

"I only used it as a means to get Kaelin to do what I asked and to follow me to safety. She can be stubborn sometimes, not wanting to do what's right for her." I had to give Bethany that one. "Plus, if we got caught, I was hoping to bluff and take a shot at the creeps when the opportunity arrived." She looked down at her hands as a few tears fell from her cheeks. "Roger overpowered me and took the gun away. I had no clue Heather brought one until it was too late."

Bethany finally looked up at me. "It wasn't Roger who wanted Kaelin dead, it was Heather. She logged on under his name and posted the death threat. She intended to push Kaelin off the building to her death and had plans to force Roger to jump as well to make it look like a murder-suicide." She started to cry harder. "I think Heather intended to kill me, too, not wanting any witnesses."

I didn't know Bethany, and I wasn't feeling a lot of love for her in this moment, but she was my wife's sister and had attempted to save her life, so I moved forward and put my arms around her to comfort her.

Her tears finally ebbed. "Where's my sister? I want to see her to apologize for everything I've done wrong in life."

"She's still in surgery. The bullet passed through you and lodged in her shoulder. She was bleeding out when we got here. As we speak, they're trying to save her and our child. I need to get back to the waiting room and see if your family's arrived."

Bethany's face reflected the panic she felt inside. The monitor started beeping at her accelerated heart rate. "Not my father."

I shook my head. "No, not him. He's left town and was spotted buying a ticket to Mexico. Apparently, he didn't pay off all his debts after all."

Just then her mother burst through the doors, coming up to me and giving me a hug before going over and surrounding Bethany in her arms. "Son, is there any word on Kaelin?"

I shook my head. "I'm headed back to the waiting room. I'll come get you when we hear something."

Several members of the security team looked up when I entered the room. "Bethany's doing well. Her lung was collapsed and the bullet grazed her heart, but she's going to pull through."

I looked over to Luke, whose arms were around my sister, comforting her. He leaned closer yet and gave her a kiss on her forehead. *Hmm. Looks like I'm going to have the brother talk with Luke soon to see what his intentions are toward my sister.* His eyes met mine, and he grimaced a bit. I just shook my head and managed a weak smile. "You'll need to get the police to interview Bethany. She has quite the story to tell and can corroborate what was recorded on audio and video, plus fill in a few gaps."

I looked around the waiting area surprised—but not really— by how many people were drawn to Kaelin's mind, her kind words, and her affection. Word had spread of the incident and members of the accounting department had come to join our vigil in the waiting area. The room was filled to capacity.

They say time moves at a snail's pace when you're anxious for news, and boy, they weren't kidding. We were going on five hours when the doors opened. Everyone was on their feet immediately, including Mrs. Richards who'd rejoined us once she knew her youngest daughter was okay.

A doctor walked out. "The family of Mrs. Meyers?"

I stepped forward. "I'm her husband. How is she?"

"She's stable but in critical and guarded condition. The bullet hit an artery in her shoulder, and she suffered a lot of blood loss as a result. Her heart stopped again on the operating table, but we were able to revive her. Thankfully, the bullet wedged up against the side of a bone, sealing off some of the blood vessel; otherwise, she would've never made it to the hospital.

"The vessel has been repaired, the bone splinters and the bullet removed. The next twenty-four hours are the most critical, as we'll watch for infection and blood clots. If she can get through that, she should make a full recovery. It's a good thing she was wearing a bulletproof vest. It stopped the path of the second bullet, which would've severed her spine. "

"What about her head? She was bleeding from the back of it."

The doctor took a deep breath in. "She's got a fractured skull and a concussion. We're keeping an eye on her vital signs. If they change any, we'll order a CAT scan, but for now, we're more concerned about the risks of surgery."

I wanted to breathe a sigh of relief that she was still alive, but remembered to ask, "And the baby?"

He nodded. "We didn't use anything during the surgery that should affect the growth of the baby. However, given the amount of trauma her body's been through, we won't know for certain for a few days if it had any affects, since the pregnancy is still in its infancy. We can do an ultrasound later to check on things."

My mother's arms came around my waist while my brother put an arm around my shoulder. "She's alive, son. You need to focus on that."

Trent nodded in agreement. "If anyone can get through this, it's our Kaelin. She's a fighter."

"Damn right she is. I didn't raise my daughter to give up. She's come too far and finally found happiness with you; no way is she going to let go of that." Mrs. Richards marched up right in front of me, pushing the doctor out of the way. "Van, you need to let my daughter know we're all here fighting for her. Do whatever it takes to convince her to stay with us to bring our grandchild into this world, to live for him and for you above all else."

My head moved up and down in agreement. "I won't let her go, not without a fight, not after all we've been through to find one another."

"When can I see her, Doc?"

"Your wife is being moved to ICU. She'll only be allowed two visitors at a time and only for—"

I shook my head and held up my hand. "I'm not about to leave my wife's side, not while her life may hang in the balance. You can threaten me and try to kick me out, but I'll go over your head to your administrator. I'm a man who gets what I want, and there's no way you're keeping me from her bedside, not until she wakes up."

To my surprise, everyone beside me and behind me nodded in agreement. My mother was already taking out her cell phone. "I'll just give Herbert a call, dear."

The doctor quickly asked her to put the phone away. *Since when did my mother know the administrator of the hospital? At this moment I didn't care.* "That's not necessary, Ms. Ellingsworth. I'm sure Mr. Stanton will allow it this one time."

We passed the twenty-four hour mark without incident. I breathed a little easier, but Kaelin still wasn't out of the woods. She did have to have a CAT scan done to see why she hadn't come around yet. It revealed some swelling on her brain. The doctors would monitor it, but it wasn't enough to cause worry, and once it went down, she should come around.

A few days later, Kaelin was still unresponsive. She was moved to a private room on a floor where they'd still monitor her heartbeat and breathing.

I hadn't left her side since day one. Luke and Trent raided my closet and brought me some clothes. Trent sat beside Kaelin, talking about all the times they'd stayed up watching crappy B movies and having a carbohydrate festival in their living room. I didn't like leaving her even for a second. I wanted to be the first person she saw if, no, WHEN she woke up. But after three days, I stunk, and who'd want to wake up to that?

I used her private bathroom to take a quick shower and shave. It felt good to be clean again, and I started to feel hopeful, but when I came out the reality of things kept me grounded. "Anything?" I asked Trent.

He shook his head. "No response. No change in her heart beat, no movement behind her eyes." He stood up to let me have the spot beside her. "I'll go get us something to eat."

I shook my head. "I'm not hungry."

His hand came down on my shoulder, giving it a squeeze. "You're not going to do her any good if you don't take care of yourself. Once she wakes up, she's going to need your help, not only to get through what happened to her but also to move forward. She's going to need you to be there for her both mentally and physically."

I let my head fall forward on the bed against her hand. "You're right. Get me whatever looks remotely appetizing."

The next two days were still the same. At some point, they inserted a feeding tube down her nose to provide the nutrition required to support her body's need to heal and the baby's need to grow. The doctor called for an ultrasound to see if her body had kept the pregnancy, and we discovered we weren't fighting for one baby but two.

We had visitors in and out of the room, dropping off flowers, cards, balloons, and food. Everyone offered to give me a break, but I wouldn't budge. Trent had taken over for me at our family's business. He occasionally sent a runner over with paperwork for me to look at and sign off on. Kaelin and I would return to work with him once she was completely healed.

By the end of a week, I was exhausted. I'd talked to my wife about everything under the sun. "I need you to wake up, angel. I want to see that smiling face of yours. I'm barely existing without you." I ended up falling asleep crying against the side of her bed, against her good arm, just wanting to feel her skin pressed against my face. I felt defeated for the first time in a long time, not sure what tomorrow would bring.

A hand ran its fingers through my hair, making me shake my head. "Cut it out, Mom."

"But I've missed touching you."

My body jumped as realization dawned on me. It was Kaelin's voice. She swallowed hard as her eyes found the water. I reached over, got the cup, and held the straw for her to take a few sips. I was surprised when she gulped it all down. "Easy there. You don't want it coming back up."

She reached up to her nose where the feeding tube was. "What is this thing? It's annoying."

I pulled her hand up to my face. "You don't know how long I've waited to see you open your sparkling emerald eyes. I've missed you, love."

Her smile was weak, but there. "I know. I don't exist without you either. You're too much a part of my soul." She looked around at all the flowers and cards covering every inch of the room. "How long have I been out?"

"Eight days."

Before I could elaborate further, the nurse walked in to do her rounds. "Welcome back to the living, Mrs. Meyers. Have you been awake long?"

Kaelin shook her head. "Only twenty minutes or so."

I looked at her questionably. "You didn't think to wake me earlier?"

"You looked so peaceful in your sleep. I didn't want to disturb you." She started to shrug her shoulders but stopped. She looked over to her right shoulder to see it strapped down against her chest. "What happened?"

"You don't remember?"

She shook her head. "Not really. I remember being in the bell tower with my sister, Roger, and Heather. She was the one behind all the accounting issues, thanks to Roger's help getting into your system."

"We know. We heard it all on audio through your watch. She's no longer an issue. Roger killed her when she threatened to hurt you."

Her eyes filled with alarm. "How's my sister?"

"She jumped in front of the bullet. Your injuries would've been much worse if she hadn't slowed it down." I gave Kaelin's hand a squeeze. "She's fine. She already left the hospital with your mom. They're staying in town with my mother and Alyssa until they know you're fine."

"She saved me?"

I nodded. "Yes. She loves you and wants to set things right between the two of you."

The nurse continued to work and take Kaelin's vitals as we talked. "I'll go get the doctor, dear. He'll want to know you're awake and check your vitals for himself. You'll probably be able to get rid of the feeding tube and a couple other items so we can get you up and moving about."

It didn't take any time at all for the doctor to show up. The feeding tube was removed, and Kaelin's first request was to go to the bathroom and brush her teeth. She wanted a shower as well, but the doctor instructed only a sponge bath until her wounds healed some more. She was still sporting stitches in the back of her head and on the front and back of her shoulder. I looked forward to giving her as many sponge baths as she wanted.

The doctor ordered some soup and juice for her to eat. If she kept that down, they wanted to increase to protein shakes and actual food. "You'll need all the nourishment you can get. Food will help you heal and—"

I cleared my throat quite loudly, and when I got the doctor's attention, shook my head. He realized what I was saying and quickly changed his statement.

"Let's just say your body needs energy to heal your wounds. Your prognosis is excellent. However, once the stitches come out and the x-rays show you're healed, you will need some rehabilitation on your shoulder to get your range of motion back."

The food tray arrived, and I was surprised by how ravenous my wife was. It was good to see her eat. "I can't believe I'm so hungry. I guess I'm making up for eight days of not eating."

She finished her meal and asked the nurse for some more. "Let's see if you keep that down first, dear. If you do, then we'll move up to more substantial foods. Is there anything I can get you?"

Kaelin reached her hand up to her head. "My head's killing me. Is there something I can take for pain?"

"I'll see what the doctor suggests. There's not much we can offer right now other than some acetaminophen." The nurse left the room while tapping something onto her tablet. "I'll be back soon."

"Why can't I take anything stronger?" I loved how my wife's mind was always working. She knew something was up.

"Remember what we planned on doing after the exam that day?" Her eyes went wide, a smile playing on her face as her good hand reached down to her stomach.

"You mean?"

I nodded. "They discovered you were pregnant when you were brought in for surgery. With the trauma your system experienced, the doctor wasn't sure your body would carry the pregnancy, so he had an ultrasound done a couple days ago."

Her hand slapped playfully at my arm. "And? Don't keep me in suspense."

I leaned over her, giving her a gentle kiss on her lips, wishing like hell I could show her just how much she meant to me. *Later, dude. Keep it in your pants for now.* I grabbed hold of her hand, placing both of ours on top of her stomach. "They're doing fine."

"They. Did you just say, they? Am I hearing you correctly?" Her voice was elated. I definitely knew the feeling. I couldn't believe we could be so lucky as to be blessed with a quick pregnancy and two kids right off the bat.

"Yes, love. We'll have two new members of the family in about eight months. That's why you need to be careful about the type of medication you put in your body and how much food you eat."

"We'll need a bigger place. We can't raise a family in your apartment." Her mind was going a mile a minute.

I held my finger above her lips to silence her. "First, the focus is on you gaining strength and getting out of here. We'll have most of our things moved to my mom's house so we have plenty of help while you recover. Trent and Mark are still there, so we'll be one big happy family."

She reached her hand up and wrapped it around the back of my neck to pull me close to her face. "I love you."

"I love you more." I responded back before sealing my lips over hers. I was looking expectedly toward the future, the bright one I'd have with my wife by my side.

Epilogue

Kaelin

Two years later...

"**Y**OU WILL NEVER TRULY know yourself or the strength of your relationships until both have been tested by adversity." It's one of my favorite quotes by the famous author J.K. Rowling.

I looked back on my life and saw the testament to the strength of my relationship with Van. We'd had our fair share of adversity, more than enough if you ask me, but we came through everything stronger and more committed to one another than ever before.

I'd almost given up on the idea of love and being loved, until he first walked into that coffee shop, several years ago.

Van captured my attention as the white knight ready to bravely go into battle to save this damsel in distress. I finally had my Cinderella moment, my happily ever after with my prince, Van. He not only rescued me, but my family, too. I thought I was alone in this world, but now I had more than enough people to love and who loved me back unconditionally.

Van and Trent had spent enough time apart that they wanted to be close again, so they ended up building houses right next to one another, just a few miles down the road from their mom and sister.

When the doctor finally cleared me to travel, Van had scooped me up and carried me away on a private jet. He planned our honeymoon, which was spent at some of the top beaches in the world. We went to Fiji, Hawaii, and Paris. I know the last one didn't have a beach, but he promised to show me some of the amazing wonders of the world, and what better place to end our honeymoon than in the City of Love.

After Paris, we jumped right back into work, until our twins were born eight months after Heather's attempt to kill me. We discovered she paid the professor off to force us to take our tests on campus, allowing her the opportunity to get to me.

Van was furious and not only had the professor fired but also sued him for personal endangerment. The campus was apologetic and tried to offer us some form of solace, but we declined. The fact that they provided us the tape from the bell tower security camera was payment enough.

The money Heather had stolen was recovered from the offshore accounts. Her father's business went bust, forcing him to sell the family's mansion and move away to start over again. Her family had blamed Van for their daughter's death, but after seeing the tape and her confession, they realized she'd been mentally unstable.

Roger voluntarily offered to testify against his father, who ended up serving life in prison for twenty counts of sex trafficking. He's serving additional years for embezzling funds against his partners, illegal gambling, and the list goes on and on. No one had any clue how horrid he'd become.

Roger didn't ask for leniency but was granted some by Van. While Roger was in prison, Van visited to let it be known that I was *his* woman. He offered to not press charges for infiltrating the computer system at work and assisting Heather in stealing money from the business, all because he saved my life. "I thought I loved her, man. I would've taken the bullet instead of her. Just take care of her. She deserves someone who can love her properly."

Wanting to put things to rest, I went with Van to the prison. He had me stand over in the corner, away from the monitor, so Roger couldn't see I was there. I loved the words Van promised. "I'll guard her with my life and love her better than any man ever has or ever will." I was surprised when he added, "Your job is gone as well as all of your possessions. I'm leaving a contact number with the warden. When he deems you worthy to be released, a probationary position will be awaiting you, providing you can prove you're deserving of a second chance."

Roger thanked Van profusely. "I'll do my best to make you proud. Please tell Kaelin I'm sorry for everything. I only want the best for her, and I know now that I'm not that person."

"I'll let her know." Van shut off the video feed, and we never talked about Roger again. I know that he's still serving his term and is due for possible parole in another year. We'll see if he sticks to his word, but until then I'm going to live each new day to the fullest.

Things at work changed considerably. Alyssa came on board as the executive assistant to Trent, Van, and myself, which freed up Luke's time to work more of the security side of things. A small romance blossomed between Alyssa and him, and they were married a couple months ago after finding out they were expecting.

Our case had ended with perfect timing for Titan Security. Apparently, someone both Van and Galen had known, who'd helped out Galen's medical missions, was in need of urgent assistance. It was some guy named Maxim up on the Jersey Shore.

It was only recently that I'd met Galen, but had been privy to the donations Van had made through the financial aspect of the business to fund Galen's cause. It always warmed my heart to see that my husband was supportive and caring for more than just his family.

I was surprised to hear that Rick, the head of Titan, along with his brother Derrick, would be heading up the latest mission. I had been under the impression that they only managed the business, not actually taking part in some of the cases. But I'd overheard them talking to Van, and apparently, they owed Maxim a favor, having known him from their past.

Van and I had received a private invitation to a party Maxim was throwing at his hotel. I didn't understand why he would be throwing a party if he was in need of security, but I guess sometimes members of the upper echelon did things in ways I was still getting used to. At the time, I'd just been released from the hospital, after being shot, so Van politely declined the invite but sent a card and present up through Rick.

It took me a while to get the strength back in my shoulder and arm. Physical therapy and rehab helped to get back my mobility, but I'd never have the strength I once did, because there was too much damage to the muscle and tissues. It is what it is, but it doesn't keep me from living life.

When the twins were born, a boy and a girl, I had a hard time leaving them behind to come into work. To be honest, Van didn't want to leave them behind either. So for the first few months, we had two portable cribs in our office. We took out the small conference table and added two smaller desks so we could all work together.

As our babies became more active, Van surprised me by opening the daycare center at work. "It was a long time coming, love. My father made this place too oppressive to work in. He discriminated against too many individuals, and it's time to set things right. I've already offered maternity and paternity leave to our employees, something he only did when he was forced to do so. Now we've added daycare with the highest trained nannies in the business. Our little ones can hang out here with the other children while we work."

My husband wasn't anything like his father. He had been an active partici-pant in my pregnancy, even attending Lamaze classes, pulling Trent along with us as backup. Every morning after the babies were born, Van was there to help me wake them up for breakfast. During the day, he helped me change and feed them, and at night, he often took some of the feeding rounds to let me sleep, especially since I needed sleep. A few months after the twins were born, he managed to get me pregnant again, blessing us with another boy.

Trent and Mark ended up using surrogates to carry each of their kids. They thought it would take a while for the process to take effect, but they ended up having two girls within five months of one another and have been looking to us for guidance on how to deal with things.

My mom and both sets of my grandparents sold their places and moved down to Orlando for a fresh start and to be closer to their grandkids. Mom now works at one of the local banks, and she's already been promoted to district manager and loves her job. She's even seeing a man who treats her right. He's a doctor.

Bethany was afraid to talk to me for a while. She felt guilty for nearly getting me killed. We had a good, long chat and laid all our cards out on the table, followed by a healthy dose of crying and hugging. We realized most of our issues stemmed from our father being an ass.

She's been going to college here and working at Mark's coffee shop part-time. She was inspired by the care she received at the hospital and wants to give back a little by becoming a nurse. She has an issue trusting men, but if Russ has his way, she'll finally break down and grant him a date.

Speaking of Russ, Peter, and the gang, they went back overseas for a new mission with the SEALs. Their unit got caught in the crossfire. They came out alive, but all of them were injured, ending their military careers a little earlier than planned.

Titan Security kept their promise to hire them on, giving them time to heal from their wounds. Peter quickly proposed to his now-fiancée, but they've yet to set a date. Michael started dating someone, but no one knows if it is serious or not. John was already married, but he and his wife are experiencing a few difficulties that will hopefully work out in the long run. Russ was the odd man out, but he keeps working on Bethany. I'm starting to see her walls begin to crumble, and she definitely has a sparkle in her eyes whenever he's around. There is a bit of an age difference there, but he's good for her. I'm keeping my fingers crossed that we have another wedding to plan soon.

As for my father, he dropped off the face of the earth. We knew he purchased a one-way ticket to Mexico, but no one has heard anything from him since then. However, through an unknown source, which I suspect is Peter still keeping tabs for us with some of his contacts, we discovered my father had been thrown in a Mexican prison for beating someone up and had his passport revoked. Karma can be a bitch sometimes and other times sweet music to our ears.

My mind kept wondering, thinking over how all of our lives were entwined with one another. I was grateful for all the new family I had and the friends I'd made through Van and Trent. My life felt complete.

I was sitting just inside the door to the apartment Van once had in his office and was breastfeeding our little Jeffrey, named after my maternal grandfather. Jeffrey's a boob-man like his father, not wanting to release them once he's done eating.

I looked around this place and thought about how far we've come, how much we've grown. We once had to hole up in here to be hidden from the public eye, but now we used the place for a quickie or to escape for a few hours of alone time since we don't use nannies at home. Sure we have help around the house, but when it comes to our kids, they are our number one priority and taken care of by us. The only other people we trusted are our family.

I heard a knock on the door. "Is he almost done?" It was Van poking his head around the corner. "I need you to take a quick look at these documents to see if this business is financially legit enough for us to invest in. The board is pressing us for a decision."

He walked over to where I was seated and cradled the back of Jeffrey's head as he moved to pick him up, getting him to finally release my breast. I watched as he talked in a quiet whisper to our youngest son. "You need to learn to share, young man. Mom's breasts don't belong to you alone."

I laughed softly. Van loved to sneak up right as I was done feeding and take a taste himself. He claimed he was deprived as a child, surviving only on formula and, therefore, wanted to get a taste of what he missed. Yeah, right. He used any excuse he could to touch me.

He burped our child and placed him gently into the bassinet just inside the door. We hadn't been able to keep Jeffrey's portable crib by our desks because he was a light sleeper.

Van walked over and surrounded me with his arms. "Have I told you just how hot and sexy you look today, angel?"

With a giggle, I shook my head. I knew where this was leading. He wanted a round in the bathroom while Trent listened for Jeffrey. "No, but I'm pretty sure you're going to try and show me."

Smiling, he lifted me up. My legs instantly went around his waist as one of his hands came down to slap me gently against the ass. "Every damn day of my life, baby." His hardened cock rocked against me, and I was instantly wet for him.

"I love you," I whispered.

"I love you more – forever," he responded.

"Forever."

Afterword

Kaelin and Van's love story was a true testament to the power of love, as they battled insurmountable obstacles to finally find their happily-ever-after. From a dangerous stalker to a financial scam that threatened to destroy everything they held dear, Kaelin and Van proved that nothing stands in the way of true love. If you thought their story was intense, you won't be able to resist the passion and intrigue of Maxim and Nathalia's fairy-tale romance. Theirs is a tale of princely desires, steamy romance, and heart-pounding suspense that will leave you breathless. Don't miss out on the next installment in this thrilling series!

Read Maxim's Needs , the third book of DOMS of Titan!

KEEP READING for a SNEAK PEEK!

Maxim's Needs

DOMS of Titan - Book Three

P RINCE MAXIM IS FACED with an impossible task - finding a suitable bride from a royal lineage before his 35th birthday. Failure to do so would mean losing his family's right to the throne and jeopardizing his country's freedoms. To make matters worse, his cousin Dalek is waiting in the wings to take over and plunge the country back into the dark ages.

Maxim isn't just looking for any woman, though. **He needs someone who can stand up to the challenges of his royal life, but who will also submit to his darkest desires in the bedroom.**

When he meets Nathalia, a woman overcoming heartache, he thinks she might be the one. He needs to convince her to take a chance on him, without revealing that he's looking for a royal bride.

In the process of gaining her trust, he uncovers a plot by her fake fiancé to destroy her. He'll protect her at all costs, wanting Nathalia to be his wife, queen, mother to his children, and a submissive to his dominant cravings.

Amidst all of this, Dalek is plotting to take the throne and destroy both Maxim and Nathalia. **Will their love be enough to save them, giving their sinful fairytale romance a happy ending or will Dalek's madness win out?** This heart-pounding romantic suspense thriller will leave you breathless and wanting more.

Maxim's Needs - DOMS of Titan, Books Three

Maxim - "Max"

"**S**AKRA. DAMN THEM." With great force, I struck the arm of my chair with my fist and threw the paper on my desk, despising what was asked of me.

"What bug's crawled up your ass today, Maxim?" Alexej asked as he came sauntering through the office door.

I didn't want his company right now but was happy, nonetheless, that he was present to prevent me from pushing everything off my desk and onto the floor. I felt the beast pacing inside me, needing to somehow let off some steam. I had eyes watching my every move, so I always had to lead by example, was never able to scream out my disgust about the ways of my world.

As Alexej strolled over to the desk, his eyebrows raised as his hand pointed to the paper I'd just discarded. I pushed it his direction, willing it to burst into flames. Who was I kidding? Unfortunately, it required an immediate reply, one I couldn't give.

I had no secrets with Alexej. We've known each other for as long as I could remember, becoming fast friends as infants. He now worked for my family as head of security for our family's hotel businesses and, more importantly, was my most trusted advisor and protector.

Alexej's facial expression fell as he scanned the letter. "Are they serious? What will you do?" His voice held great sadness for my predicament.

I let my shoulders slump, as I was forced to admit, "My moment of freedom will soon expire. There are no foreseeable options. You know the love of my family, friends, and people comes first in my life."

After taking the paper from Alexej, I let my fingers graze over the embossed seal atop the page and then closed my eyes, remembering the long history of our family's crest. A few moments later, I scanned over the letter once more, not sure what I was looking for.

The words were those of my father:

> My son, you are hereby given notice that you are less than eight months from reaching your thirty-fifth birthday. According to our laws set forth by your forefathers, you are to be married and take over the family business at that time.

> We've attempted to find you suitable women to court, but you refuse to return home in which to do so. If you insist on staying your course, you will be required to find a woman that meets all the criteria of your ancestors, or we will arrange for you to marry someone we deem suitable.

It is expected that you will wed no
later than the month prior to your
thirty-fifth year. At that point, you
WILL return to your land of birth
and assume your role as head of this
family and all that it entails.

You hold the fate of our family and
our land within your hands. If you
fail, your cousin Dalek will assume
your duties and, with them, attempt
to destroy everything we've built to
date.

The letter went on to include some extra fluff and circumstance, reading
more like an order than a request. What I wanted to do was rip the damn thing
up and throw it in the nearest fireplace. But I knew I'd never be able to say
I didn't receive it. The final lines of the correspondence stipulated I respond
posthaste.

Reaching up, I rubbed my eyes with one hand and shook my head. "I need
you to send a response back to my parents letting them know I'll do what is
expected of me. But I want it known that I will search for a bride of my choosing.
However, if I fail, then I'll agree to their terms. I won't let Dalek ruin what it
took centuries for my family to build. Even if I have to sacrifice my happiness
in the process."

Throwing the paper back on the desk, I reached up to pinch the bridge of my
nose, feeling the onset of a stress headache. Why did life have to be so fucking
complicated?

Alexej called out to my secretary. "Gloria. Could you be a dear and bring Max something for a headache and maybe some lunch for the two of us?"

Her soft voice drifted in through the open door. "I'm on it."

Looking up, I could see the worry evident on Alexej's face. "I'll send your message, but I have to ask, how do you intend to find your bride?"

The idea of being subjected to an arranged marriage turned my stomach. Exasperated, I replied, "Have your men speed up their search. We know for a fact that several families fled the surrounding countries of our homeland to escape persecution. You've tried finding them in the surrounding nations but have been unsuccessful to date. I suspect the promise of a new land, where one could gain independence and freedom, may have lured some of them here to America."

Looking up to Alexej's sympathetic face, I added, "My fate is in your hands. Find someone that fits the bill, someone I can grow to love over time."

Alexej moved to the edge of his seat. "You do realize you're asking me to find the impossible. What expression is it that Americans use?" He pondered the question for a moment. "You're asking that I find a needle in a haystack. You do realize what era we live in, where men and women no longer wait until marriage to satisfy their carnal desires."

I nodded my agreement. "Just assure me you'll find the treasure I so desperately need, even if you have to bribe your way into finding it. We've got six months in which to locate my virgin bride and even less time to convince her to marry me. I just hope she's . . ."

Words suddenly escaped me. One minute I'd been looking Alexej's direction, discussing a possible plan for my future, and the next I was captivated by a beauty with long, flowing locks of chestnut hair framing a face that could only be described as an angel incarnate, who now appeared on the wall of monitors across the office from my desk.

Her simple sundress floated out around her as she sauntered into the hotel foyer. I couldn't pull my eyes away from the monitor as she stopped to examine some of the art on the walls.

I stood up and walked over to the bank of monitors and reached out for the screen she was standing in, running my hand over her image, wanting to commit it to memory. I couldn't understand why I was drawn to her or why her eyes seemed so wistful and sad.

She kept grasping the charm on her necklace, and as she walked a few feet farther into the hotel, continuing to peruse the décor, she occasionally reached out to touch something, as if to see if it were real.

To anyone else, it would look like I was stalking every person in the facility. However, as head of the hotel chain and its manager, I needed to have eyes on everything that transpired, especially within the confines of the main floor where the casino and the boardwalk were located. Alexej's security crew had the same set of monitors, and more, to ensure the safety of anyone who entered our establishment, whether they were a guest or just spending the day gambling.

Gloria's knock on the door broke the spell I was under, causing me to turn around. She entered my office, pushing a food cart, and produced a bottle of aspirin. "For your headache, sir."

"Thank you," I offered, taking the bottle from her hands before quickly downing a couple pills with a bottle of water from the cart.

"Will there be anything else, sir?" Gloria queried.

"If you'd be so kind, tell people I'm not in right now or that I'm in a meeting and cannot be disturbed."

She nodded her head in understanding. "As you wish. Have a pleasant lunch, and let me know when I can expect you back in."

"Of course."

Once the door to my office was closed, I turned to the monitors and saw that my sweet angel, můj sladký andílek, had vanished. I quickly searched each screen, trying to discern where she'd gone, only calmed when I'd located her on the back of the pool deck overlooking the Atlantic Ocean, looking like she'd lost her only friend.

Alexej began to laugh as he came up behind me, giving me a slap on my back. "You've got it bad, my friend. Remember, you can look all you want, but your focus needs to be on finding your intended."

Agreed. "Souhalísm." Turning around, I ran my fingers through my hair in frustration, before admitting, "I don't know what it is about this young woman" —I pointed at the screen she currently occupied—"but she's caught my attention each and every time she's been here."

Alexej's brow furrowed as he began placing our meal on the conference table in my office. "The woman, she's been here before? Why?" he asked, taking a seat.

Sitting down, I nodded. "She comes at least once a week, always looks at the décor throughout the hotel's lobby before proceeding to the pool's deck or out onto the beach."

Looking down at the food, I found the cooks had sent up one of my favorites, a medium-rare filet mignon, with diced potatoes and a side of vegetables. I took a bite or two and then pushed it away, unable to take the food in front of me, with the weight of an entire nation resting on my shoulders.

Alexej pushed the plate back in front of me and pointed his fork my direction. "You need to eat, Maxim, to keep up your strength. That headache will only get worse if you allow yourself to dwell on all that has transpired."

Taking a couple bites of food, he added, "If you'd like, I can try to find out whom the fair maiden is. It would be no trouble."

I took a deep breath, before finally stabbing my fork into one of the pieces of potato. "I admit, she appeals to me greatly, but it would be a waste of our time to expend resources on trying to figure out who she is. If she is fated to me, then she'll come up in our searches, if not, then she was never meant to be mine."

Taking a bite of my food, I looked up to the monitors and saw she was finally leaving the establishment. In my mind, I quietly wished my fair angel well on whatever was troubling her. I knew nothing could ever come of us, since my destiny had been decided for me. "Just find someone I can tolerate and keep your search as quiet as possible. You know I can't risk Dalek finding out until it is too late for him to do anything about it."

Alexej nodded, knowing exactly what I meant. The candidates my parents had found had offered to come to me in order for us to meet and potentially court. The only problem was my cousin Dalek. Someone had leaked private information about these women, and each one had been intercepted en route to America.

My heart ached for what my cousin had done to all of them. They'd been taken captive and whisked away to areas unknown, only to reemerge married and pregnant, ending all potential of becoming my bride.

I wanted to curse my family for having such stringent rules in regards to whom I could wed. It was hard enough to find someone with a lineage comparable to my own, but to find someone who'd saved her innocence for marriage was even harder. My father could've easily changed these rules to meet modern-day society, but he had not acted in a timely manner. Now it was too late.

"Maxim? Max?" Alexej's words brought me back from my thoughts. "Are you okay?"

After nodding, I admitted, "I'm just going over things in my mind, realizing the great task that lay before us." Taking another bite of food, I added, "Have you any word on the culprit who's been leaking information to that kretén (asshole) cousin of mine?"

I watched as a mischievous smile spread across Alexej's face, knowing that he intended swift punishment for anyone who dared go up against my family. "It was one of your father's secretaries. She'd been the one handling the travel plans for all of your potential candidates." He shook his head in disgust and grunted. "The woman was seduced by one of Dalek's men. She currently resides in the country's prison while your father decides the course of punishment he wishes to take."

I cringed at the words. Our nation's penal system was not far removed from that of a concentration camp. The conditions were harsh and the punishments even harsher. It was rare for anyone to be placed into the system, because most of the citizens strived to maintain peace and happiness. I guess that's why the crime rate was nearly nonexistent, until Dalek decided to tamper with things.

My cousin had shown his hand early: he had every intention to use any means necessary to take the position I'd been born into. That's why I had to oblige my father's orders and take over the family business whether I wanted to or not.

Dalek already resorted to various levels of treachery, but the men who stood around him took the fall, claiming they'd acted of their own accord. I wondered why they were so loyal to him, a man who wanted to destroy years of technological advances our family had made and, instead, give rise to the barbaric practices of yesteryear. The only consolation I had was in knowing that any attempt on our lives, by him or a member of his team, would be considered a heinous crime immediately punishable by death.

We finished our lunch and parted ways, as Alexej promised to continue his quest to find a suitable woman my family would approve.

I continued to work, looking over the recent figures for our hotel franchise. The numbers were all within the range we'd been expecting. The most promising was our newest hotel—the one I currently resided at in Atlantic City, New Jersey—the Palace by the Sea. It was our highest-grossing entity to date, one I didn't want to leave. Sure I missed my family and my homeland, but I found happiness in my work. I often worked long hours to avoid going back to my suite, where I was alone and had everything to myself. I prayed for Alexej's success in finding someone who would fill the loneliness, challenge my mind, and arouse my sexual desires.

Dear Reader,

I HOPED YOU ENJOYED diving into my world of romantic suspense, where love is hard-earned, and danger lurks around every corner. Kaelin and Van's story was just the beginning of the thrilling DOMS of Titan series, and the next installment promises to take things up a notch.

Are you ready to join the next journey and experience the intense romance and thrilling suspense that the DOMS of Titan series has to offer? Max and Thalia are willing to do whatever it takes to secure their future and a kingdom they love, even if it means putting themselves in harm's way. This is not your typical fairytale with princes and knights, but a story of passion and resilience in the face of adversity, where love and loyalty will be put to the ultimate test.

Titan Security is expanding, introducing new characters who will steal your heart and take you on thrilling adventures. Peter, Russ, Michael, and John are just some of the names you'll want to remember as they prepare to embark on their own journeys of love and danger in upcoming Titan books. The series is not for the faint of heart, but for those who crave adventure, danger, and, of course, steamy love.

If you enjoyed Van and Kaelin's story, please remember to leave an honest review.

Keep it steamy,

Cynthia

Sign up for my newsletter and get free reads and so much more delivered to your inbox. It's a chance for us to connect!

About the Author

I GREW UP IN a small town in South Florida and moved to Central Florida to attend college. I married my friend, love, and soul mate and still reside in the area with our amazing son, and a feisty, four-legged little doggie boy.

In my books, I draw on my background in healthcare, business, and science, along with my husband's engineering and wireless technology knowledge.

I love to cook and create in the kitchen and on the bbq grill. I sometimes lose myself in a song at the piano. I enjoy crafting, amusement parks, and the beach!

Let's connect and get to know each other. Find me at: www.cynthiaponeill .com

Books by Cynthia P. O'Neill

*T*HE *NEED* *SERIES*

Dangerous men with hearts of gold seeking submission loving women. In this dominating series of standalone romances, the men are the alphas and the women take control of their hearts. Start with book 1, I Need You Always , and get caught up in need and the satisfying happy-ever-afters.

The Titan Security Series

In this Need series spin-off series, the Titan heroes are the security guards you crave knowing. In their pasts and futures, they deal with wounds that carve out pieces of their hearts that only their women can heal. Start with book 1, Derrick's Choice, and fall in love all over again.

DOMS of Titan

In this Titan Security Series spin-off, friends of Titan reach out seeking guidance to protect the women they love, who are in danger. These men are dominant in their own rights, but will stop at nothing to protect the women who own a piece of their heart. Start with book 1, Galen's Pursuit , and fall in love with this series.

The Learning Series

When Laurel and Garrett try to get past the stalker in her past as well as the dangerous enemies he's collected over the years, there's more between them than mind-boggling passion and romance. Can they help each other overcome their demons and find happy-ever-after in this steamy romantic suspense series or will

Garret learn there's nothing more important than love on his own? Start with book 1, Learning To Trust .

<u>Stalk Me Online!</u>

Bookbub

Facebook

Website

Amazon

Acknowledgements

I would like to thank, first and foremost, all my followers, fans, bloggers, and friends. Without all of you, my books would not be possible. Keep spreading the word. Hugs to all!

To my family – All I can say is I love you all and I'm thankful for your support in pursuing my dreams!

To Mia Mincheff, my good friend, editor, and fellow book enthusiast, I'm at a loss for words. Your belief and encouragement in my dreams means more than you'll ever know. You help make me a better writer with your knowledge and guidance. I'm forever grateful our paths crossed.

To Mandie Stevens and Bonnie Paulson. I'm glad our paths crossed. You have both been patient and helpful guiding me in a new direction of my authoring journey. I'm forever grateful.

To Stacy Nickelson. You're a friend, confidant, and beta reader. I don't know how I can repay you for encouraging me to follow my dreams.

To Marisol Taveras-Magrans, a beta reader and friend – our paths crossed, thanks to Lisa, and I'm so happy to have you as part of my beta team. Your encouraging words and pointing out any issues with the books mean the world to me. You help make me a better writer.

Above all, thanks to God, for giving the ability to write.